The Golden Scepter

By Alex Zabala & Dyego Alehandro

Now contains the free short story The Missing Capstone, *featuring* Chauncy Rollock and Jake Thrasher

DESTITUO OMNIS TUI ANTE FALSUS COGITATUM

Abandon all of your previous misconceptions
A Latin inscription engraved on a granite spire in Meteora, Greece

Prologue

Babylon, 539 BCE

The last boulder fell into the river with a violent splash. Almost before it hit the water there were men rushing to surround it with mud. For several heart-stopping moments it looked like the river would win the battle; the waters were low, it was true, but that didn't make them any less powerful. The torrent had swept away four men but finally the mud and timber were in place. The water level downstream of the boulders was lowering and the dam showed no signs of failing. The majority of the river had been successfully diverted in a new direction, down a different river bed and into an open field.

King Cyrus grinned broadly, a rare show of emotion for the young conqueror. This was it. The mighty Euphrates river, the defender of Babylon, was reduced to a slow trickle. He had successfully overcome one of the largest hurdles in his path. This would be a night to remember.

***

The Medo-Persian army moved cautiously through the stream that had once been the Euphrates. The sound of their advance was masked by the loud music of a celebration within the city walls. There was no celebrating for the Medo-Persians yet, however. The river might not be an obstacle but there was still the wall to consider. The Babylonians bragged about their wall; it was wide enough to host chariot races and would not be easy to surmount, but Cyrus was confident. Already he had made more progress than armies prior to this. They would climb the walls or break through the heavily-guarded gate, whichever appeared less hazardous upon arrival.

The first soldiers, silent as ghosts in the night, climbed up the causeway walls to scout the gate. To their immense surprise they found the gates wide open. The guards were in a drunken stupor, obviously too caught up in the festivities to care about security. The Babylonians had trusted in their mighty river and their gods to keep them safe.

The soldiers moved through the city and the members of the Babylonian royalty were dead before they realized their mistake.

After the battle, King Cyrus stood on a balcony atop a ziggurat and raised his arms to the heavens. The populace below, his loyal soldiers and his new subjects, bowed low as he spoke. "I am Cyrus, king of the world," he announced in a loud voice. "Great king, legitimate king, king of Babylon, king of Sumer and Akkad, king of the four rims of the earth, son of Cambyses, great king, king of Anshan, grandson of Cyrus I, descendant of Teispes of a family which has always exercised kingship!"

He lowered his arms and basked in the cheers and adulation. This was a glorious moment, one that would live forever. He had conquered the great world power of Babylon, whom many had said would never be subdued. He would have enjoyed celebrating for much longer, but he knew he could not fall into the same trap as the people he'd just conquered. The job of administering the kingdom had to begin in earnest. There were many treasures of Babylon that needed to be found and added to the coffers of the new Medo-Persian empire. He tasked one of his greatest generals, Kambashi, to find and collect these treasures. Every empire needed money, after all.

***

General Kambashi finally reached a point where he could see into the plain of Dura and he felt his breath leave him. His entourage made startled exclamations as they, too, saw the enormous golden statue that cast a shadow across the entire valley. Fifteen men standing on top of each other would barely have reached the top of the statue and they would have looked tiny in comparison to the man the statue represented. The locals had spoken of this image, erected in honor of King Nebuchadnezzar. The statue was an effigy of the illustrious king and great care had been taken in the details. It was clad in the best royal Babylonian robes, with multiple layers and garments clearly visible. The face was slanted upward in arrogance, giving the typical cylindrical helmet a slight tilt. Clutched to its chest was a noble scepter. The craftsmanship was magnificent, but even more impressive was the sheer amount of gold involved. There was no point in honoring the long-dead king and the wealth of the statue would make Kambashi a favorite in the empire for his entire life.

It took twenty horses and dozens of ropes but they finally managed to dislodge the effigy. It fell to the earth with a resounding crash. The fractured chunks of gold would be easier to transport back to the capital, but that would have to wait until morning. Twilight had crept upon them while they worked and it was time to bed down for the night. The general set up a rotating guard and was about to enter his tent when he noticed the dust cloud on the horizon.

He had not sent for reinforcements and was therefore wary of the horsemen that were approaching rapidly. He pulled out his sword when they showed no sign of slowing down.

"To arms!" he ordered, but it was already too late. Arrows whistled through the air as the horses thundered past.

Kambashi fell to his knees and looked around him, choking on the stirred-up sand. Most of his men had been slain in that first pass and the workers had already scattered. He had to get to his horse. He stood no chance on the ground. He pushed himself up and sprinted for the closest animal.

He never made it. The unknown attackers came again and this time their arrows found Kambashi. He fell to the earth once more but he would not give up.

"This wealth...belongs to Cyrus!" he shouted with all of his strength.

The enemy, dressed in flowing black robes, ignored him. They came to a stop and began searching through the rubble of the fallen statue. Kambashi pulled himself along the ground, duty and honor driving him to ignore the pain and weakness that enveloped him. The Medo-Persians had conquered the strongest city on earth and Kambashi would not allow simple pillagers to rob the kingdom of its glory.

The looters picked up a fragment of the statue and it glittered in the fading sunlight. "That belongs...to King Cyrus," Kambashi said again with difficulty.

The man holding the fragment stopped and walked over to

Kambashi. The general could see that the fragment was the upper part of the statue's scepter.

"The Divine Flame does not belong to Cyrus," the unknown man replied. "It did not belong to the Babylonians before him. It belongs to us and we are retaking what is ours."

General Kambashi, favorite commander of Cyrus the Great, collapsed before he could ask the meaning of those words. The horsemen left as quickly as they'd arrived and silence once again enveloped the plain of Dura.

Chapter One

Ankara, Turkey
Present Time

The well-dressed man paused for a moment and stared up at the magnificent structure before him. Its stately design blended in with the historic architecture of downtown Ankara and yet it stood out as different, as spectacular. It was only fitting that it was a building designed to house some of the greatest antiquities known to mankind. Two different styles were combined for excellent effect: the ubiquitous Muslim minarets and the classic Ottoman vast inner spaces.

If it had been designed by someone else he would've been jealous. As it was, he was immensely proud of his Institute of Antiquities of Ankara.

He walked swiftly to the rear of the museum. Even before he opened the door he could hear the festivities inside. It was the night of a gala ball to thank the primary benefactors and financial contributors of the museum. A smile spread across his face. The sound of music, laughter and conversation only intensified as he walked down the narrow corridor leading to the main auditorium. He almost ran his fingers along the walls as he went. They looked like ancient, sculpted stone as old as the city itself, but they were little more than precast cement.

He knew what to expect as he entered the auditorium, and yet he felt a momentary shortness of breath. The high dome above, the many dimmed alcoves, the sheer grandeur of the museum was increased by the event held below the dome. Women wore the most elegant evening dresses and the men were in fine tuxedos. The laughter and conversation was flowing as freely as the best French Champagne.

The chairman spotted him and clapped his hands together. "Ladies and gentlemen, the museum director would like to say a few words. Please give your undivided attention to Dr. Faruk Mayal."

The audience clapped politely as Dr. Mayal bowed his head and approached the lectern. He was a tall man, but he felt taller as he stood at the head of the crowd. He was in his late forties. He kept his curly black hair short and wore a neatly trimmed beard that grew along the contour of his jaw. His dark complexion, prominent nose and black eyes made him look like a hawk as he surveyed the crowd in front of him.

"I would like to thank all of you for attending this event and I hope you are enjoying yourselves," he said. "On behalf of the Institute of Antiquities of Ankara, I would also like to thank you for your generous contributions. Without your support and backing, this magnificent museum and its many displays would not exist. You have allowed us to reach our goal: showcasing the treasures of the Middle East and showing the world the rich culture that we possess. Soon everyone will know what our history is all about. We can even give our competition, the Anatolian Ankara Museum of Antiquities, a run for its money."

He paused for dramatic affect. "Therefore, I invite all of you to roam the museum. Take in the displays and see for yourselves what we have procured. Enjoy the delicious feast that has been prepared. After all, you paid for it."

A polite chuckle murmured through the crowd and was quickly replaced by gasps of amazement as the lights of the museum slowly increased in intensity. Curtains rose from the alcoves as their own interior lighting switched on. The many displays were now shining in their full glory and it was truly a sight to behold.

Dr. Mayal walked off the podium and mingled with the guests, shaking hands and joining in their laughter and conversation. An aging man he recognized as a noted professor of Middle Eastern archaeology approached him.

"I noticed a statue of a worshipper from the Temple of Abu from Tell Asmar," the professor said in a quivering voice. "Is that authentic or a replica?"

"I assure you that all of the displays are the genuine, original articles," Dr. Mayal said in a voice loud enough to be overhead. "There are no replicas here."

"Even the golden helmet of King Meskalamdug, from the cemetery of Ur?" the professor persisted. "Surely that is a replica."

Mayal bowed his head in an honoring gesture. "You are most

10

astute, professor, in your identification. Yes, even the golden helmet of Meskalamdug is the bona fide article."

The professor expressed his amazement before wandering off to partake of the exquisite catered buffet. Another man, this one much younger, approached Dr. Mayal and shook his hand. "I have a question for you, Doctor, if I may. I have studied Ottoman architecture and know that the main cupola does not need a supporting beam, and yet this museum has such a pillar. What is its purpose?"

"An excellent question, young man. We have reserved that pillar for a special display. The main dome has a retractable door that will permit a shaft of light to shine down on a platform on the main level."

Those nearby perked up at the mention of such a feature. "What will be displayed in such a fashion?" a woman asked.

Mayal put his finger to his lips. "Ah! For the moment that is to remain a mystery. Mysteries are the spice of life, after all."

He moved through the crowd again and answered questions ranging from the simple to the complex. He confirmed that the museum was only at sixty percent capacity and that there was plenty of room for future expansion. He identified several of the more obscure artifacts. He even promised to name a display after one of the most generous contributors.

The orchestra finished its last song for the evening and he returned to the lectern for one final announcement. Everyone became silent and all eyes were on him.

"This museum will be filled with the glory of our past. I am confident that it will soon become the Mecca of museums displaying our history. As I speak, I have a series of archaeological groups scouring the Middle East, composed of only the best professionals that money can buy. We are leaving no stone unturned in our quest for greatness, our duty to find the most precious antiquities in existence!"

Chapter Two

The Zakhu Mountains
Northern Iraqi Desert
(Near the border of southern Turkey)

He could handle rainstorms and thunderstorms; during his work in the Yucatan he'd often had to. Living in Wyoming he knew exactly how to deal with sleet and blizzards. He'd even survived hurricanes, typhoons and tornadoes through the years. But he was sick of sandstorms.

He was huddled in a small alcove as he tried to clean his hands so he could rub his eyes. He knew this was the worst possible time but he couldn't help it. His eyes were red, tired and itchy and somehow rubbing them helped. He only managed to let in more sand before he replaced the goggles.

Four months. Four long summer months in the desert. It didn't seem right to say the dig was in Iraq; he was practically a stone's throw away from Turkey and Syria, and was suffering from all the inherent heat and dryness of the region. Today was a day of the Shamal, the local name for a powerful windstorm. It was the second Shamal since summer had started and he was roundly sick of it. The winds would last from three to five days and everything would grind to a halt. He'd studied the local culture for many years now and an ancient song came to his mind. '*The Shamal, the Shamal! Oh how your winds discipline us! How they teach us and chastise us. But we are hard-necked as we lean into you. We get slapped by you, yet we laugh, like a mother who punishes us, we get slapped, yet we laugh.*' Except he wasn't laughing anymore.

"Chauncy!" a voice shouted through the wind. "Get inside!"

He squinted through the sand and could just make out a silhouette. It was a large, portly silhouette and that meant Hakan, the dig leader. Chauncy Rollock gave a thumbs-up to the man and then waved him away, smiling. Hakan Ramush was the most distinctive of the dig's workers, but Chauncy came a close second. He wasn't tall like Hakan, more on the shorter side if anything. But his barrel chest and powerful body, made even more powerful by the years digging dirt in every imaginable situation, made him larger than most of the dig workers. Add to that his slightly graying blond hair and light blue eyes and he was easy to spot.

He might not be laughing at the Shamal like the song he remembered, but he was definitely excited and didn't want to take shelter just yet. Against all odds they had unearthed a small collection of ancient grain storage buildings barely two months ago. Dr. Faruk Mayal had selected Hakan as dig leader because Hakan had a reputation for having infallible instincts; it turned out to have been a very wise decision. Hakan might be a bit gruff and brooding but he'd personally led the digging and had found the first storage bin. He'd also silenced all opposition when the workers had complained. "We are looking for our history," Hakan had said loudly. "This is part of it. You never know what you might unearth that will someday be the prize of any museum." He'd then proceeded to curse and swear at the workers for being so lazy, but Chauncy had already stopped listening. He hadn't even needed the original pep talk.

Through the long dry spells, the lack of academic interest and funding, and yes, even through the sandstorms, *this* was the reason he had become an archaeologist. Revealing a piece of the past and trying to fit it into the puzzle of history. It was the closest he'd ever get to a time machine. In the coming hours and days he would catalogue each object, each piece of art and writing and learn much more about the society that had used this grain storage site. Earlier today they had unearthed a long series of rooms that had proven Hakan's words and instincts right again. These rooms had well-built archways, exquisite carvings on ivory pillars and plenty of evidence of long-gone Babylonian decorations. That meant these rooms hadn't been built for simple peasants or grain farmers, they had been built for royalty or a high-ranking dignitary. The things found in here could very well end up bringing a wealth of knowledge and prestige.

The sandstorm could rage its heart out; he was going to explore a little more today. There were nineteen rooms so far discovered and each one had been filled to the brim with rocks and rubble but had been devoid of artifacts. The ivory pillars and carvings were a delight, of course, and each was carefully catalogued. But there was nothing else here and that bothered him. Rooms of this magnitude should've had beds and benches, vases and pedestals, *anything* to show off the obvious wealth. It seemed like the rooms were emptied of their treasures and then filled up with rocks. It couldn't have been tomb raiders, he knew. They never would've bothered to put in the stones after they'd looted.

They'd dug out a new room today and there was something about it that was tugging at his mind and that was why he was braving the sandstorm. The rooms were buried beneath the desert sands and so technically he was standing on top of the building right now. He tried to wrap his cloak tighter but the wind wouldn't let him. He leaned into the wind and counted off the steps it took him to go from one end of the roof to the other. Several times the wind gusted strongly and he almost fell off. It was worth it, though, because he finally pinned down the problem: the room below was smaller than the others had been. The size of the roof, equal to all of the others, proved it. He'd paced off the room earlier in the day and there was a six-by-eight section in the back unaccounted for. That meant the room was extra reinforced, the missing space was purely aesthetic, or there was a hidden area back there.

Pictures of a gleaming hoard came unbidden to his mind and he chuckled softly. *Been chasing treasure in the Yucatan too long,* he chided himself with a smile. There were a dozen possible explanations for why the room had forty-eight square feet missing.

A figure loomed suddenly out of the sandstorm and Chauncy fell back with a curse. He cursed again when he saw who it was. "Abdul!" he shouted over the wind. "What are you trying to do, scare me to death?"

The short man smiled his idiotic grin. "No, no, Mr. Rolly, I come help."

Chauncy sighed. He'd tried a hundred times to get the little man to recognize that the name was *Rollock*. Or even to just call him Chauncy. It didn't work. But he had to give Abdul credit. While all the other workers had retreated from the storm, Abdul had braved the winds to come out and give him a hand. Maybe he wasn't so bad after all.

"You came just in time," Chauncy said with a rueful smile. "I do need your help. C'mon down and out of the wind."

They climbed down the ladder and retreated into the newly-opened room. It was cooler than the surface and there was no danger of death by sand particles. He pulled off his goggles and blinked several times. The reliefs and art on the wall were still present. It wasn't like they would have magically disappeared. He pulled out his flashlight and played the beam slowly over the back of the room. It was like a lot of Babylonian art and told the tales of various military conquests, most obviously embellished.

"What looking for, Mr. Rolly?"

"I'm not sure," he answered honestly. "This room should be bigger but it's not. I need to find out why."

Together they examined every inch of the back end of the room before finally finding the slight indentation of a hidden door. Abdul was suddenly apprehensive and refused to help open the door.

"What are you afraid of?" Chauncy asked. "The dead can't hurt you. My mother always told me to be afraid of the living, *they're* the ones with guns and bombs. Come on."

Abdul still hesitated. "You go first," he said finally.

Chauncy agreed and brought out a small crowbar. His heart was pounding as he worked the door open. He couldn't help the vision of treasure that floated in his mind this time, nor did he want to. It was like all the great movies and books. He wasn't in it for fame and fortune but it never hurt when such things came along. The find behind this wall could change history. He pulled the door open fully and stopped in his tracks.

"Grain baskets?!"

He stood there for several long moments, the shock rooting him in place. A laugh finally exploded from him as he shook his head. This is exactly what he deserved from all of his daydreaming. He moved his flashlight beam across the inky blackness. These walls were not filled with art or writings; they were instead whitewashed plaster. Due to the centuries of dust buildup they looked grimy instead of the pristine shine they would've had on the day the room was sealed.

Abdul, not afraid of ancient baskets, was moving quickly in and around the containers, grinning widely. Chauncy followed at a more subdued pace and tried to piece together the puzzle in his mind. The baskets were made of a wood or reed that wasn't local,

16

otherwise they wouldn't have lasted so long. He carefully opened one of them and nodded. Their contents were long gone, stolen by insects or simply disintegrating with time. Why would these baskets have been sealed off from the rest of the room? Why were the other rooms filled with rocks? It didn't make a whole lot of sense. Such efforts were usually done to protect something, but what could possibly have been so important about grain?

A sudden commotion and rattling snapped his attention elsewhere. "Sorry, Mr. Rolly, I trip."

Chauncy tried not to roll his eyes and waded through the sea of containers in order to help the assistant. Abdul had managed to trip on a basket and knocked several of them over. So much for the integrity of the find. Chauncy leaned over to pick up one of the baskets but stopped suddenly. Out of the corner of his eye he spotted something that was emphatically not a grain container. He kneeled down and had to blink several times to convince himself this wasn't a hallucination brought on by months of desert living.

A semi-large wooden chest lay toppled on the floor. It had been hidden in one of the baskets but Abdul's carelessness had brought it to light. The wood was a rich dark brown and it was definitely not local. It was probably imported from even farther away than the grain basket material. It was three-and-a-half feet wide and one-and-a-half feet deep and tall. Every inch of the wood was covered with artistic carvings and he felt his pulse racing again. He didn't immediately recognize the symbols. They were very similar to the Babylonian influence seen everywhere else in this location, but they were also different. He dug through his mental memory banks, trying to come up with a match. His heart really began pounding as he realized it was unlike anything he'd ever seen before. It had touches of Sumerian on it, as well as a possible Elam connection.

His hands were shaking so hard he couldn't hold the flashlight straight anymore. He handed it to Abdul and noticed for the first time that the other man's hands were shaking as well. He took one look at Abdul's face and knew it wasn't excitement that caused the tremor.

"What's the matter?" he asked sharply. Perhaps the little man had seen something he hadn't.

"Me scared," Abdul said, his throat working rapidly. "Box is

17

bad. Me go now."

"It's just a box," Chauncy said. "What makes you think it's bad?"

Abdul refused to answer so Chauncy leaned forward and carefully felt along the edges of the lid. There were four metal latches, probably iron, one on each side. None of the latches felt locked or trapped, however, so he carefully worked them all open. He could scarcely hear anything over the drumming of his pulse as he slowly lifted the lid. Once again he felt a sharp tug of disappointment.

"Nothing but cloth," he said. Still, the material would be ancient and might give some clues about whoever had built this grain storage. He reached in to grab the fragments and instead found himself holding something else. He rearranged the fabric and this time he wasn't disappointed. A golden cylinder lay amidst the rags, thick and elegant and ending in a conical shape. He peered closer and realized that the cylinder was made up of stacked rings, each with exquisite symbols carved on them. He lifted it up and was surprised at just how heavy it was. Both ends appeared to be broken. It was lovely, truly beautiful, and would be worth one heck of a sum to Dr. Mayal.

The beam of the flashlight was now dancing all over the room. "Abdul, keep your hands still, I need to see this!"

"Golden scepter," the other said, his voice sounding like he was walking through a graveyard on Halloween. "We must go! You die, Mr. Rolly, you go or you die. End of world!" Abdul jumped to his feet and dropped the flashlight. Its lens shattered and the room was plunged into twilight. Chauncy dropped the scepter in the box and snatched at the little man.

"What's the matter with you?" he demanded as he grabbed Abdul's tunic. "Have you gone insane?"

"It end of world. Hakan will kill you! He wants golden scepter, I heard him. He want end of world."

He stood up, gripped Abdul's shoulders and shook them lightly. "Pull yourself together and breathe. When did you hear this? Why would Hakan want the end of the world?"

"Evil...evil thing...end of world! Run, Mr. Rolly! Run!"

Abdul broke free of his grip and ran screaming from the room. Chauncy debated whether or not to chase after him but finally decided against it. Some long-held superstition or a misheard phrase had obviously convinced the crazy little man that this was the end of the world. Chauncy groped around in the dark and picked up the golden relic. Every culture he'd ever come across had stories and legends about the end of the world, from Armageddon to Ragnarök. None of them involved golden Babylonian scepters. Perhaps Abdul had cracked after all these months in the desert, or maybe he'd just been crazy all along.

He wrapped the scepter, placed it carefully back in the box, and lifted the whole thing under his arm. He paused and looked back around the room, thinking of how strange this dig site was. The hundreds of grain bins, the tons and tons of rocks and identical rooms...somebody in ancient times had gone to an incredible amount of effort to keep this scepter hidden. He felt a cold snake slide up his spine and shivered.

End of the world. Maybe he'd wait until tomorrow to tell Hakan about this new find.

Chapter Three

The bearded and portly Hakan Ramush was eating in the mess tent when he heard the wailing. At first he thought it was simply the wind, but several of the workers also lifted their heads up and looked around. "You hear that as well?" he asked.

They all nodded and began to speculate as to what the sound could be. Hakan, always a man of action, decided to find out personally. He strode from the tent and pulled his long shirt up over his face as he exited into the shrieking sandstorm. It took him several minutes but eventually he stumbled over the wretched little figure of Abdul lying on the ground.

"Abdul, you fool," Hakan shouted over the wind. "What are you doing? Get up!"

He leaned over to help the fallen man but Abdul shrunk away from him. "You kill Mr. Rolly," the idiot shouted, his hands shaking as he pointed at Hakan. "You kill him. It is end of the world!"

"What the devil are you talking about?"

"Mr. Rolly find golden scepter. I hear you say you kill him if he do!"

Hakan clamped down on the words he really wanted to say and quickly composed himself as a worker came out from the mess hall. "Quick, get the medic," Hakan ordered. "Abdul is having fits of hysteria. We cannot afford to dampen morale any further."

The medic arrived quickly while Abdul was still babbling and administered a strong sedative. "This is all I have at the moment. It will wear off in a few hours."

"Take him to his tent," Hakan said. "I'll deal with him later." He walked swiftly to his own tent, the largest one on the dig. Chauncy Rollock had found a golden scepter and not reported it, had he? Well, it was definitely a good time to pay a little visit to the archaeologist. He grabbed a few supplies that he would need and then ducked back into the howling wind.

The storm hadn't eased a single bit as Chauncy retreated into his tent. Thankfully no expense had been spared with the equipment for this dig; otherwise he might have worried that his domicile would blow away in these conditions. The ropes that held his tent in place were humming loudly and the extra rope was flapping in the breeze like a frightened pigeon. The noise would get distracting very soon so he went straight to his earplugs. He could still hear the wind and the flapping but at least now he could also hear himself think. He set the box on his field desk and dug around in the drawers. He brought out a couple of maps, a magnifying glass and two reference works. Only then did he open the box and really begin to scrutinize this strange scepter he'd discovered.

It was two feet and eight inches in length, and eleven inches in diameter. It was about the size of a loaf of French bread. The conical end, with the slightly-overlapping rings, reminded him of a reverse rattlesnake tail with a broken end. At the other end of the rings protruded part of a golden rod. He felt the jagged edge of the conical side and peered down inside. A plate beneath the broken last ring indicated that there was a chamber inside the end. He shook the object very carefully but there was no rattling sound. Whatever was inside the chamber was not loose, so it couldn't be jewelry or gems. He shrugged mentally and brought the magnifying glass over to examine the symbols on the rings.

There were winged lions and bulls with human heads, the typical Babylonian lamassu that were ubiquitous with the culture. But there were other creatures present, tigers, eagles, even crocodiles, and none of them were distinctly Babylonian in style. Other shapes and symbols were also visible, a cuneiform writing that looked to have features of several of the earliest languages, including Sumerian, Akkadian and Hittite. There was a definite mixture of cultures here, just like the box the scepter had been inside. He'd never seen anything quite like it. He would need to do a lot more research before he could attempt to decipher the meaning of the symbols and writing.

He decided to leave the symbols for later and returned to the physical makeup of the scepter. He carefully inserted a knife between the tapered rings but made no progress. He then tried to rotate the rings. The outer ring, the broken one, moved about an eighth of an inch but the others wouldn't budge. A pity. He really would have liked to see what was in the chamber. It was obvious that time, dirt and sand had rendered the object inert.

It was equally obvious that this scepter was not going to end the world. He shouldn't have listened to the idiotic superstitions of Abdul. This scepter was an astounding find, more than worthy to be shown in Dr. Mayal's museum. The combination of symbols from different societies might even help shine some light on early cooperation between the ancient Mesopotamian people. A stray thought latched into his brain and he grabbed his Bible. This scepter looked like it might once have been part of a much larger object, and with the obvious Babylonian influence he had an idea as to what that much larger object would have been...

A smile spread across his face as he came to the book of Daniel, chapter 3. He read aloud the first two verses: "Nebuchadnezzar the king made an image of gold that was 60 cubits high and 6 cubits wide. He set it up on the plain of Dura in the province of Babylon. Then King Nebuchadnezzar sent word to assemble the satraps, prefects, governors, advisers, treasurers, judges, magistrates, and all the administrators of the provinces to come to the inauguration of the image that King Nebuchadnezzar had set up."

His smile only grew larger. The plain of Dura was right here in Iraq. The giant golden statue of King Nebuchadnezzar had never been found but Chauncy knew he was now holding a part of it. This was the golden scepter that the image of the king himself would have been clutching. But what was it doing here, practically a stone's throw from Turkey? And how had Hakan known it would be here? Why didn't he tell him beforehand that there was a very good possibility something this grand would be found?

Because it was evident that Hakan *had* known. The fervor and drive that had accompanied this dig was way out of line with the simple grain storage they'd found. Chauncy had thought the large man was simply passionate about antiquities at the time, but now it was all coming together. Abdul *hadn't* been crazy; not about this, at least. His heart began thudding in his chest again.

Hakan will kill you. The words of Abdul echoed through his mind as he began to panic. There were no vehicles at the site; they only came every couple of days with supplies. He was in the middle of a desert that was in the throes of a deadly sandstorm that would last God-knew how long. He could try escaping but where would he go? He didn't have enough water to last him more than a handful of days. But he had to do *something*. He couldn't just sit and wait for Hakan to kill him. He would have to pack up a small suitcase with only the bare essentials and get out of here.

Then another thought came to him. He would need help. There was no other solution. But who on earth could he contact? Chauncy nervously searched through his wallet as he pulled out various business cards, tossing them one by one to the floor. He finally found the one he needed. The person he was looking for was living in Turkey. He fumbled for the satellite phone and dialed the number. After ringing a few times he heard an answering machine with a voice explaining how to leave a detailed message.

Blast! Chauncy thought. *I need a live person, not a recording.* He left a message anyway and quickly started looking for his luggage.

A heavy hand landed on his shoulder and he jumped from his chair, his shriek matching the wind. He twisted around and felt his throat tighten as he caught sight of Hakan.

"I see you have been keeping secrets from me," the large man said quietly. "You are a gifted archaeologist, Chauncy, but no infidel may touch the Golden Scepter and live."

Chauncy never saw the blow coming. His world melted into darkness as the windstorm bellowed and raged outside.

Chapter Four

Several hard jolts penetrated the darkness in his mind. His eyes creaked open and he noticed that he wasn't in the middle of the desert anymore. Sensations flooded his body and he realized that he was incredibly stiff, very sore, quite hungry, and had one *heck* of a headache. Those aches and pains only served to drive home the fact that he was, in fact, still alive.

He tried to sit up but discovered that he was tied securely. Well, that would go well with his last memory. But why hadn't Hakan killed him? He'd said that infidels couldn't hold the scepter and live, hadn't he? Chauncy searched carefully through his memory, ignoring the fresh headache that erupted because of his mental activity. Yes, that's what was said. It had been a clearly stated death threat, and yet here he was, still quite alive.

The big question now was how much longer he would stay alive. Another jolt ran through him and he realized that he was in the back of a large truck or van. The jolts were caused by bad road conditions. That also explained why his whole body was shaking: just the vibrations from travel. But his mind kept drifting to the undeniable fact that he was still alive and that he didn't have a clue how long it would last. The dryness in his throat and emptiness of his stomach meant that he'd been out for at least a day. He didn't want to die of thirst, and certainly didn't want to be in this predicament when Hakan decided to finish the job.

Wiggling around didn't seem to loosen the ropes any, but at least he figured out where the knots were. He was tied mummy-style, from his feet up to his neck, and there were five knots that he could find by the way they dug into his skin when he moved. Hakan had left nothing to chance. Sweat broke out all over his body and it was only partly due to the sweltering desert heat.

This wasn't looking very good at all. The ropes around his feet and around his hands, crossed behind his back, were looped around each individual limb instead of in the easy-to-loosen broader loop. He peered about in the darkened space to see if there was anything sharp enough to cut the ropes, but he knew within seconds that it was futile. There wasn't even anything abrasive nearby, let alone something sharp. The entire interior was covered with some sort of truck bed armor. He sighed heavily as he realized he was also tied to the bed itself so he wouldn't have much room to maneuver.

Well, at least he could spend the time analyzing his prison. He refused to think of it as his tomb. It looked like the surplus military trucks that brought the dig its supplies every couple of days. There was a large bed with a framework of metal poles that seemed like a cage, and over that cage was a tightly-wrapped dark tarp to block most of the sunlight. That was a bit heartening. If he could get unhooked from the bed he might be able to break through the tarp. That was the first good news he'd had since waking up.

He heard the telltale squeaking of brakes and felt his body being pressed against the head of the bed. They were stopping. That couldn't be good. He desperately tried to strain his way out of the ropes but it was pointless. He was hungry, overheated and weak, and he couldn't even turn far enough to try chewing any of the ropes. He heard doors slam and there was muted speaking that sounded oddly like Turkish. The conversation was interrupted by a sudden explosion that rocked the truck.

A beam of light stabbed into his eyes and his whole body tensed up. This was it. This was the end. He hoped it didn't hurt.

"C'mon Chauncy, at least move an inch," a gruff, hauntingly-familiar voice grunted at him. He opened one eye and stared at the figure that was climbing into the back of the truck. It was a man, that much was clear from the voice, but his face was covered in a full sand-mask complete with goggles. But the sound of gunfire outside, as well as a second explosion and possibly some drugs Hakan had given him confused Chauncy.

"C'mon, Chauncy!" the man ordered again as he brandished a knife. Chauncy tensed and squeezed his eyes shut again. Maybe it wasn't a rescue after all. The knife slit through the ropes holding him and hope returned once again to his world. He could barely move but didn't have much choice in the matter. His rescuer helped him get up and out of the bed, where the brilliant sunlight did its best to melt his eyebrows and singe his skin. He stumbled after the figure, barely noticing the other trucks around him, barely even hearing the gunshots in the distance. His rescuer said something that Chauncy couldn't hear but he sensed the urgency involved and tried to pick up the pace. His muscles were stiff from being tied up for so long and his legs were being rebellious.

An old Jeep was waiting down in a gorge near the road and the rescuer hopped into it. Chauncy fell into it, but that was good enough for the moment. He didn't even have a chance to buckle in before the Jeep roared to life and sent up a spray of rocks behind it. The rescuer was saying something but again Chauncy couldn't hear him.

"Get those plugs out of your ears!" the man shouted and finally he understood. No wonder everything had been muted. He dug the wax out of his ears and was blessed with a full auditory system again.

Chauncy slowly slid up to a sitting position. "Who are you?" he asked.

"I know it's been twenty-odd years," the man said as he removed his mask and goggles. The thin, sixty-something year old man was smiling from ear to ear. "But surely you remember Abydos. You just called me."

Chauncy let out a big sigh of relief. "Jake Thrasher, you old banshee, you slimy old goat, you! I was so out of it, I totally forgot I called you."

The man straightened up. "Ha! You haven't changed much from the young graduate who hired me to excavate Abydos. Well, you *have* gotten old."

"Yeah right," Chauncy snorted, rubbing his hands where they'd been bound. "Look who's talking."

Jake kept his eyes on the dirt road as he spoke. "So how did you know I was in Turkey?"

"At my going-away party my colleagues gave me your business card. Boy, was I shocked when I saw your name. That's how I knew you were still alive and kicking. Yet who knew I would be meeting up with you like this?"

"Well, I'm more kicking than alive these days," Jake chuckled as he surveyed Chauncy. "You look like a sheepherder who hasn't slept in days."

Chauncy gave Jake a sad smile. "I smell like one too. Plus I have a thundering headache from being hit on the head."

Jake took a quick glance at his cracked rearview mirror and

grimaced. "You may not have a head left unless you put it down!'"

Several bullets whistled past the vehicle and Jake turned the Jeep into a new direction. He reached under the steering column and pulled out a pistol, which he handed to Chauncy. "Use this!"

Chauncy stared at the unfamiliar weapon and felt a hollowness in his stomach. He wasn't used to shooting at people.

Jake must have seen the expression on his face. "These men will kill us, if you have a problem shooting at people who shot at you first, then shoot their tires."

Another stream of bullets ricocheted off their truck. Chauncy swallowed and turned around in his seat. *Shoot their tires*. Yeah right. He was in a rickety old jalopy careening across the desert and he had no proper firearm training. How was he supposed to shoot out tires on a truck that was also moving haphazardly about?

"Shoot, Chauncy, shoot!"

He took a breath, steadied the weapon, and fired off a couple shots. They didn't go anywhere near the other truck. He had the deep satisfaction of seeing the other driver swerve to avoid being shot. Maybe that would be good enough. He aimed toward the hood and squeezed the trigger five times. The other vehicle twitched violently and bounced off a rock. Even at this distance the sound of a tire blowing out was distinctive. He watched in equal parts horror and fascination as the truck spun out before flipping and digging itself into the ground.

Chauncy turned around and handed the pistol back to Jake. "Where are we going?" he nervously asked, trying to forget what he'd just done.

"Someplace safe," Jake answered.

"Safe? Are you sure?"

Jake shrugged. "I hope so."

Chauncy tried to get his ragged breathing and racing pulse under control. He sighed, looked out over the vast desert and marveled at its beauty. There were people who hated the desert and people who loved it but Chauncy was firmly in the middle. After spending too many winters snowed in at his Wyoming ranch he was glad to see a land devoid of moisture. There was a stark splendor to the mountain ranges on the horizon and the endless expanse of dirt and sand about them. It reminded him of an Ansel Adams photo: dark, foreboding and gorgeous.

The Jeep swerved a little and brought him back to reality. "What are you doing?" he asked in exasperation.

Jake was trying to drive with one hand while digging around in the back with his other hand. "I'm looking for something," he answered.

Chauncy rolled his eyes and turned around. "Why don't you just concentrate on driving and I'll get it for you. What are you looking for?"

"A sword."

It only took a few seconds for Chauncy to pull out a hefty sword. "Where did you get this?" he asked as he studied the weapon. The blade looked like it was made of solid gold and the hilt was made of carved iron covered in fading silver.

"I grabbed a few things from one of the trucks before I found you," Jake said, acting innocent.

"You wasted time picking up your fee first, before you rescued me?" Chauncy asked, glaring at Jake.

"A fee? Oh no, I found this on my own here. You didn't give it to me. You still need to pay me for your rescue. Those trucks we blew up as a diversion and hiring thugs to do it weren't exactly free, you know. Tell me about this weapon. It looks valuable."

Chauncy grumbled for a minute longer while he analyzed the sword. It was hard to think with a thundering headache. "Well, the design is pretty ancient and the hilt looks like it could be original Babylonian. The blade is not original, though. Gold is a poor metal to make anything that needs to withstand shocks."

"Couldn't it be ceremonial and still be original?" Jake asked.

"Oh, it's definitely ceremonial, but it's not original. The hilt has Akkadian and Sumerian symbols, and the blade does too, but the blade has a Latin phrase etched into it. '*Flamus Divinus.*'"

Jake looked deflated. "And Latin is definitely not as ancient as Babylonian. Why do you think they etched 'Divine Flame' on the blade?"

Chauncy raised his eyebrows at Jake. "You know Latin?"

"I'm Catholic."

"*You're* Catholic?!"

Jake shrugged. "Non-practicing. Now answer my question."

Chauncy looked back at the sword. "I don't know," he said slowly. "This worries me, Jake. These Akkadian and Sumerian

29

symbols are the exact same ones on the Golden Scepter."

"There's a golden scepter, too?" Jake asked, sounding excited. "Is it worth something?"

"It was worth killing me," Chauncy said grimly. "I'm still not sure why Hakan didn't just chop my head off after he called me an infidel."

"That's not an original insult around here, Chauncy."

"Yeah, but now I think it means something, especially with this Divine Flame business." Chauncy leaned back in his seat and closed his eyes. He was exhausted straight down to his core. "I only wish you'd gotten the scepter too. I don't like the idea of it being in Hakan's hands."

Jake chuckled and Chauncy cracked open an eye. "What's so funny?" Chauncy demanded.

"You mean the golden scepter that's in the box in the back of my Jeep?" Jake asked, his tone all innocent again.

Jake now had Chauncy's attention. "You banshee!" he said as he whacked Jake's shoulder. "Weren't you going to tell me about that?"

"Just thought it was another part of my fee," Jake said, still smiling. "We can talk terms."

Chauncy closed his eyes again. "No, no, the scepter isn't for sale. Once we get to our destination we can discuss your fee. Where are we going, anyway?"

"My place in Ankara, it should be safe."

"How are we going to get past the Turkish border?"

Jake laughed. "You forget who you're dealing with. The border has more leaks than my faucet; how do you think I got down here to begin with? No, Chauncy, it won't be a problem. Always have a back door, that's my motto."

Chauncy nodded and closed his eyes, his head pounding. He was so very, very tired.

***

Hakan stood with his arms folded across his stomach and glared at the seven men kneeling before him. "Who is in charge here?" he asked in Turkish. He repeated the question in Arabic, Kurmanji, three other variants of Kurdish, Zazaki and Armenian before switching to several European languages. There was no answer and he sighed, growing impatient. He stepped back and nodded at one of his armed assistants.

The sound of the gunshot hadn't even died down when one of the six remaining men answered. "We were hired for the job," he said in Turkish.

"Who hired you?"

There was silence again. Hakan was interrupted by two of his assistants driving back from the truck wreck. They were carrying the driver, who was in pretty bad shape. "Did you see who the rescuer was?" Hakan asked his injured assistant.

"I saw only that he wore a mask, Great One. I am sorry to have failed you."

Hakan rubbed his forehead. This was turning into a disaster. He'd had the Golden Scepter and he'd had Chauncy Rollock. He'd acquired everything he needed to bring glory to his people once again. Now the threads were unraveling. "I am going to ask one last time, gentlemen," he addressed the prisoners. "Who hired you?"

One of the men stirred. "Jake Thrasher."

Hakan hissed through his teeth. He knew that name. Thrasher was a minor black marketer who was occasionally helpful in acquiring certain things. Hakan would never have guessed that Thrasher was capable of this kind of operation. He walked back to his truck and signaled to his personal assistant. "Eliminate the prisoners and the incompetent driver," he ordered. "And alert every Ember. I want Chauncy Rollock back alive."

"And the other man?" an Ember asked.

Hakan held up Chauncy's satellite phone and glared at the last number Chauncy had dialed. It would take a while but he would have the number traced to the owner.

"Jake Thrasher will die," Hakan said.

Chapter Five

The name of the city that the Hittites gave it was *Ankuwash*. The Galatians and Romans named it *Ancyra*. During the classical Hellenistic and Byzantine period it was known as *Ankyra*. The Armenians called it *Enkare*. The Europeans knew it as *Angora* when the Seljuk Turks conquered it in 1073. It wasn't until 1930 that the Turkish Postal Servicer Law officially named it *Ankara*.

Chauncy already knew that it was a large city, second only to Istanbul, but he didn't know that it was filled with so many serpentine streets. He looked around as much as he could, his hooded robe obstructing his peripheral vision. The old was mixed with the new here. Jutted stone and brick buildings shared the same streets as sleek steel and glass constructs. The streets were packed with buses and cars and even an electric train.

It was giving him a massive dose of déjà vu. Twenty years ago he'd walked the dark side streets of Cairo with Jake Thrasher and had looked out at the mixture of ancient and modern. Back then he'd simply been a college student looking to impress a girl and prove his doctoral thesis; now he was trying to stay alive long enough to see that same girl again when he returned home.

He and Jake ducked down several side streets before stopping in front of an old dilapidated building with a wooden staircase leading up the back. "So this is your grand palace, huh? I see your tastes haven't improved since Cairo," Chauncy quipped.

"Like Cairo, Chauncy, this is just a front. My operation is much bigger than it was back then, but I don't flaunt my success here. Not in Turkey. There are too many hungry eyes."

Chauncy looked around at the lines of decaying structures, broken windows and piles of trash. It was just like any city anywhere else in the world: if you have money, you'd better not show it in front of those who *don't*. "I understand completely."

The ancient wooden stairs they climbed were so rickety that the squeaks could be heard over the traffic. A dark hallway awaited behind the door at the top. Loud music and conversation could be heard from behind poorly-sealed doors, and the stench of cigarettes and cigars was as permanent a fixture as the floorboards. They walked down the long hallway and stopped before a door that was as equally old and worn as the others. Jake knocked in a specific pattern and a few seconds later the door was opened by a man who was as old and worn as the door.

An exchange of Turkish went between Jake and the older man as Chauncy followed slowly. The decor was not what he expected. Large, heavy curtains were draped over the windows, blocking out all street lights and even most of the outside noise. Puffy, dark-colored pillows adorned the comfy-looking sofas. The wallpaper had Moorish motifs of faux mosaic interlocking tiles. Chauncy felt like he was walking on clouds as he made his way across the thick carpet.

Chauncy sank into one of the sofas while Jake held a conversation with the attendant. "So what are you doing in Turkey?" he asked as soon as Jake was finished.

"Business, what else? Things weren't going so well in Egypt so I moved here when the war started in Iraq. I've negotiated trade from Turkey to Iraq, stuff that is high on a soldier's want list. Cigarettes and whatnot."

Chauncy couldn't help but chuckle. "It's the 'whatnot' that you excel in, Jake."

Jake smiled and waved his hand dismissively. The attendant returned with a couple of Jake's signature drinks as well as an electronic tablet. Jake immediately began reading something on the tablet while Chauncy took a gulp of scotch-on-the-rocks.

"Well, this is interesting," Jake said suddenly. "Did you know that you're dead?"

Chauncy arched an eyebrow. "I'm way too sore to be dead."

Jake wordlessly handed the tablet over and Chauncy felt a strange sense of surrealism as he read the headline: *Thirty workers dead or missing in Turkish dig site disaster.* He looked up at Jake but the other just shrugged. Chauncy returned to reading the article, the sense of detachment growing with each paragraph that detailed the horrible fire that broke out at the Zakhu Mountains archaeological dig. All workers, including dig leader Hakan and consultant Chauncy Rollock, were burned alive during a sandstorm that knocked over a malfunctioning stove. The site was closed by the government pending further investigation.

Chauncy looked at the time and date of the article. It was posted four hours prior and already the international papers were picking up the story. There was even an opinion piece by some 'expert' windbag on how safety standards had been slipping recently due to budget cuts. He felt numb as he handed the device back to Jake and tried to start a conversation. He sank even further into the sofa.

"I can't believe it," he said slowly. His eyes were having difficulty focusing on anything. "Is Hakan really dead? And all the workers?"

"Not a chance that Hakan is dead, Chauncy. That's just the story he cooked up to cover his butt. He probably *did* kill all of the workers, though."

"Anita!" Chauncy said suddenly, standing up as the thought struck him like lightning. "My wife will read this and be heartbroken. I have to call her."

"You can't," Jake said, standing up and blocking his path. "Chauncy, use your head. Hakan will be tracing any calls made to your family."

"I don't care," Chauncy said as he desperately tried to get around Jake. "I can't have her thinking I'm dead. And Troy! He can't lose his father, not at his age."

Jake grabbed his shoulders and shook him. "Try to think, Chauncy. If you call your family you'll be putting *them* in danger. You'll be putting *us* in danger. Do you want to *really* be dead after Hakan finds us?"

He took a deep, shuddering breath. "Have you ever been married, Jake? Or even in love?"

"Thought I was in love both times I was married," Jake said as the attendant appeared, also blocking Chauncy's path. "I turned out to be wrong."

"Then you don't know what it's like. I can't put Anita or Troy through this kind of pain. I love them, Jake, more than I love archaeology or anything else."

"But you aren't putting them through this pain. Hakan is. I can get a message to your wife and son but you can't ever call them."

Chauncy collapsed onto the sofa and rubbed his eyes. "But she's going to be so upset."

"She'd be even more upset if Hakan catches up with us. This way it will only be brief, until I can get word to her. Trust me, Chauncy."

"You're asking an awful lot of me. Why should I trust you? You tried to sell me out in Abydos."

Jake rolled his eyes and spoke quietly. "That was twenty years ago, Chauncy. You keep forgetting that I saved you then and I saved you now. I'm an underworld scoundrel but I have a *little* honor. Besides, Hakan needs to be stopped."

"Why?" Chauncy asked, trying to get his mind to work properly. "How do you even know him, anyway?"

"He's an extremely ruthless and cunning man," Jake answered. "I've had my eye on him for a few years now. He's at the top of the underworld game in Ankara. He's behind a whole lot of quiet murders, black market rings, thefts, abductions, bombings...you name it, he's probably done it."

"I don't believe it," Chauncy said quietly. "I always thought there was something a little off about him, but never would have guessed it was this bad."

"Like I said, he's cunning. He uses a string of aliases and I doubt that there are even a handful of people who know his real nature. His public profile is exactly why he was in charge of your dig: he's fluent in almost all the Middle Eastern languages and his academic record is amazing. He's almost a genius and happens to be evil."

Chauncy felt a shiver go through him. He'd been on that dig for several months, never more than a hundred yards away from Hakan. It was like suddenly finding out your next door neighbor was a wanted serial killer. "Why is he so evil?"

Jake shrugged. "Why is anybody evil?" he asked in return. "Might have something to do with Babylon. The sword I found was in his personal truck and obviously meant a lot to him. And he just killed himself off, so to speak, in order to get his hands on a Babylonian golden scepter. *That's* something I need to look into."

"Do you think Hakan would have killed me? And if so, why didn't he just toss me in the fire with the other workers?"

Jake smirked. "Oh, he would've killed you. Why he didn't in the first place, it's probably because he thought you might still be useful. You *do* have a pretty good reputation as an archaeologist.

Hakan is not in the habit of destroying things until they have ceased being important. Maybe he thought he could torture some information out of you."

"I need to find out why, Jake," Chauncy said with conviction. "Why is this scepter so important? He gave up an extremely prestigious and lucrative job with Dr. Faruk Mayal for this scepter. He's cut himself off from the future, gambling everything on this. There's got to be one heck of a reason for that and I'm determined to find out what it is."

Jake leaned back in his sofa. "What's your game plan? I don't have the space for a roomie, you know."

"As long as you get word to my wife and son, I might as well take advantage of being officially dead. I need to move undercover and try and figure out what's so important about this scepter. Nobody tries to kill me and gets away with it."

"Even if it ends up killing you for real this time?"

Chauncy tried smiling. It seemed to help a little. "I've dealt with Mexican cartel lords, Mayan kings and *you*. What could possibly be worse?"

"It's not a laughing matter, Chauncy. What's your next step?"

"I know a man who might be able to help me. Only problem is that he's in Germany."

"That means you'll need a fake passport and the services of a smuggler."

"Any of your acquaintances do that kind of work?"

This time Jake smiled. "You're looking at him."

"You branched out, huh?"

"I have a bad habit to support: scotch ain't cheap. Speaking of cheap, how do you plan to pay for all of this?"

"You've got the sword for starters," Chauncy said. Somehow, Jake's refusal to do anything for free only made Chauncy feel better. His worldview might have received a severe shock recently but some things would never change. "Once we figure out what the scepter is we can sell it to Dr. Mayal. That should keep both of us rich for a long time."

"Assuming we can evade Hakan and get any proof we need to expose him, right?"

"Assuming that, yes."

Jake looked at his watch. "The sun will be up in about four

hours. Get some rest while I arrange some details."

"So you're going to help me?"

"For the right sum I'll do just about anything, Chauncy, including smuggling you to Germany. Now get some sleep."

Chauncy followed the attendant to a small side room. He felt comforted and hopeful for the first time since he'd found the scepter.

Chapter Six

The black curtains had been pulled back to let in the morning sun as Chauncy shuffled to the dining table. He could smell exotic spices wafting out from the kitchen and the wonderful aroma of *coffee*. His body practically ached for the black gold as he sat down at the table and poured a steaming cup. He drank slowly, allowing the hot drink to work its magic on his sore and tired muscles.

Jake was nowhere to be seen so Chauncy took a few moments to look around. The place looked different with fresh sunlight streaming in. The colors and motifs that had been dark and foreboding last night were now bright and cheerful. The artwork now seemed inspiring instead of depressing. He wasn't sure if it was the sunlight or simply the improvement in his own demeanor that wrought this change in the decor. Maybe it was the coffee. He didn't know but he liked the change.

The code-knock broke his concentration and the attendant opened the door for Jake. The older man smiled and sat down at the table with Chauncy.

"Got some great news for you," he said without preamble. He opened a folder and slid a small card across the table. "You're a brand new man."

Chauncy picked up the photo ID and stared at a picture of himself from many years ago with a different name next to it. "Sidney Morrison?" he asked, incredulous. "Isn't Sidney a girl's name?"

"I knew a hitman who would take issue with you on that," Jake said with a broader smile. "Cheer up, it's not like it's your real name. It also has some of the same phonetic sounds as yours so you'll react to it quicker. Chons-*ee*, Sidn-*ee*."

"Yeah, that's real easy," Chauncy said with a rueful smile. "I guess I'll get used to it. Where'd you get this picture?"

"From your driver's license, of course. You were sleeping like a log."

Chauncy wanted to protest; it wasn't right to take somebody's stuff while they were sleeping. But the job was done and he didn't have to wait, so there wasn't any real point in making a fuss about it. "Don't they hang people for forgery around here?" he asked instead.

"Yes, and it would be *both* of us swinging by our necks. Both the forger and the customer are liable, and you, son, are my customer. I've been doing this for six years now without an incident. I don't think they'll catch on just for this case."

"I hope not. What's the plan, then? How are you going to smuggle me into Germany?"

"By ship," Jake said, getting up and going over to a nearby cabinet. He pulled out an electronic tablet that displayed a map. "You'll be on a merchant ship. There's one leaving from Istanbul tomorrow night that will be loaded to the gills with frozen fish and other seafood. You're already on the employee roster, and if push comes to shove you can hide out in the freezer. It won't be comfortable but you'll survive. The ship will head out to the Mediterranean, make deliveries in Italy and Spain, and then head up the English Channel to its final destination, Hamburg. Where are you going after that, anyway?"

Chauncy smiled. This was working out perfectly. "That *is* where I'm going."

"What do ya know, I'm better than I thought I was. I'm going to have to go over a few of the finer points with you, but for the most part you'll be fine as long as you don't draw attention to yourself."

The attendant came from the kitchen at that moment, bearing a large china tray with excellent-smelling food. He passed in front of the window and a burst of gunfire shattered the tray and ended his life. Chauncy stared at the fallen man in shock, his mind not accepting what had just happened. The silence was broken by a barrage of bullets and he dropped to the floor.

A dull thud sounded from the doorway and his pulse spiked. Somebody was trying to break in! A crack appeared in the wood as the thud was repeated. Bullets flew sporadically into the room from the street below. Artwork, decor and drywall crashed all around them, kicking up white dust that flew into his eyes.

"Where's the back door?" he shouted at Jake, who was also on the floor.

"I don't have one!"

"What? Are you kidding me? You, Mister-Always-Have-A-Back-Door? What do we do?"

"Follow me."

Jake got up on his hands and knees and scurried to the bedroom, Chauncy barely a second behind him. The older man dug around in a large dresser, pulling out money and passport. Chauncy was relieved to discover that he was still carrying his new passport. Jake then grabbed the sword and the case with the scepter. "Carry these!" he ordered as another thud rocked the house. Jake turned and headed toward the closet.

"Oh, this is original," Chauncy said, his heart in his throat. "They'll never think of looking in the closet!"

***

The reinforced door splintered into a dozen pieces as the battering ram connected for the fourth time. The two men with the ram immediately forced the splinters out of the way and entered the room, their rifles at the ready. Hakan entered the room after another four men rushed in. Long gone was his look from the dig; now he was dressed in full ceremonial attire: a long black robe and a golden turban. He ignored his robe as it tried to catch on all of the debris and bent over the dead man near the window. He scowled heavily. This was neither Chauncy Rollock or Jake Thrasher. His marksmen in the street below had killed the wrong person.

He stood up just as his attendant entered the room. "There is no one here," the attendant announced. "Nor is there any sign of the scepter or your sword, Great One."

Hakan clenched his hands into fists and swore quietly in four languages. "Tear the rooms apart," he ordered. "Leave nothing untouched."

The attendant bowed and barked the order to the others as Hakan strode purposely to the largest room in the house. That Chauncy Rollock had been here was evident from the clothes in the smallest room. This large room obviously belonged to Jake Thrasher. Hakan studied the room carefully, his eye not missing any detail. There was no back door to this building, and all of the

41

windows had been covered by his snipers. Jake and Chauncy couldn't possibly have disappeared into thin air. A man like Jake would never have a domicile without a retreat. Nobody survived more than a year in the black market without a rabbit hole.

He walked over to the main closet, which had been wrenched open by his men. They had torn the clothes to make sure nobody was hiding behind them, but they had failed to notice the most important part of the closet. Hakan kneeled down and pursed his lips. The dust pattern was wrong and it only took him a second to locate the trap door.

There had been a hand-cranked elevator here, but now there was not. He pulled out his handgun and yelled for his attendant. He was not going to lose the scepter again.

***

Chauncy breathed through his mouth as they moved quickly down a tunnel. He really wished he had a hand free to cover his mouth, but the wooden box that contained the scepter was heavy. "An escape elevator is a great idea," he said, his voice muffled. "It really is. But why did it have to lead to the *sewer?*"

"If it led to the ground level," Jake said, splashing swiftly through the smelly muck, "we would already be dead. What's the point of an elevator that leads you right to your enemies?"

"Yeah, but the sewer?"

"Just be quiet and keep moving," Jake said. "It won't take Hakan long to find this getaway."

"I'm sorry about your attendant," Chauncy said after a moment of silence.

"So am I. He was a wise and discreet man."

"What do we do now?"

Jake shook his head and paused in a shaft of light. He peered up through the grate on the street above but couldn't quite tell where they were. "I have some friends who can pick us up, but I don't want to do it in broad daylight. The question is if Hakan will charge into the sewer after us, or whether he will stay up top and wait for us to reappear."

A distant splash echoed through the tunnels. "I guess that's our answer," Jake whispered. "C'mon, Chauncy."

Chauncy tried to move quickly without making noise. It wasn't easy. Jake switched to an outright run and Chauncy followed suit, giving up all pretense of being quiet. He had to give up trying to take small breaths as well. The stench overwhelmed him and it took a supreme effort to suppress his gag reflex. *It's better than getting killed, it's better than getting killed, it's better than getting killed* he repeated to himself.

A gunshot echoed through the tunnel and Jake made a hard turn left. He pointed at the ladder barely visible on the wall. Chauncy grabbed his shoulder and pushed him to the ladder. Another gunshot roared in the semi-darkness and ricocheted off the bricks. Jake moved up the ladder at a speed that was impressive for an older man and Chauncy had a hard time keeping up.

Jake pushed open the grate and a blinding ray of sunlight streamed in. Chauncy jerked his head aside and felt a sudden rush of heat on the back of his head. Adrenaline kicked in and he threw himself up the last few rungs. He looked around frantically while Jake tried to catch his breath. They were in a small back alley somewhere, with huge apartments in front and back and two major roads to the left and right. A small metal pipe caught his attention and he rammed it in the handles of the sewer grate.

Jake grabbed Chauncy and pushed him toward the street. "That's not going to hold them for long," he said. "We need to get out of here."

"But where to?" Chauncy protested. "In case you hadn't noticed, this is broad daylight; you know, where we don't want to be running around!"

"Does it look like we have a choice?" Jake snapped.

They were about to exit the alleyway when a man with a rifle rounded the corner. He barely got out a Turkish expletive as he tried to raise his rifle. Jake's right arm shot out and crunched the man's nose. He didn't stop for even a second to see what he'd done, he simply turned and ran into the street.

Chauncy jumped after him, his heart thumping an unhealthy number of times. Cars honked and screamed past them but somehow they made it to the median. Various groups of people on the sidewalk were staring and pointing. The rifleman with a broken nose opened fire and the pedestrians scattered for cover. Jake dove into the traffic again. Chauncy swallowed hard and followed.

The shots were being fired blind and none of them came close as Jake and Chauncy ducked into another alleyway. He was too out of breath to ask Jake what the plan was. He was just going to have to trust the old scoundrel. He didn't realize he was praying until that very moment.

They ran for fifteen minutes, ducking in and out of alleyways and shops. No other gunmen appeared and no bullets came near them during that time. Jake exited the rear of another shop, went up to the street and hailed a taxi. Jake gave directions and then collapsed into the back seat, where both men tried desperately to catch their breath. Five minutes later the taxi came to a stop and both men got out. Jake led the way down yet another alley and then into a small brick building. A few minutes later they were beneath the streets.

"Why are we down here again?" Chauncy asked, trying to catch his breath while not breathing.

"They'll never think of looking for us down here twice," Jake said.

"You sure about that?"

The older man shrugged. "Worth a shot, anyway. This part of the sewer system isn't connected to the other, and it leads to a few places where we can lie low until night." Jake paused and turned around. "I'm not as young as I used to be," he said quietly. "I hope Hakan doesn't chase us all the way to Germany."

"'Us'?" Chauncy asked. "You're coming with me?"

Jake managed a thin smile. "I'm not sticking around; my cover's been blown. I guess you could say my Ankara office location is officially closed."

Chapter Seven

Hakan was fuming as he drove back to his apartment in Ankara and the thick traffic on the streets wasn't helping his mood either. He had failed twice in securing the scepter. Chauncy and his friend were turning out to be rather challenging. But Hakan had faith. He knew the scepter would eventually land in his hands and no infidels were going to thwart the plans of his true god.

Since there was nothing better to do in the traffic, Hakan reflected on how this had all started. Two years ago he was in Saudi Arabia looking for work as a supervisor of archeological digs. That was when he met Bahir Hashimi.

Mr. Hashimi had invited him over to his estate for dinner. It was during dinner that Mr. Hashimi confided to Hakan that he was a member of an old religious sect known as the *Flamus Divinus Adventum*. His boss then explained the history and prophecies of the sect, including details about the Golden Scepter that would bring the *Flamus Divinus* into ultimate power.

Hakan had expressed his disbelief at the whole story. But when Mr. Hashimi thoroughly explained the scientific principles of the scepter, Hakan was ready to change his mind. He needed the job, too, so he joined the Divine Flame and worked hard. Over time he became a believer and rose rapidly in rank until his current position, that of the Great One. It was a heavy responsibility but a great honor.

A great honor that might come crashing down if he didn't get his hands on that scepter. Everything he'd learned and all the prophecies were coming true, except for the fact that he no longer had the Golden Scepter.

His cellphone rang and he took a deep breath. He'd been expecting this call.

"What is the status?" The voice on the phone did not sound amused.

Hakan tried to keep his voice from shaking. "Exalted One, they have escaped. We lost the battle but the war is far from over."

There was a brief silence. "You had the scepter in your hands Hakan!"

Hakan eyed the traffic while he spoke. "I know, Exalted One. But we have many Embers who will track them again."

"You have one more chance, Hakan." A second later the line went dead.

Hakan threw the phone onto the seat next to him. Even if it cost him his life, he was going to make sure the scepter was back in his possession.

Cheyenne, Wyoming, USA

It was a truly beautiful day, a cloudless jewel that was rare for this time of year. It was cruel to have such a pretty day on such a sad occasion. Anita Rollock looked out at the small sea of people gathered for the funeral and felt her throat tighten. It simply wasn't true, she kept telling herself. Chauncy couldn't be dead. They said denial was unhealthy, but they hadn't faced a loss of a spouse when *they* had said that.

She had ignored the sermon that was given; she'd heard the words many times before for others and it changed very little. Instead she thought about her loving husband and how he was still alive. It wasn't just denial that told her this. The official report from Turkey left much to be desired; there were all sorts of unanswered questions. The small box of ashes they'd sent back could have been from anyone or anything. She was going to keep convincing herself that her husband wasn't dead.

She also needed to be strong for Troy. She looked down at the boy—no, the young man—that was her son. He was twelve years old, about to be thirteen. She knew that the death of a parent aged children rapidly and she couldn't bear to think of how this was affecting him. What if Chauncy really was dead, and she planted false hope in her son's mind? Would that hurt him worse?

It was overwhelming. For seventeen-and-a-half years she'd had the warmth, love and support of a truly wonderful spouse, a man who'd considered her his equal and his best friend. It still took her breath away to think about how he'd been so suddenly and brutally taken from her. Now she was going to have to fill out a whole heap of documents and try to piece together a life without the man

46

who'd made life worth living.

She pushed that out of her mind and put her arm around Troy. He didn't squirm away as he normally would, ashamed to be seen hugging his mother. "Life is ironic, son," she said softly. "Way too ironic."

"Real ironic or Alanis Morissette ironic?"

She had to smile at that. It was something he'd been saying for several years now and it buoyed her spirits to hear him making a joke at a time like this. "Probably a little of both. You remember when your father was working with Dr. Sova in the Yucatan, right about when he was kidnapped? After that ordeal he confided to me that all along he'd really just wanted to be a Biblical archaeologist, and so that's what he specialized in. He said it would be safer. He was chosen for this job in Turkey because of his knowledge of that part of the world...all because he is a Biblical archaeologist."

Troy looked off into the distance at the Medicine Bow mountains. "That's close enough to real irony, I guess. Mom...do you think Dad's really dead?"

Her heart skipped a few beats. His thoughts had been mirroring her own. For a moment she was paralyzed. Should she confide her hopes, and risk crushing him? "I don't know," she said honestly. "I really don't know. The official report from Turkey has so many holes in it...I don't know what to think. I hope and pray he's still alive."

"Me too," he confessed. "He made it through Mexico alright, and that was drug lords. If he died saving the world it would be different. I don't want him to have died in a stupid accident."

She didn't know what to say to that so she hugged her son tighter. Her close friends Gloria and Marlo Gund were still steering the guests and media away from her, and for that she was very grateful. She was having a hard enough time just talking to her son. She was watching the parking lot which is why she saw the black limousine drive in and come to a stop.

Nobody she knew had access to a limousine. She didn't think anybody in the whole town had access to a limousine. She groaned inwardly. It was probably lawyers or somebody equally annoying coming to pester her about Chauncy. Didn't anybody have any decorum?

The driver stepped out and opened the rear door. The man who emerged was not what she was expecting. He was tall, judging by how high he stood next to the limo. His suit looked expensive even from this distance. Thankfully, Anita's friend, Marlo, was right there to redirect this odd visitor and Anita smiled in relief. She wouldn't have to talk to whoever he was.

She turned her attention back to her son. Troy was gazing off into the distance, an intense look on his face. "What is it?" she asked quietly.

"In the old days, I would be the man of the house, wouldn't I?" he asked with a catch in his voice.

She smiled even though her heart ached. "That phrase isn't really used anymore," she said. "Why?"

He looked at her for a moment before turning his gaze back to the mountains. When he spoke, his voice was very quiet. "I'm not ready to be the man of the house."

She closed her eyes against the tears and held him close. Of course he wasn't ready. He wasn't even a teenager yet. She hoped that he would make it through this okay.

Somebody cleared his throat and she blinked, startled. She looked up to see a tall, dark man standing nearby. "Mrs. Rollock?" he asked, peering at her over the rim of his expensive-looking spectacles.

"I don't know how you talked your way past Marlo," she said angrily, "but I'm not in the mood to talk. Can't you see I'm consoling my son?"

"I am very aware of that," he said, his tone apologetic yet firm. He spoke with a thick accent that she couldn't identify. "And I am so sorry for your loss. This world needs all of the archaeologists it can get so we can learn from the mistakes of the past. However, I have some vitally important information about your husband."

Her heart seemed to lift a few feet. "What information? What do you know?"

The man looked over his shoulder. "I do not feel comfortable discussing it here. May I meet you at your house?"

"What kind of information is it, mister...?"

"Doctor," he corrected with a smile. "Doctor Faruk Mayal, director of the Institute of Antiquities of Ankara. I see you recognize the name. It was I who hired your husband for the dig. I presume you have read the official report on the so-called accident?"

She squeezed her son's shoulders and stood up. "Yes I did. It was filled with gaps."

"Precisely. That is why I am in your country. The Turkish and Iraqi governments are collectively refusing to give me access to my own dig site, or any more in-depth information about what went wrong. I have many friends in academia here and some of them even have political power. I have spent the last week trying to pull every thread I can. I have not uncovered much, I'm afraid, but I what I have found out I think you deserve to know."

This was the chance she'd been waiting for. A quiet fire had been burning in her as she'd continually been denied access to information about her husband's fate. She'd first learned of his death in the newspapers, for crying out loud, and that just wasn't fair. But standing here in front of her was one of the most influential men in the world of archaeology. If anybody could get answers, he would.

"As soon as everyone else is gone, I will be leaving for home. You may follow me."

He bowed his head low. "Thank you."

***

It was evening by the time they made it back to the house. A wave of melancholy washed over Anita as she looked at the place she'd called home for nearly a decade. She and Chauncy had designed it together and had it custom-built to spec. He'd wanted to add influences from all sorts of cultures and even now, so many years later, she could identify which parts of the design were inspired by which ancient societies. The block entryway she led Dr. Mayal through was definitely Egyptian. The sofas and chairs in the living room were Byzantine and the tea set she used to serve was covered with Scandinavian runes.

"I assume the designs in here were selected by your husband?" Dr. Mayal asked after sipping the tea.

"We selected them together," she answered. "But they were mostly his idea."

"You both have exquisite taste," Dr. Mayal complimented. "Your husband's reputation is why I selected him for the dig."

"Speaking of which...?"

His face became serious and he set his cup down. "Are you sure you want your son to be present for this? It might not be easy to hear."

She looked at Troy. He was sitting in the large chair, ignoring his tea as usual. He showed no signs of wanting to leave and confirmed it with a small shake of his head. "He'll be fine. What do you want to tell me about my husband, Dr. Mayal?"

"Please, call me Faruk," he said before taking a deep breath.

Anita nodded. "And please call me Anita."

Dr. Mayal continued. "I have managed to look deeper into the circumstances of the accident that claimed the lives of all of my team. There are a few things about it that do not make sense, and everything looks far more sinister now that I have discerned information about my dig supervisor."

"What do you mean? Who was your supervisor?"

"I hired a man named Hakan Ramush because he is an intelligent man well-known in archaeology. He supervised over two dozen prior digs in Turkey and the Middle East. However, this appears to be a front. Only yesterday I learned that there is a collection of brutal illegal operations in Turkey that might be associated with Hakan. He pulled the wool over the eyes of the archaeological community for years. Do you really think he would allow himself to be killed in a fire?"

Anita shivered involuntarily. "You're saying he started the fire." It wasn't a question.

"It certainly seems that way."

"But why would he kill all of the workers? Why would he kill my husband?"

"That is where things become less clear, Anita. I chose his team to search in an area that was rumored to hide a Babylonian golden scepter of immense value. I picked him, and your husband, for this project because their reputations were excellent. If the Golden Scepter were found it would be an incredible boon for me, and for Turkey and the Middle East as a whole. We have a rich and varied history, a history that is being forgotten in today's world, buried beneath senseless wars, terrorism and religious zealotry. My museum aims to bring that history once again into the mind of the world, to show East and West that we are not simple, violent brutes. Mesopotamia is the cradle of civilization and I hope one day we can bring that to the world's notice once again. That is why I have nearly three hundred men on digs throughout all of the Middle East."

"It certainly is a noble mission," Anita agreed. "But why would Hakan kill for the Golden Scepter?"

"In my research I came across a mention of an ancient religious cult surrounding this scepter. It is possible that Hakan is either part of that cult, or more likely he is working for them. However, my research suggests that the cult began dying out about the time that Rome fell. If Hakan is not associated with them, then he would steal the scepter for its worth on the black market. In either instance he would not hesitate to murder anyone in order to get his hands on that scepter."

"And you think Chauncy found the scepter?"

"It is very likely. That is one of the reasons I wanted to speak to you in your home. Did you receive any emails or messages from Chauncy regarding his work on the dig? Did he mention finding a scepter?"

She shook her head. "He only sent me a couple of emails and none of them said anything about finding something important." Anita was having intense thoughts about the injustice and wasn't particularly interested in the scepter. "If Hakan murdered my husband I want him brought to justice."

Dr. Mayal nodded emphatically "I share the same feelings, Anita. Hakan was in my employ; that does not bode well for my reputation or my museum, does it?"

"I suppose not."

"I have spent millions of dollars to make my museum a success. I am not going to let a foolhardy criminal such as Hakan ruin things for me. I will fight to my last kuruş to get justice...both for myself and for you."

"But what can we do, Faruk?"

"We are not without options, Anita. Knowledge is our ally. I will be speaking with some more of my friends tomorrow and see if I can get access to my dig site. If I can see what was going on I might be able to decipher whether or not the scepter was found. I do not wish to raise false hope within you, Mrs. Rollock, but if your husband found the scepter it is entirely possible that Hakan kept him alive. Every piece of information I can get about this debacle will increase our chances of bringing Hakan to justice. Are you absolutely certain he never sent anything to you?"

"I'm positive," she said. "What can I do to help?"

Dr. Mayal seemed frustrated. "If any of your friends or your husband's colleagues have political power, now would be a good time to start calling in favors."

"I don't think we have any political pull," Anita said. "But where are my manners? Would you like to stay here? We have a guest suite in the east wing to accommodate both you and your chauffeur."

"I would hate to impose upon you and your son. This is a difficult time for you."

"You're helping me find out what happened to my husband, Faruk. There is no imposition. Please, it would be a great honor if you would stay."

Dr. Mayal bowed his head like he had at the funeral. "Then I graciously accept. Your hospitality and generosity will not go unrewarded. I will send my chauffeur back to the hotel so as not to be even more of a burden. Let us hope that, together, we can decipher this riddle and bring justice to all parties involved."

Chapter Eight

Hamburg, Germany

"Quit fidgeting!" the voice of Jake Thrasher hissed near his ear.

Chauncy Rollock tried to stop twitching, he really did. But he'd been stuck in the bottom of a merchant vessel for what felt like forever and now he was cooped up in the backseat of a tiny European car. The seat wasn't big enough for one person, let alone two. He wasn't usually claustrophobic; he'd crawled around in tunnels barely larger than a coat hanger on expeditions. Maybe it was nervousness. He didn't believe for a second that Hakan had lost their trail, no matter how many times Jake tried to convince him otherwise. The thought of a dangerous man determined to capture him and regain the scepter was more than enough to set him on edge.

The car came to a stop and the driver said something in German. Jake paid the fare and finally they got out. Chauncy looked around with a distinct feeling of disappointment as Jake herded him into the tiny shop. No matter where he went in the world he ended up in the bad part of town. Of course, it was usually in the bad part of town where Jake operated so that probably shouldn't have surprised him. The shop was old but not nearly as old as anything in Turkey. Germany had a lot of history to it, a history he found intriguing, but he was used to dealing with the ancient as opposed to medieval. He knew that all of Europe had some pretty ancient history as well, but it wasn't something that leapt to the front of his mind when he thought of ancient history.

He almost walked into a display case near the register and shook his head. If he didn't get his head out of the archaeology clouds *he* was going to be history. The display case had several types of briefcases in it and one of them would be large enough to house the Golden Scepter. He unwrapped the box and pulled out the phone that Jake had given him. It would be significantly less conspicuous to carry the scepter in a metal briefcase than in an ancient, carved wooden box...but that didn't mean the symbols on the box were no longer important. He'd had experience with symbols in the Yucatan and knew that anything could be a clue. He took pictures of the box from every angle, inside and out, upside down and right side up. He then wrapped the scepter in the rags and rushed over to where Jake was haggling with the store owner.

"Can't you see I'm busy?" Jake growled when Chauncy pulled on his sleeve.

"Here, can you sell this fancy wooden box, too?" he asked without apology. "Just make sure and get enough to buy that large metal briefcase over there."

Jake nodded and Chauncy went back to looking around the shop. The fine layer of dust that lay over everything went well with the musty smell that seemed to hang about the place like tapestries. It was all a facade. The items for sale here in this 'antiques' shop merely had the appearance of old. He peered closely at one of them, a clay teapot claiming to be Scandinavian. It was a cheap modern knock-off from China, just with added dust and scrapes to make it look old. The rest of the shop was exactly the same. He wondered if the shop ever made any real sales to curious but ignorant tourists, or if it was funded entirely by the type of transactions Jake engaged in.

He found a chair that was supposed to be of Grecian origin and sat down very gingerly. It didn't collapse under his weight but he wasn't sure how long that was going to last. He partially unwrapped the scepter and looked intently at it. *What is so wonderful about this?* he asked himself. *Why is this worth killing for?* Maybe it was solid gold, but even that didn't seem a good enough reason. He was an archaeologist, not a murderer or a thief. His reputation was as golden as the relic he held in his hands, which is why he was chosen to help find it. Why would simple knowledge of this artifact be a death sentence? Why would a man as brilliant as Hakan be willing to throw away the rest of his life just for this one piece of history?

There was obviously a reason, he just didn't know it. He stared at the Akkadian and Sumerian symbols on the scepter, willing them to give away their secrets. There was not yet a rhyme or a reason to the carvings that he could make out. He would match his archaeological knowledge against just about anybody's in the business and he was fairly certain he could at least give them a run for their money, but this? This was getting out of his depth and he was humble enough to admit it.

How did he keep getting mixed up in these kinds of things? He'd only ever wanted to pursue his love of antiquities and the past while providing for his family. He never wanted to get involved with Mexican drug lords or deadly Turkish imposters.

His self-pity party was interrupted by Jake, who was grinning from ear to ear. "Great call on that box, Chauncy. It more than doubled what I was going to get for the sword alone. Get that scepter into the briefcase and follow me to the back of the store."

"Why, what's in the back of the store?"

"The *real* store. Clothes, equipment, computers, everything you're going to need to survive."

Chauncy went over and pulled the largest briefcase from the display and carefully, almost gently, put the still-wrapped scepter inside of it. He snapped the latches shut and felt more secure. He followed Jake to the back of the store, through a convoluted hidden doorway, and stopped short, his jaw falling open. The room was about two-thirds the size of the main store and was absolutely crammed full of every type of merchandise. "Where did all of this come from?" he asked, stunned.

He immediately closed his mouth and nodded. "Never mind." If Jake Thrasher was anything to go by, he knew where everything had come from. He hesitated for a minute. He wasn't entirely comfortable purchasing stolen goods.

Jake must have read his mind. "You weren't ready to shoot people either, Chauncy. Your life is on the line here. Now get some clothes and anything else you think you'll need."

"How much of an allowance do I have?" Chauncy asked with only a tiny bit of sarcasm.

"As much as you can carry."

So Chauncy went and bought several changes of clothing and a new pair of shoes. Jake paid for it all and before long Chauncy was decked out in his new clothes and feeling better for it. He still needed a shower, but that could wait. He sat back down in the allegedly Grecian chair in the front of the store and pulled out his phone.

"What's your game plan now?" Jake asked.

"There's somebody in town that should be able to help me with this...problem," he said. He put in a few search terms and a street map of Hamburg showed up.

"You know somebody in Hamburg? Someone you can trust?"

"Why do you think I wanted to come here? It certainly wasn't for the food."

"Come on, there's nothing wrong with German food," Jake said with a smile. "Who's your friend?"

Chauncy looked around. "I don't want to discuss that at the moment. I have the address." He handed his phone to Jake, with the map and address clearly visible.

Jake studied the phone for a minute before handing it back. "Won't take long to get there. I'll get us a cab."

"Shouldn't you be heading to America with a certain message?" Chauncy asked.

"Only after I see you safely to your destination," Jake said with a mischievous grin. "You might find trouble if I'm not around."

Chauncy was going to fire off a sarcastic retort but it died on his lips. He *had* managed to get into a whole mess of trouble and couldn't blame it on Jake. He owed his life to Jake, in fact. "You're probably right," he said instead.

Jake called a taxi service and they stepped outside after a few minutes of waiting. The sky was overcast and dark, with the kind of clouds that spelled certain rain soon. Chauncy shivered from a cold burst of air but suddenly felt great. After being stuck in the deserts of the Middle East for so long, it would feel good to experience some rain.

After they'd crammed into the backseat and Jake had given directions they resumed the conversation. "Who are you going to see that you think will help you?"

Chauncy shrugged his shoulders uncomfortably. "His name is Erick Hausen. He's the CEO of Future Engineering Technology."

Jake lifted his eyebrows. "How do *you* know the CEO of a high-tech company?" he asked incredulously.

"When I was in the Yucatan I was mentored by Doctor René Sova."

"Who?"

"He was an incredibly intelligent man. He single-handedly deciphered some Mayan glyphs on an ancient temple."

Jake shrugged. "So, what does that have to do with this guy in Germany?"

"Dr. Sova belonged to a group called SSOSA, the Secret Society of Savants Association. Erick Hausen is a member."

Jake laughed and looked out at the city they were passing through. "A secret society of eggheads. I've heard it all."

"There are secret societies for killing people," Chauncy said defensively. "Or ruining lives or hoarding money. Why not one where the people try to better themselves?"

"Take it easy. What does this SSOSA do?"

Chauncy was still rankled. "Every three years they'd have a Mind Game. The position of initiator would rotate and the initiator would send out symbols that the others would have to try and interpret. Dr. Sova took me along and showed me one of the games, which is where I met Erick and the others."

"What was the point?"

"To test their intelligence. Bragging rights. These men are incredibly intelligent, Jake. Normal people like you and me wouldn't stand a chance in their games."

"So basically, they just want to be reminded that they are superior to everyone else."

Chauncy bit his tongue and thought of a diplomatic way to respond. "They wanted a challenge. There is a small reward for winning, but it's insignificant. It was the pursuit of knowledge that they cared about, not showing off. If they wanted to show off they would have joined MENSA and made fun of the name."

"What's wrong with MENSA?"

"It means 'stupid girl' in Spanish. Smart people calling themselves a stupid girl? Not very smart."

Jake chuckled for a moment. "Why do you think this Mr. Hausen will be able to help you? Just because he's smarter than MENSA?"

"He's a brilliant engineer with access to a huge amount of technology, most of it not available to the general public yet. I think he should be able to at least point me in the right direction. And if not, he's about the only person that I can trust with this."

"You're forgetting about me."

"Do *you* have any idea what this scepter is?" Chauncy countered.

"Haven't a clue."

"Well, then, there you go."

He felt Jake studying him for a few minutes. "You've grown up more cynical than I would have expected," Jake said finally. "You were bright-eyed and naive when we last met."

"I was in my twenties and nobody had tried to kill me yet," Chauncy said heavily, closing his eyes against the stream of people and cars outside.

"Yeah, that'll do it to you. Let's hope we can keep that to a minimum from here on out, right?"

Chauncy grimaced. "Yeah, right."

***

The video screen flickered in and out of focus before resolving itself into a picture of two very familiar men.

"Are these the ones you spoke of, Great One?" the voice on the other end of the connection asked.

Hakan's smile lit up his face. "Yes, those are the targets," he said with great enthusiasm. "When did they leave?"

"Five minutes ago, Great One. I made sure the briefcase they bought had an activated GPS tracker. Was that the right course to take?"

"It was indeed. You will be richly rewarded, Ember. Keep up the good work."

Hakan closed the connection and quickly went over the information he'd just received. So, Chauncy and Jake had run all the way to Germany, had they? He'd anticipated them going to Europe and had flown to Rome in preparation. He could be in Hamburg in less than two-and-a-half hours.

He closed his laptop and moved quickly. This was his chance to get the scepter back. Once Chauncy and Jake were dead, and the scepter was his, glory could finally return to his people.

His smile widened. History was about to be rewritten, and it was going to be his hand that did the writing. He couldn't wait.

58

Chapter Nine

The fire alarm screeched through the house like a wounded banshee and Anita catapulted right out of bed. Her heart pounded furiously as she reached for her robe. She grabbed her cellphone and scrambled madly for her wallet as she headed for the door. She paused for a moment and felt the engraved wood; it was cool to the touch so she opened the door. Her face was immediately assaulted by a heavy layer of smoke. She coughed and dropped to her knees, vague emergency training piercing into her mind. "Troy!" she shouted at the top of her lungs as she scrambled down the hallway.

There was no immediately visible fire and she wondered where it had started. She felt along the wall and flipped the light switch. The kitchen was devoid of fire. She dug frantically through the linen closet and got out two towels. She took a deep breath and stood up, plunging the towels into the sink. Her lungs were just starting to ache when Troy crawled into the room.

"Mom, I have a fire extinguisher."

She got back down, crawled to her son and wrapped him in a quick hug. "There's too much smoke," she said over the sound of the alarm. "We need to leave. Take this towel."

Troy looked aghast as he covered his head with the wet towel. "But...but—"

"Don't argue," she said ordered sternly, her pulse quickening as flames crept into her peripheral vision. "What is more important: your stuff, or your life?"

Troy obeyed and Anita quickly scrambled to a nearby desk. There were some things that were worth saving, so she pulled out a leather attaché case that contained their passports and birth certificates. "Let's go!"

Troy grimaced but nodded. She turned to crawl to the back door when a sudden realization hit her like a lightning bolt. "Dr. Mayal," she yelled, horrified.

Contingency plans raced through her mind as she thought of the house layout. The fire was creeping slowly toward the kitchen from the living room and the front office; it might have reached the hallway leading to the guest suite already. If she went that way she might not make it safely. But she couldn't just leave a guest to burn, either, especially one who might know what happened to her husband.

Her husband. Her mind suddenly became crystal clear with a clarity she hadn't known since he'd been reported dead. This fire was no accident. Whoever had killed, or tried to kill, Chauncy was now coming to get her, her son and the only link they had to answers: Dr. Mayal. That meant they might have already killed him. She prayed that they hadn't, but now she suddenly knew what to do. She herded her son quickly out the back door and into the night. The cold air bit into her skin and managed to find its way through her robe. She ignored it and made sure that Troy was safe in the gazebo before taking the fire extinguisher from him. She sprinted to the east wing of the house and smashed the guest suite window open. A thick cloud of smoke came boiling out of the window and she had to step back, coughing.

"Dr. Mayal!" she shouted, praying desperately that the poor man was still alive.

There was no answer and she climbed through the window, covering her mouth and nose with the wet towel and breathing slowly. She strained to see through the darkness and was thankful that at least the fire hadn't yet reached this room. There was, however, a glow underneath the doorway and she knew her time was short. She went straight to the bed and shook it.

"Over here," a muffled voice came from underneath the covers.

Anita wrenched the covers off the bed to find Dr. Mayal huddled in a ball, his hands covering his face and head. She took a deep breath and gave him the wet towel. The glow under the door was getting brighter and the smoke was really starting to sting her eyes. She grabbed his arm and pulled him along with her, moving as quickly as possible to the window. It took a lot of trial and effort to get the doctor through the new emergency exit, but she managed it. She had to half-drag, half-push him to the gazebo where Troy was waiting anxiously.

"I called 9-1-1," Troy said, holding up his cellphone. "They should be here in soon."

A few minutes later they heard a distant siren. Anita made sure that Dr. Mayal was breathing properly and checked his pulse. He'd probably inhaled a lot of smoke. He tried to say something but she ordered him to conserve his lungs. She fussed over him for a moment, making sure that he would survive long enough for the paramedics to take over. She then sat down heavily next to her son and wrapped him in her arms, tears streaming down her face as reaction and emotions finally hit her.

She'd lost her husband and now she was losing the house they'd built. The black smoke billowing into the black sky perfectly mirrored her feelings. Everything was going up in smoke. Her hopes for the future, her thoughts of the past, everything was a twisting vortex of darkness. The pain threatened to overwhelm her, to choke off her oxygen as the smoke had. She couldn't give in to depression; she had a son to take care of. She had a guest to look after. She was all that was left to hold back the tide and keep her family together. She shouldered the burden with difficulty as the tears continued to fall.

The firefighters came less than ten minutes later but it was ten minutes too late. They did their best, of course, but the fire was simply out of control. She'd had to retreat further back from the gazebo to avoid the sparks and the smoke that continued to flow from the place she'd called home. The medics gave them fresh oxygen and strapped Dr. Mayal to a gurney.

"He inhaled a lot of smoke," one of the women said, confirming Anita's earlier diagnosis. "We're going to take him to the hospital. Is he family, or..."

"He's a friend," she answered. "Can we come with him?"

She suddenly realized that she really wanted to go to the hospital with Dr. Mayal. There was nothing left for her here. It would be better to just go to the hospital where she could not see the ruined husk that used to be her home. She would also feel like the worst host imaginable if she didn't accompany him. And so they piled into the back of the ambulance, a medic, Dr. Mayal, her and Troy.

It was a tight squeeze but Troy didn't seem to mind. He looked about at all of the instruments and high-tech gadgets with a look of wonderment. That was good. She didn't want him focusing on what had just happened. She'd tried to instill in him the importance of not getting too attached to *things*, but that didn't mean the training had held. She snorted softly as she looked out the back window of the ambulance and saw the fire still consuming the structure. She had always tried to not be attached to things, and yet here she was, sick to her stomach over the loss of her house.

Dr. Mayal held on strongly, even improving slightly, on the twenty-minute ride to the hospital. They wheeled him into the ER and told Anita and Troy to get checked out. One of the nurses gave her a medical gown to put on under her robe, apologizing that they didn't have anything better at the moment. The nurses checked her and her son and deemed them both to be okay, remarking that they were lucky to not have gotten any smoke in their lungs. By the time they were released, another nurse came and told her that Dr. Mayal was being admitted for overnight observation. He had urgently requested their presence.

He smiled weakly as they entered. "It is good to see you," he said. His accent was deeper and he was harder to understand, a testimony to how much he had recently suffered.

"I'm glad you pulled through," Anita said, a genuine smile on her face. "I'm sorry to have been such a bad hostess."

"What do you mean?" he asked, puzzled. "You saved my life."

"After inviting you to stay and then letting my house burn down," she answered with a laugh.

He shook his head and motioned for her to come closer. "That fire was no accident. Remember what happened at the dig?"

The hair stood up on the back of her neck. The dig in Turkey had been consumed by a fire. The man trying to find out what had happened had stayed at her house, and then her house was burned to a crisp. It was obvious that Faruk did not believe it was a coincidence and neither did she. She spun around suddenly, half-expecting to see armed men barge in on her. But there was no one there but her son, who was hunched over in a chair.

"Can you walk?" she asked quietly, leaning in closer to Dr. Mayal.

"With a little help, yes," he answered. "I think we should do this quickly."

She went over to Troy and whispered some instructions. He was half-asleep but he nodded and shuffled out into the hallway. Moving swiftly she went back to the bed and helped him up, first to a sitting position and then standing. He had to lean heavily on her at first but was determined to keep moving. She walked to the door and peeked out. The hallway was deserted and Troy was lingering near the end of the hallway, ready to provide a distraction if necessary. He held up four of his fingers and pointed down the hall and to one side. Her heart swelled with pride at her young man. Four doors down on the left there was an empty room.

Troy was walking over and she gave him a quick hug. Her mind raced furiously. She'd worked here for a few years, but that was before Troy had even been born. The hospital was an old building, however, and it was unlikely that they would have changed things all that much. That meant the break room and the lockers would be down the hall and to the left.

Her heart pounded with fear and excitement. She knew that what she was doing was technically illegal but it didn't matter to her. Five minutes later she was dressed in scrubs and felt much better. Stealing clothes barely qualified as a crime; she had friends still working here and could just say she was borrowing them until something better came along. The next part, however, was going to be very difficult. She would have to steal an ambulance or other emergency vehicle in order to escape, and she would have to do so undetected. She'd never done anything like this in her life. The adrenaline pumping through her was making her feel shaky, but at the same time this was so much fun. It was like *The Fugitive*, just with no Harrison Ford or Tommy Lee Jones in sight.

"You do not need to do that," Dr. Mayal said when she outlined her plan. "My chauffeur is still at the hotel, remember?"

"Can you trust him?" she persisted.

"He has been with me for three decades. I have trusted him with my life before."

She felt a little bit cheated, but mostly relieved. She didn't want to get caught stealing an ambulance.

"You were going to steal an ambulance?" Troy asked, his eyebrows practically touching his hairline. "Who are you trying to be? Doctor Richard Kimble?"

She felt even sillier but also impressed. Her son had followed her exact reasoning and even located where she'd gotten the idea. He was going to be a genius when he grew up. "It was just a thought."

"And if my chauffeur were not available, or otherwise

untrustworthy, it would have been our only hope," Mayal said, wheezing slightly. "I have already called him. He will be here in five minutes."

"It will be less suspicious if I push you around in a wheelchair," Anita said. "We will be practically invisible here."

Dr. Mayal nodded. "That is a good idea. I am not so sure I can walk all that far just now."

"Are we going to talk more about what happened?" Anita asked, looking over her shoulder. She kept expecting dangerous villains to be stalking her. Probably just a lack of sleep.

"I do not think it is safe to do so here," Dr. Mayal said, closing his eyes and leaning back in his new bed. "Wait until we are safely on the road."

Anita nodded and sat down heavily on one of the chairs. It felt like there was a heated metal ring of pain around her head at about eyebrow level. Rubbing her temples seemed to help relieve some of the pressure, but not much. She was still in shock. Her house had burned down less than an hour ago. Her husband had been reported dead less than a week ago. Things were moving too rapidly for her to keep up and react to them. She still hadn't properly grieved for her husband because she was still in denial. Her house, however...there was no denying what her own eyes had witnessed. She kept thinking she was going to wake up at any minute and it would have just been a spectacularly bad nightmare.

"What are we going to do now?" Troy asked.

Anita nervously toyed with her cellphone. "I need to tell our friends, Marlo and Gloria that we are okay. And I need to talk to the fire officials, I don't want them to think we started the fire."

Dr. Mayal shook his head. "You do not have time, Anita. Do you realize what you are up against?"

Anita stopped what she was doing and looked at Dr. Mayal, she was nervous and scared but now she was angry. "No I don't. Who are these people anyway? I want answers and I want them now."

A small beeping sound brought her back to reality. Dr. Mayal pulled a small cellphone from his pocket and glanced at it. "He is here. Let us talk in the limo."

She took a deep breath and steeled herself as she helped Dr. Mayal into a wheelchair. Getting him out of the hospital without incident was going to be tricky. If anybody stopped her she was going to have to spin some kind of story to get them off her back. But what story would she concoct?

She never had to figure it out. The hallways were mostly empty and when they got to the south entrance the receptionist merely waved at her with a cheerful smile.

Once they were in the limo Dr. Mayal ordered the chauffeur to drive out of the small town.

Anita was still furious. "I need closure," she said..

Dr. Faruk turned to look at her. "What did you say?"

"I said I need closure. I want to know why my husband died," she said, raising her voice.

"How do you plan on doing that, Mom?" Troy asked.

"I'm going to the dig site."

"Anita, do you realize what you are saying?" Dr. Mayal asked, his tone incredulous.

Anita clenched her fists. "Of course I do. I want to personally see the camp with my own eyes. I can't and won't believe Chauncy is dead until I see the scene myself."

"Anita, this cult is dangerous," Dr. Mayal said in an attempt to dissuade her. "Look what they tried to do to us here in the United States!"

"Who are these people? Who is this cult?"

"They are known as The Divine Flame. They get their name from the Latin *Flamus Divinus.*"

"Who cares about the name? Why did they want to kill my husband? Why couldn't they just get what they wanted and let him go free?"

Dr. Mayal looked genuinely frustrated. "Who can understand the minds of people like that? Look, Anita, I understand the life of a human is more important than any relic I can fill my museum with. But do you really want to risk your life, and the life of your son, for this?"

That thought made her pause, but only for a second. "They've already   tried   to   kill   us," she said, her voice strong. "I don't think they're going to give up, so we're in danger no matter where we go. I need to see the dig site, Faruk. I need proof, one way or the other, about my husband's fate."

Dr. Mayal sighed. "I can see that there is no dissuading you. To tell the truth, I am grateful. You and I have the same goal: justice. I believe it will be in our best interest to travel together to the dig site."

"I appreciate the offer, Faruk, but I can do this on my own."

"I have no doubts about that, Anita, but I urge you to think about it. I know the authorities in and around Turkey and Iraq. I have the legal right to access my dig site, even if they do not want to grant it to me just yet. You are an American and a woman and it will be difficult for you to get anyone to listen to you in that part of the world. If we work together we can both get what we want."

They argued back and forth about the details all the way to the Denver airport. In the end, Anita relented. All that really mattered was that she was going to Turkey, and she was going to get answers.

Chapter Ten

The glittering stainless steel and glass structure towered above the Hamburg city skyline, a sleek yet imposing symbol of the power of its owner. Erick Hausen had designed the building to be a perfect representation of the business and computing world. The security system of the building exceeded what would normally be expected in a business, even a technology business. Before Chauncy made it fully into the lobby there was a small beeping sound from the floor and two guards appeared from thin air.

They spoke a warning in German. Chauncy must have looked as lost as he felt, because one of the guards switched to English.

"All recording, tracking or otherwise traceable technologies must be checked at the main desk."

His heart rate returned to fairly normal levels. "Oh, okay," he stammered slightly. "Where is the—never mind, I see it."

The guards escorted him to the main desk where both he and Jake deposited their respective cellphones. The receptionist held out his hands expectantly and Chauncy looked at his briefcase. "Oh, there's no technology in here," he said as firmly as he could. His hands were shaking now and that was not a good impression to be giving. He tried to steady his hands.

The receptionist narrowed his eyes. "That is not what the security panel is saying. You have a GPS device in there."

Chauncy looked at the briefcase, utterly baffled. "All I have is an ancient archaeological relic," he said slowly. "From long before satellites were invented."

"There is a broadcasting GPS device in your briefcase," the man said, his voice suddenly turning as hard as the building's steel. "You can either relinquish it, or you can leave the building immediately."

Broadcasting GPS device. Reality hit him like a ton of bricks and he exchanged a glance with Jake. The older man had apparently just reached the same conclusion. They were being tracked by Hakan.

"Uh-oh," Jake said.

The two security guards reappeared and took a firm hold on his shoulder. "Tell Erick Hausen that Chauncy Rollock is here," Chauncy said as quickly as he could. "My life is in danger. *His* life might be in danger."

"Mr. Hausen does not have time to meet people who do not have appointments," the receptionist said, his voice even firmer than before. "And we do not waste time with persons who do not sequester their technology."

"*Einen Augenblick*," a voice said from the intercom. "Is that really you, Chauncy?"

Chauncy looked toward the intercom. "It's really me, Erick," he said, smiling despite the danger they were in. "I'm in a bit of a bind at the moment."

"*Ach so*! It is better than being dead as I thought you were. *Friegeben!*"

The guards immediately let go of Chauncy and Jake, but one of them objected to Erick. A conversation in German ensued that Chauncy didn't have a chance of even trying to understand.

"Chauncy," Erick said, startling him. "Do you need that briefcase?"

"It is very important that the object within doesn't fall into the wrong hands," Chauncy said, trying not to look accusingly at the guards or receptionist.

"Did you activate the GPS tracker?"

"No."

"Is there sensitive equipment within the briefcase?"

"Sensitive to what?" Chauncy asked.

"I plan to disable the GPS tracker with EMP. Do you have a laptop or computer inside?"

"No, nothing like that at all."

"Please put the briefcase on the blue countertop."

Chauncy did as instructed. A moment later there was a quiet whining sound and the tiniest spark came from the briefcase. "*Vollbracht*," Erick said. "Is the man with you coming along?"

"If we've been tracked here then I'm in trouble too," Jake said. "Erick can surely deliver the message for me so I can stay."

"Please move quickly," Erick said before launching into a short German speech. The guards stepped into escort position and pointed to a row of elevators. Chauncy walked toward them, managing to admire the interior design of the building as he walked. Everything was smooth and elegant, including the elevators. The guards pointed them to a specific elevator, one that had EH in a fancy monogram on the doors.

Once inside there was only one button to push, so Chauncy pushed it. It was one of those express elevators that were so smooth he didn't even realize they'd started until they'd stopped and the doors opened. There was a very short hallway leading to another engraved elevator. The doors opened as they approached and it lifted off without their input.

The doors opened and Chauncy gasped. The view was *amazing*. The Elbe River and Hamburg's vast port was less than a mile to the south, and beyond that were trees and smaller cities. Coming into the city he'd been struck by the vegetation and the predominance of green, but up here it was even more startling. He could almost feel the dust and grime of the Iraqi desert melting away from his memory.

Erick Hausen stood up from behind his desk and smiled. He was tall and lanky and looked a decade younger than his sixty-seven years. "Why are you not dead?" the German engineering genius asked.

"Sorry to disappoint you," Chauncy said, returning the smile and looking around. The art and furniture matched the lobby and the building: stainless steel, glass, and modernism.

"Oh no, my friend, it is not disappointment," Erick said, coming around the desk to grip Chauncy's hand in a firm handshake. "We did not spend much time together, but René Sova's trust in you spoke volumes about your character. When I read that you had perished, *Lieber Gott*! I was dismayed. Who is your friend?"

"Erick Hausen, this is Jake Thrasher."

The two men shook hands before Erick peered closer at Chauncy. "You have a lot of explaining to do, but allow me to fill in some gaps." Chauncy felt like he couldn't keep any secrets from Erick's grayish-blue eyes. "You are legally dead, which means that you traveled here using a fake passport, probably being smuggled in through the port. I am assuming that Mr. Thrasher here supplied one or both of those services. That means you are on the run, since you are a man of good character and not the type of person who would normally engage in such illegal operations. Your alleged death occurred on an archaeological dig, which coincides with the gold rod-type object in your briefcase. You could have been smuggled inconspicuously without said rod. Therefore, I can safely assume that the rod is, in fact, related to your troubles and is probably the reason you are here."

"What do you mean, a man of good character wouldn't do illegal operations?" Jake objected. "Are you saying that I'm not a man of good character?"

"You aren't," Chauncy said, looking at Erick with awe. Listening to that summary made him think of Dr. Sova and a flood of memories came to him. He felt privileged to once again be in the company of a SSOSA member. "How did you know there is a golden scepter in my briefcase?"

Erick's smile grew broader. "Standard security process, Chauncy. All briefcases and purses are scanned and analyzed as they are brought into the building. The golden scepter, as you called it, was deemed to not be a bomb. Otherwise, you wouldn't have even made it to the lobby. May I see the scepter?"

Chauncy placed the briefcase on the desk and unlocked it. "Before we begin talking about the scepter, I have an urgent request to make."

"Please, proceed."

"I need a message delivered to my wife and son, informing them that I am alive."

Erick rubbed his chin. "I assume you want this message to be as private as possible?" he asked.

"I can't have anyone else intercepting the message or they will be put in danger."

"It will be difficult. I would normally initiate a secure email, but I am assuming that you do not have either of the programs I normally use for such a conversation. With a message of this importance it is generally best to deliver the message by hand."

Chauncy grimaced and looked back at Jake. "That's what I was going to have Jake do. I thought maybe you could arrange something instead."

Erick rubbed his chin. "I have one or two colleagues in America that might deliver the message, I suppose," he said

70

slowly, obviously thinking hard. "Is there anything that you would say to your wife, a private code or something that only she would understand?"

Chauncy perked up. "Yes, and it's only three words. *'My little Xochitl.'* It means flower."

Erick tilted his head slightly and smiled. "That sounds like Aztec. What is that language called? Nautle?"

"Nahuatl," Chauncy corrected, smiling as well.

Erick sat down at his desk and began typing. He asked for clarification on the spelling and pronunciation of the Aztec word and then pressed several buttons. After a moment he stood up with a look of satisfaction. "It is done. A colleague of mine should be delivering that message to your wife within several hours. Now, may I see the scepter?"

"Thank you so much," Chauncy said as he handed the object to Erick, who took it as carefully as if it were fine china. "You've lifted a great weight off my shoulders."

"I am happy to help," Erick said as he ran his fingers over the conical rings of the scepter. He was obviously interested in the object. "This is constructed extremely well. The symmetry and ergonomics are obviously a part of the design. These rings intrigue me."

"I was able to move the top one about an eighth of an inch when I first examined it."

Erick glanced up, his eyebrows rising. "Really. That is an interesting piece of information."

"Why?" Jake asked, stepping a little closer to look at the scepter.

"Well, the top ring is jagged, obviously a result of being damaged. But if you look inside you will see a plate that prevents us from peering into the interior."

"I noticed that plate as well," Chauncy said. "I thought there might be jewelry or something inside the scepter."

Erick shook the device slightly. "No, it is unlikely to be a holder of jewelry. Do you see the line in the plate?" He held it up so that the other two men could look at it.

"Huh," Chauncy said. "It looks like an overlap. I didn't notice that when I first examined it."

"Does that mean there are two plates?" Jake asked.

"Or perhaps even more," Erick answered. "This overlap means that if the top ring were to move a certain amount of degrees, it would open and reveal the section beneath."

"Why don't you think the scepter holds jewelry, then?" Chauncy asked.

"Because I am fairly certain that the rest of the rings are movable as well, which means there is very little room at the bottom of the scepter to hold jewelry, even though the bottom does appear to be a reservoir. In addition, I sincerely doubt that this was a typical way of securing ancient valuables."

"You're right on that account," Chauncy said.

"What are the markings for, then?" Jake asked. He appeared slightly more interested than usual.

"Here is a question: what did Chauncy use to open his briefcase?"

"A code. Are you saying the symbols are part of a code to unlock the scepter?"

Erick shrugged. "It is not impossible. The fact is that there are different symbols and animals on each ring, and that each ring apparently moves to reveal the next layer. If you know the right symbols and animals to align, you would get to the bottom."

"The first Rubik's Cube," Chauncy said with a grin. "Except with something in it."

"Wouldn't you simply have to rotate each ring until you found the next section, and then repeat until you got to the bottom?" Jake asked.

"That depends entirely on how it is constructed," Erick replied, turning the scepter over and over in his hands. "If it is a simple half-plate turning design, then yes that is possible. If it is more complicated than that, however, you would need to have the proper sequential order. It would be more like a rotating combination lock in that regard. Also, look at the top. It has been broken off, allowing us to view the plate that has opened. I assume that when it was intact you would not have been able to see your progress, and therefore it would have taken a lot longer even with a half-plate design. This item intrigues me greatly, Chauncy, and I thank you for bringing it to me."

"If the rings can't be moved, we can't get to the bottom. What do we do now?"

"There must be something of great value in the reservoir," Erick said, speaking mostly to himself. "Something that the designers did not want the wrong people to access. Yes, this scepter very much intrigues me. There is much to be learned. Come along, my friends, to my laboratory and let us see what secrets this scepter shall reveal to us."

Chapter Eleven

The elevator plummeted toward the bottom of the building and Erick finished making an announcement in German. "I have cleared out the laboratory of all personnel, so we may research this in private."

"You sure you want to stop all work? Won't that look suspicious?" Jake asked.

Erick shook his head. "There is no other way to ensure confidentiality when you have a large number of scientists and engineers running about. Do not worry; I have evacuated the premises before, usually during a Mind Game. The employees are accustomed to my eccentricity."

"So what were these Mind Games about?" Jake asked. "Chauncy mentioned them to me. They sound like a waste of time."

"Jake!" Chauncy said, aghast.

"*Nein*, it is okay, Chauncy," Erick said, holding up his hand to stop the argument that might have ensued. "To the layman it is indeed a waste of time. Those of us in SSOSA think otherwise. We never consider it a waste of time to exercise the brain. The Mind Games are part competition, part education, where we all learn from one another. We do not do it for bragging rights necessarily; otherwise we would make it a public thing. The betterment of oneself and one's world view, Mr. Thrasher. That is the essence of the Mind Games."

Jake seemed to absorb that information. The elevator reached its destination and the doors opened to reveal a very long, well-lit tunnel. "This is my private entrance to the laboratory," Erick said as he exited the elevator and walked over to a golf cart. Chauncy joined Erick in the front seat while Jake had to sit on the back bench. They rode in silence for several minutes before coming to a large, reinforced door. Erick parked the vehicle, walked up to the door and pressed his palm against a biometric scanner while speaking a German phrase. The doors slid open whisper-quiet to reveal a massive collection of machinery.

Chauncy stepped forward slowly, his eyes wide, his mind almost numb. "This is amazing," he said in awe. Everywhere he looked there were humming machines, large screens with information on them, and items that looked like they belonged in a science-fiction movie. He would never, not in his entire lifetime, be able to figure out how to use even a tiny fraction of this much equipment.

"Yes, it is amazing," Erick said with pride evident in his voice.

"What goes on down here?" Jake asked, and there was no mistaking the awe in his voice either. There weren't many things that could impress Jake Thrasher, Chauncy knew, but apparently Erick Hausen's laboratory was one of them.

"Everything," Erick answered with a chuckle. "Or at least, everything that has to do with technology. This is where my products are invented, researched, prototyped and tested. There are only one or two locations in the entire world that have this amount of analytical and manufacturing power. If you think this is a lot, you should see the other four sublevels."

"What do you plan to do with the scepter? You aren't going to break it open, are you?" Chauncy asked, clutching the scepter closer to his chest.

Erick's eyes widened. "*Nein*! That is so primitive. You are here, surrounded by amazing technology that is years from being on the market, and yet you think I will act like a Neanderthal? *Lieber Gott*."

"I'm sorry," Chauncy said. "I didn't mean it like that."

"I know. What we need to do is non-invasive research. We need to look inside of the object without physically opening it."

"You going to use X-Rays?" Jake asked.

Erick motioned for them to follow him. "In a way, although these are nothing like the machines you would find at your local hospital. Even the machines that scan you at ports are nothing compared to this."

"Um, Hamburg doesn't have any of those machines in its port, does it?" Chauncy asked.

"Fortunately for you, they do not have any yet that would have detected you. I am sure Thrasher was aware of that. You know of MRIs, correct? Those require living tissue to work so we will not be using them here. We are turning to a prototype Industrial Radiography machine of mine that combines several different types of scanners. There is no other like it in the world."

"How does it work?" Jake asked.

Erick smiled. "You would require several degrees in electrical engineering before you would understand."

"I've just been insulted again," Jake said. There was a smile on his face, so Chauncy knew he hadn't taken offense.

Erick led the way through the maze of equipment. It took several moments for them to reach the opposite wall. Erick stopped in front of a large steel-reinforced door that was covered in warning symbols and messages. Most of them were in German, as was to be expected, but a couple of them were in English. Chauncy had only a moment to read two of them. *Warning: Authorized Personnel Only* and *Danger! Extreme Radiation Hazard* were not exactly heartening signs to see. He didn't get a chance to read any of the others as Erick performed a security ritual and the door slid open.

They entered a narrow rectangular hallway. On the left the hallway opened up into a larger room that had the most extravagant and complicated control section Chauncy had seen yet. There were seven monitors on the wall and at least four different types of keyboards or controlling devices. Behind the chairs was a large square pedestal that was a mystery to him. The far end of the hallway terminated at another heavily-reinforced door that had even more warning signs on it. Erick led the way to the reinforced door and turned a locking wheel to swing the door inward. As Chauncy passed through the doorway he noticed just how thick the wall was. His attention was immediately arrested by the enormous cylindrical device sitting squarely in the middle of an octagonal room. It was almost two stories tall and there were thousands of cables connected to it. Most of them were the diameter of telephone wire, but there were at least a dozen that were the size of his legs. Two of the cables were big enough for him to crawl through if they were cut open.

"Here it is, gentlemen," Erick said with pride. "This machine uses every type of ionizing-radiation-scanning technology and several types of Ultrasonic Holography. Any object placed inside can be viewed at any angle. We can even use the computers back here to virtually manipulate the item as if we were holding it in our hands."

Chauncy was too impressed to speak but that obviously wasn't a hindrance for Jake. "What is the purpose of this machine?" Thrasher asked.

"I currently use it for reverse engineering," Erick answered. "But the ultimate use will be finding structural weaknesses in nuclear engines and other complicated machinery. I believe that different space industries will also want to use it to make better components to send to the ISS."

Chauncy shook his head. "Dealing with the International Space Station," he said. "You've moved up in the world."

"Yes, I have. Please open that bottom door, the smaller one, and place the scepter within."

Chauncy did as he was instructed, opening up the door and placing the scepter very carefully on a glass plate. He then returned to the rectangular command area as Erick shut and locked the heavy door.

"Why are the doors and walls so thick?"

"For something as small as this scepter I probably did not even need to close the door," Erick said as he sat down at the computer. He began to turns dials, push buttons, and flip switches. "When running at full power, however, the radiation level approaches what a very small nuclear weapon would emit."

Chauncy moved instinctively away from the door and the computer. "Has the radiation seal ever broken?"

"No, and it will never do so," Erick said. He was still manipulating the computer controls. "I personally designed this room with the help of Alexander Yubarov. Do you remember him, Chauncy?"

Chauncy snapped his fingers. "Of course. He's another SSOSA member. He's a nuclear physicist, isn't he?"

"Indeed."

"You said the radiation approaches a small nuclear weapon," Jake said, interrupting. "What kind of power bills do you have?"

"I was among the people who helped investigate the problems that the Krümmel Nuclear plant was having. I am also one of the designer/consultants for the new Moorburg coal plant. I do not want for energy. Okay, everything is in place. It will probably take an hour or so for the scan to complete. Would you two care for some lunch?"

Chauncy and Jake looked at each other. "Yes, please," they both said at the same time.

"Come along, then. My private lunchroom is very well-stocked."

***

Hakan leaned forward and adjusted the zoom on his binoculars. The GPS signal had ended rather abruptly after it entered the glass-and-steel fortress of Future Engineering Technology. His reconnaissance from a nearby rooftop had identified two, and only two, weaknesses. That alone was impressive. Most skyscrapers and corporate buildings were riddled with security holes and possible attack points. The only possible points of entry at Future Engineering were the front lobby and the large shipping/receiving area in the back. The front parking lot that was attached to the lobby was the only part of the building that was not surrounded by a large concrete wall. He had scanned the wall for weaknesses but had only discovered a complicated security system that would not be easy to circumvent.

He turned to his attendant, who was just now walking onto the roof. "Here is the report you requested, Great One," the man said, bowing low.

Hakan snatched the document and stroked his scraggly beard as he read it. When he was finished he swore. "This is just what we need," he said. The report stated that Future Engineering Technology was owned and operated by one Erick Hausen, an engineering genius who was well-connected in the industrial and political world of Germany. He was even an international figure and his products were often regarded as the best of the best.

"What is your plan, Great One?"

Hakan stared at the report as if the heat of his glare could turn the facts into falsehoods. "We are dealing with somebody whose death would cause a real stir. A Bible archaeologist dying was a curiosity. His wife and son burning in their house was a touch ironic. But a chieftain of engineering? That will not be so easy to sweep under the rug. We will need to handle this delicately."

He lifted the binoculars again and gazed at the building. The goal of the Divine Flame was noble, of course, although most of the world would not see it that way. At the moment they were surviving because practically nobody knew they existed. If they moved too early and revealed their hand without having the Golden Scepter to back them up...well, it would make things difficult. As things stood, the world was reacting slowly to their presence and it might take months for a full retaliation to come. Hakan would have to make his boldest move at a point where the world reacting to them would not make a difference. He needed that scepter.

Risk versus reward. That is what all warfare is, Hakan reflected. The reaction of the world's governments would be much swifter and deadlier if they killed a well-known international man of industry. He could not risk that, not yet. While the reward of the scepter was well worth any risk it would be foolish to ignore the danger.

"We will do an extraction," Hakan ordered. "Prepare the Embers. Mark at one hour."

"Yes, Great One," his attendant replied. Hakan caught the look of exultation on the man's face before he turned and rushed out.

And why shouldn't he be excited? The Golden Scepter was the key to everything. Babylon would rise to power once again and those who helped to usher in its birth would be richly rewarded.

Chapter Twelve

The private lunchroom was everything Erick had promised and more. It was bursting with a huge variety of food, both local and imported, and Chauncy immediately began filling up his plate. He hadn't eaten well in what felt like a long time. The food on the dig was pretty good; it had been better financed than most of the digs he'd worked on, so the equipment and basic ingredients were better. The cooks, however, had left much to be desired. The few meals he'd had in Turkey were tasty but rushed. Here, finally, after several long months he was going to be able to sit down and enjoy a fine meal.

As he filled his plate he talked with Erick. It was good to be back in the presence of a SSOSA member, somebody who was always striving to improve his mind. They reminisced about the first time they met in Ecuador, during Dr. Sova's final Mind Game. A conversation that normally would have made him melancholy actually made him happy. He was glad to see that the death of Sova had not ended the SSOSA group.

"We are planning another Mind Game," Erick said as he drank a big cup of black coffee. "It will be different without René, but we plan to press on."

Chauncy sat back and enjoyed his meal and the feeling of security that was coming over him. He was in the presence of one of the smartest men alive; not only in the presence, but in his guarded research lab. The threat of Hakan and the Divine Flame seemed to be fading. Even if Hakan tracked them here, which was almost guaranteed, the man would have a hard time finding any weakness in a building designed by Erick Hausen.

They continued to talk about the Mind Games and SSOSA, and even Jake seemed to be getting into the conversation. The more they talked, the more at ease Chauncy felt. It had been a good idea to come to Erick; it probably saved his life. He would never be able to repay this genius.

Erick looked at his watch after they finished lunch. "The scan is complete. Shall we?"

They returned to the imaging room. The largest screen had an image of the Golden Scepter on it that looked more real than the actual object.

"That's amazing," Jake said as he sat down. "What kind of resolution is that thing running?"

"You would know it as 4K, even though that name is a bit of a misnomer. All of these screens are 4K. At least until I finish my prototypes. As you can see, this is only the exterior of the scepter. I can rotate the image in any direction I choose."

"I didn't even notice those scars on it when I first found it," Chauncy said, pointing at the rod part of the scepter. "This is very impressive. But why isn't it in 3D?"

"It is about time that you noticed," Erick said with a conspiratorial grin. "Turn around."

They all swiveled in their chairs. The large black table at the other end of the room was suddenly awash in bright color. Within a few seconds a large holographic image of the Golden Scepter appeared. It rotated in mid-air and looked nearly as real as the 4K screens had portrayed.

Jake whistled. "You were saving this part to really impress us, weren't you?"

"I am guilty," Erick said, his grin growing wider. "Come, move your chairs closer and let us examine the insides of this intriguing scepter."

Erick manipulated a few more levers and the scepter slowly turned into a ghostly mirage of itself. The rod portion was solid, as expected, but the scepter end looked a lot more complicated.

"*Ach so*! I was correct. Look, each of the rings is part of a simple combination lock. You could rotate the rings for many years before coming across the right combination."

Chauncy stood up and leaned over the aluminum railing that separated the black pedestal from the room. He gazed closer at the internal structure of the scepter with a growing sense of awe. "The earliest known combination lock was traced back to the Roman era, if I'm not mistaken," he said, adjusting his view to take in all of the object. "This scepter predates that by at least five hundred years. What are we *dealing* with here?"

"I am not a scholar of antiquities like you, Chauncy," Erick said, shaking his head. "I do not know. Is not ancient man supposed to be barely above cave drawings?"

Chauncy snorted. "That is what most of my contemporaries would have you believe. That's why so many people like to say aliens built the pyramids. They simply cannot grasp the fact that ancient man was *smarter* than we are, because they were closer to perfection."

Erick shrugged again. "I cannot argue with you, Chauncy, for I do not have the necessary facts. But look, the bottom of the scepter is a reservoir as I surmised."

"Why is it blacked out?"

"There appears to be an inert liquid or gas contained within. It does not appear to be explosive or incendiary in nature, otherwise my lobby security would have identified it. Let me see if I can open it."

Chauncy looked back at Erick. "You can do that?"

"Virtually, yes. The scepter was scanned by three separate super-computers that have analyzed it down to the last detail, allowing us to simulate anything we wish. This is how the device will be used to determine if new nuclear reactor designs are safe. I even included some sound effects. Chauncy, I will begin to move the first ring. Please tell me when the plate is open."

The holographic ring began to turn slowly in the air and Chauncy watched, mesmerized. The sound of metal scraping against metal could be heard softly in the background as the virtual rings grinded against each other. "It's open," he said at the right moment. The ring was showing that a small triangular-shaped hatch had opened near the bottom of the device.

There was a pause for a moment before the second ring began to move. Once again, Chauncy called out when the hatch opened. "You were right, Erick," Chauncy said with growing enthusiasm. "The rings are part of a combination lock. Each part is slowly opening at the right moment so that there is access to the reservoir."

"*Ach so!* It is a brilliant design, this scepter. Let us see what the simulation says is in the reservoir."

The operation was continued until they reached the last ring. "Well, here we go, gentlemen. We are about to see what ancient men of old considered important enough to lock away inside this scepter. Virtually, of course."

The final ring slowly rotated into place. A blinding flash and thunder filled the room. Chauncy threw up his hand to protect his eyes but it was too late. Dark, purple spots filled his vision completely and his ears were ringing. The three men stared at each other as their vision slowly cleared, each of them wondering who would be the first to react.

It was, unsurprisingly, Jake Thrasher who spoke first. "Would either of you mind explaining to me," he said slowly, stressing each word carefully, "what in God's name just happened?"

Silence descended on the room for several heartbeats. "I do not know," Erick said finally. "The computers simulated what would have happened if the scepter had been opened."

"What was that, then? An explosion? How could that be?" Chauncy asked.

"It cannot be an explosion," Erick said firmly. "My security would have picked up anything like that. Perhaps the simulation made a mistake. I need to look at the report."

"You sure it wasn't some type of ancient gunpowder?" Jake asked. "One that your scanners wouldn't be aware of?"

"Impossible!" Erick said. "The history of gunpowder only goes back fifteen hundred years or so. Besides, anything that is capable of causing an explosion will have a distinctive chemical signature, which, again, my security would have spotted."

"Then what was it?" Jake demanded.

"Let me read the report," Erick said irritably.

There was silence again while the German engineer read the computer report. "*Ach du lieber!*" he exclaimed, leaning back in his chair and rubbing his eyes. "This cannot be so."

"What? What's the problem?" Chauncy asked.

"All three supercomputers report the same thing, independently of each other. That means that it was not a mistake in the calculation. It just...it is impossible."

"What does the report say?" Chauncy asked, growing ever more impatient.

"That is the problem: I do not know what I am reading."

Chauncy and Jake exchanged startled glances. "*You* don't know what you're reading?" Jake asked, his tone almost mocking. "I thought you SSOSA guys knew everything."

Erick glared at Jake for a moment. "The analysis of what is in the reservoir is written in the language of quantum mechanics. I am an engineer, not a nuclear physicist."

"You realize what you're saying, right?" Jake asked, standing up and looking at the report. "You're saying that something as old as Babylon has something quantum in it."

All three men stared at each other. "How?" Chauncy asked to nobody in particular. "How does something so ancient have a material in it that only a nuclear physicist would understand?"

"You explained this machine with nuclear terminology," Jake said. "Ions and radiation and all of that. How come you can't read this?"

"I designed this with the help of my on-staff nuclear physicists," Erick answered. "I know enough about the math and processes to help design more efficient reactors, but I do not know this much. This would require an expert in a field where there are very few who can claim that title."

"Why don't you just call in your on-staff physicist?" Chauncy asked. He shook his head almost instantly after asking the question. "No, that wouldn't work. He would start asking questions that we wouldn't want to answer."

"Exactly. There is, however, a man who can answer these questions and can be trusted with the highest of security."

"Alexander Yubarov," Chauncy said, smiling fondly as he recalled the talented scientist. "Yes, he could answer this in a heartbeat. But he is in Russia, isn't he?"

Erick reached over and switched off the scanning computers. "That will not stop us from contacting him. All of the SSOSA members have a secure computer connection. We use it for the Mind Games. Mine is in my office. We will take the scepter and the report back with us."

***

The man who got out of the nondescript car took a deep breath. The imposing structure of Future Engineering Technology stretched up into the sky like the tower of Babel. It cast a heavy shadow across the land, a shadow that did not reach to his heart. He was ready for whatever should occur to him. He was an Ember, and the divine fire that burned in his soul could not be darkened by the constructs of man.

He adjusted his belt and the hidden weapon more comfortably on his body. He let out his breath very slowly and offered up a silent prayer to his god. He looked over at his companion and saw the same determination on her face. There would be no stopping them.

They walked swiftly toward the front door and the lobby beyond, but not so swiftly that they looked suspicious. Their dress was normal street attire, the expressions on their face were bright and excited. To all outward appearances they were just a German couple who wanted to visit the technological wonders of Future Engineering Technology.

They stepped through the front door and the man immediately assessed the situation. There was a long, thirty-foot-long glass corridor leading from the front doors to the open lobby. Now that they were inside they would need to be hyper-alert for the security systems. If those systems were as good as was claimed, they would be activated at any moment.

Two more steps was all it took to activate security. Two massive, steel doors slammed shut and blocked off the lobby and exit. At the same time the glass walls of the corridor were blocked by equally thick steel plates that appeared almost out of nowhere.

A warning voice could be heard in the hallway in several languages. "Do not move. Illegal weapons have been detected on your person. Do not move."

They were trapped in the entryway, but they had prepared for that. They ignored the warning and within seconds they reached the far end of the corridor and were carefully placing small packets of C4 on the barrier. This was the only way to see just how strong the security was. They would likely be beyond the blast radius but they did not care. They were Embers. They were driven to a higher calling.

They didn't even hear the hiss of the gas as it filled the room. They collapsed unconscious to the floor before they could finish their mission.

***

A klaxon blasted through the lab and Erick slid to a halt. His face registered disbelief and surprise for a split second before

86

being replaced by determination. He walked over to a nearby computer and immediately punched in a code.

"What's happening?" Chauncy demanded, clutching the scepter case closer to his chest. "What's going on?"

Erick held up a finger, signifying that Chauncy should wait a moment. He held a quick conversation with security.

"We are under attack," Erick said grimly as he turned from the computer. "Two persons, a man and a woman, attempted to use C4 to blast into my lobby."

"Hakan," Jake and Chauncy said at the same moment.

"He's here," Jake continued, stepping closer to Erick. "And he will stop at nothing to get this scepter. He's already tried to kill both of us, several times in Chauncy's case."

Erick smiled thinly and without humor. "He is no match for my security. We are safe here."

Jake shook his head. "Don't underestimate him," he said urgently. "I did that, and I lost my office in Ankara. He is ruthless and unstoppable."

"No man is unstoppable, Jake Thrasher. Your Hakan has never faced off against a SSOSA member. I believe that you will find him grossly outmatched."

"But—"

"Enough," Erick ordered. "We will return to my office and orchestrate security measures from there. You will see."

Chauncy followed closely behind Erick. He was heartened by the German's confidence...and yet he felt a shred of doubt slithering in like a snake. Erick Hausen was undeniably a genius of engineering, and his security was among the best in the world. And while Hakan had never faced off against a SSOSA member, Chauncy sincerely doubted that any SSOSA member had ever been challenged by a man like Hakan. The weight of the Golden Scepter in his hands seemed to triple as they made their way to the elevator.

Chapter Thirteen

The trip to the Denver airport was a long and nerve-wracking experience. Troy managed to fall asleep in the plush seats of the limousine, but Anita could not keep her eyes shut. She alternated between staring at her son and scanning the sparse traffic visible through the tinted rear window. It was too dark for her to positively identify anything, let alone notice if they were being followed, but she couldn't stop herself.

Her husband had been killed and the same maniacs had now tried to kill her. Not just her, though. She would not worry too much if it was only herself being threatened. But her son was in danger, as was her only chance of getting answers.

As the minutes dragged on, she agonized over the proper course of action and whether she had taken it. She tried to assess the situation from a logical point of view, but her emotions kept interrupting. Part of her desperately wanted to keep Troy away from Turkey, to keep him away from the place where his father died. He was a strong young man, stronger than she realized, but she didn't want to put him through this torture. To prevent Troy from seeing the scene of his father's death however, would have required leaving him with Marlo and Gloria.

She trusted the Gunds implicitly. They had been the best friends that she and Chauncy could have possibly had. But leaving Troy with them meant he would have been out of her sight, out of her immediate zone of protection. As long as she could see him or be near him, she could fight to protect him. But how much danger was she putting him in by taking him to Turkey? The cult had already killed in Turkey. They had already tried to kill in Wyoming.

Nowhere was safe, she finally realized. Nowhere was safe, so the only place for Troy was by her side. She just hoped that he would have the fortitude to withstand this trip. Maybe by going to the scene of the crime they could both find answers. She didn't know what awaited her; she didn't know what, if any, answers she would find at the dig site. Maybe it was closure she was seeking. Or maybe, just maybe, she would find some clue about her husband's demise that would lead to justice. At the very least she would gain knowledge about the dig. That would be nice. *"Knowledge makes everything brighter,"* she heard Chauncy say in her memory. He was quite fond of saying that. She missed him terribly.

The process of boarding the private plane was excruciating. There were always people at the airport, no matter what time of day or night, and she tried to analyze every single one of them as they passed through the terminal toward their destination. None of them seemed out of the ordinary to the logical part of her brain, but she was tired, frightened and feeling very illogical. The elderly couple sitting close together on a bench were only *pretending* to rest their eyes. The businessman typing away on his laptop was obviously chronicling her every move. The three Hispanics were hiding weapons in their pockets. The distinguished-looking doctor who was staring at her was trained to kill. The security guard was crooked. The flight crews were sinister. Nobody was innocent or who they appeared to be.

Her paranoia lasted well past the time she boarded the private jet with Mayal, his chauffeur and her son. She kept watching the runway, expecting somebody to come charging at them with a bomb or rifles. She kept her eyes peeled for danger throughout the flight. She didn't blink more than twice the entire time.

The landing at JFK airport was even worse. There were a hundred times more people milling about and she tried to watch all of them at once. She blamed the resulting headache on lack of sleep but deep down she knew better: she was trying to protect herself and her son from a thousand different threats at once while her body dragged from lack of sleep. There was only so much that adrenaline could do.

Her body's supply of adrenaline ran out about thirty minutes after they left JFK. She was looking out the window, imagining F-15s coming to shoot them down, when her eyes finally shut.

***

The rising sun cast long shadows from the mountains of Wyoming as the doctor came to a slow and startled stop. The

90

address he'd been given on a secure pathway from Erick Hausen led to a still-smoldering husk of a house. Emergency and cleanup crews sifted through the debris, applying flame retardants at strategic places.

"Excuse me, what happened here?" he asked the closest official-looking person.

"Place burned down last night," the man replied, looking up from his clipboard. "Sorry, we aren't allowing any press in here."

"I'm not press, I am a colleague of the Rollocks," the doctor replied, his eyes going wide as he stared at the remainder of the house. "Was anyone harmed?"

The man peered closer. "No, Anita, her son and an unidentified male were admitted to the hospital last night. If you need to speak with them you can try your luck there."

The doctor got directions to the hospital and drove off in a cloud of dust. Erick had said the message was vital and urgent. He sincerely hoped that the house burning down wasn't a result of a failure on his part to deliver the message on time.

The hospital only increased his fears. The Rollocks and the man, identified by the staff as Doctor Faruk Mayal, were no longer present. They'd disappeared sometime in the night and absolutely nobody on staff knew what happened. Apparently, the disappearance had created quite a stir since the local police and the fire marshal wanted to question Anita Rollock over the cause of the house fire.

He returned to his office as swiftly as he could and made a beeline straight for his secured workstation. His fingers shook as he dialed in the international number.

"Erick," he said without further preamble. "There's a problem."

Chapter Fourteen

The ride up the elevator seemed longer than before, but Chauncy knew it was an illusion. They entered Erick's office, where he strode to his desk with purpose. His hands flew over the keyboard and touchscreens and within moments there was a display of the building visible on the screens.

"There are only two access points to this structure," the German engineer stated with authority. "I designed it that way. Corporate espionage and sabotage are not things of the past, gentlemen, and there are hundreds of people who would love to steal my designs or destroy the prototypes. This building is a fortress to prevent those things from happening."

"Didn't you say C4 was used?" Jake asked. "That should have put a dent in your lobby, for sure."

Erick smiled. "They didn't make it to the lobby. There are hidden scanners as you walk through the entryway and if anything explosive is discovered, the entryway closes off with steel. As a last measure, an incapacitating agent is pumped into the room to prevent further attacks and keep the assailants in place until GSG-9 can arrive. Here they are now."

Chauncy turned his head slightly to look at another monitor, which showed a live video feed from the exterior of the building. Several large, military-looking vehicles were pulling up into the parking lot. "GSG-9?" he asked, not quite believing it. "Aren't they the elite German SWAT team who stopped that plane hijacking in '93?"

"More or less correct," Erick said, his smile broadening. "I am considered an indispensable part of Germany's technological world. A VIP, as you Americans would say. The security of this building is a top priority in Hamburg and nearby locations. Please be silent."

Erick began a conversation with several different people while Chauncy motioned Jake back a few steps.

"Do you think we'll be able to get away from here without

Hakan finding us?" he whispered.

Jake shrugged. "I really don't know, Chauncy. I'm spooked by how fast he found us. He must have a larger network than I imagined."

Erick snapped his fingers to get their attention. His face was ashen and Chauncy immediately knew that something was wrong. "I have bad news," Erick affirmed, his voice a husky parody of its usual self. "Chauncy...your house was burned down and your wife and son are missing."

His knees inexplicably buckled and he almost fell to the floor. He righted himself almost immediately and bolted forward. "What? When? Why?" he asked.

"My colleague in America made inquiries at the hospital," Erick explained. "Your wife and son were admitted with a third man, a Doctor Faruk Mayal. They then disappeared and nobody knows where they are."

Doctor Faruk Mayal. "Of course," Chauncy said slowly. "Doctor Mayal is the man who hired me for the dig. He's a huge name in the antiquities arena. I wonder what he was doing all the way in America? And more importantly, what was he doing at my house?"

Erick looked back at the screen, thanked his colleague, and closed the conversation. "I can find out for you," he said. "The GSG-9 are securing the front entryway right now so I have a moment or two." His fingers once again flew over the various command surfaces of his computer.

"Dr. Mayal was at a fundraising dinner a day after your alleged death. There is a newspaper article interviewing him where he states that he will, quote: 'leave no stone unturned until the truth about Chauncy Rollock, and my dig site, are known and revealed to the world,' unquote. He has apparently declared a private war on the Turkish government to give him access to, again I quote: 'the dig site that is rightfully mine, and the information that belongs to Chauncy's widow,' unquote."

"But my house burning down?" Chauncy asked. He put the scepter case on the desk and rubbed his temples. "Jake...you don't think?"

"Hakan," Jake said, and there was no questioning the tone in his voice. "His network truly is larger than I imagined and what better opportunity would he have to kill Anita, Troy and Dr. Mayal?"

Chauncy swallowed past a thick lump in his throat. "Their disappearance from the hospital...are they dead?"

"Take heart," Erick said suddenly, his eyes scanning a page full of obscure computer code. "A private plane was chartered by Faruk Mayal from Denver to JFK, and from JFK to Istanbul. Three other passengers were with him, including an Anita and Troy Rollock."

Chauncy felt life flowing into him once again. "They're alive," he said, letting out a breath he didn't realize he'd been holding. "But why are they going to Istanbul?"

"You keep asking questions that we can't answer," Jake said, sounding annoyed. "It's your wife. Why do *you* think she's going to Turkey?"

He forced himself to think rationally. Obviously, she hadn't received word that he was alive. What would she do? She would try to find out what happened. She would be relentless in her efforts to find answers and the only place to get answers was the dig where he 'died.' He told the others as much and they agreed that it made sense.

"GSG-9 has removed the attackers and have checked their prints and identities," Erick said as he turned back to the monitors. "They...this is odd."

Jake and Chauncy both moved closer to Erick. "What's odd?" Jake asked.

Erick shook his head, a puzzled frown on his face. "They are both German citizens," he said slowly while the officer on the other end of the communication rattled off words in German. "Neither has a criminal record. They have no relatives or ties with any known terrorist groups. They are probably the last people who would be involved in this."

A stray thought hit Chauncy like a runaway semi. "Check their academic records," he said. "Look for anything involving archaeology or Latin."

Erick translated and then began typing away. "I can perform that check faster than they can, probably," he said. "I keep an eye on all of the major universities, looking for potential employees. *Einen Augenblick, bitte...*"

One moment later he leaned back. "Your hunch was correct. The man took an archaeological class specializing in the Babylonians, and the woman took several semesters of Latin. What does this have to do with—"

"*Flamus Divinus*," Jake said, snapping his fingers. "Of course. And the scepter markings are Babylonian, aren't they?"

Chauncy nodded. "Mostly Babylonian, yes. That's it, then. These two are definitely linked to Hakan."

"You two keep mentioning Hakan. Are you referring to Hakan Ramush, the dig master who is dead?" Erick asked.

"The dig master who died in the same fire that killed me?" Chauncy asked with a heavy layer of sarcasm.

"*Ach so!*" Erick exclaimed. "Of course. Layers of lies surround this man, I see."

"You don't know the half of it," Jake said. "I'm convinced that he's behind a whole slew of deadly and illegal activity in Turkey. I just can't prove it. And now, with this Divine Flame business, it looks like he's increasing his efforts."

"We need to do two things," Chauncy said, holding up his fingers and ticking them off as he spoke. "First, we need to find out more about this scepter. If Alexander can help us figure out its secrets, we might get a clue as to why Hakan is so obsessed with it. Second, we need to figure out what *Flamus Divinus* is. Is it a group? A cult? An Internet forum?"

"I concur," Erick said. "I must speak with the GSG-9 commander. After that I will initiate a conversation with Alexander." He glanced at one of his digital clocks. "There is only a two hour difference; he will not have gone to bed yet."

Jake paced the room, Erick returned to his conversation with the counterterrorist commander, and Chauncy finally sat down in one of the chairs. Alone with his thoughts, he was in turmoil from the news about his family and his home. He'd designed that house with Anita, every detail and every design discussed, selected and implemented with great care. And now it was gone up in smoke, literally. *My wife and son on their way to Turkey, of all places!* he thought. Dr. Mayal really went out of his way to help, but they were heading straight into the lion's den. Hakan might personally be here in Germany, or he might not, but his network in Turkey was still more than enough to capture or kill his family and his good friend.

"I need you to go to Turkey," Chauncy said as he leaned in toward Jake. His voice was carefully controlled. "I need you to keep an eye on my family."

Jake nodded, his eyes searching Chauncy's face and seeing the resolve there. "I was planning to make a trip to give them the good news about you anyway. Now it appears they'll need it more than ever."

"Don't let them charge back to the U.S. though," Chauncy warned. "If Hakan is watching them, and I have no doubt that he is, a sudden change in their plans will be a dead giveaway that they know I'm alive. Once they know I'm alive..."

"Things become more complicated," Jake agreed. "They're a huge target if Hakan can get to them and then make sure you know about it. I'll bet he's already planning it. I'll be on the next plane out of here."

"It will be a private plane," Erick interrupted from the side. Chauncy jumped; he hadn't realized that Erick had been listening. "I have a plane on standby at all times. It will take you fifteen minutes to get to the airport."

"Thank you," Chauncy said, and he meant it. "This means a lot to me."

"How should I do this?" Jake asked. "Do I wait for GSG-9 to clear the building? Or do I sneak out while everyone is looking at the front door?"

"Speaking of sneaking out while everyone is looking at the front door," Chauncy said suddenly, his gaze darting over Erick's shoulders to look at the monitor, "Why is there a GSG-9 team in your private elevator?"

Erick spun around instantly, his hands already reaching for the keyboards. Before he could begin to type there was a sudden power surge and everything electronic in the room went black.

"Chauncy Rollock and Jake Thrasher," the deep and haunting voice of Hakan said from the intercom. "I know you are here. I know that my Golden Scepter is here. Deliver it to me and no one gets hurt. You have five minutes."

Chapter Fifteen

Erick immediately got up and went to one of his cabinets without speaking a word. Chauncy looked to Jake, who shrugged. "It's not my scepter to give away," Jake said simply.

And that was really the crux of the matter. With that simple statement, Jake had helpfully placed full and total responsibility of this mess squarely onto Chauncy's shoulders. He didn't need this right now. He looked down at the container that held the scepter. The scepter was impossible; it had power in it that was far beyond his understanding. He knew what kind of man Hakan was. How could he simply hand this much power to that kind of man?

The simple answer was that he couldn't. This was bigger than him, bigger than SSOSA, bigger even than his family. Hakan had killed all of the dig workers and had tried to kill him. If he got his hands on the scepter, what was stopping him from going after the rest of the world? He was just going to open his mouth and say that but Erick returned from the cabinet and interrupted his thought.

"Follow me," he said grimly. He was carrying a black tablet and a small metal briefcase. It was dark in the room and difficult to see his full expression, but Chauncy could tell that it was set in a grim mask. Chauncy didn't hesitate to stand up and step into line behind Erick, with Jake right behind him.

Erick walked swiftly to his private elevator and flipped open a hidden panel on the wall. A red lever was inside and he pulled it down. The elevator doors opened with a mechanical grinding noise and Erick didn't hesitate. He went straight to the side of the elevator and pulled open another hidden panel. Chauncy stepped inside and made sure that there was plenty of room for Jake to stand and for Erick to work.

Erick set the metal briefcase on the floor and unwound a long, thick cord. He plugged that cord and a cord from his tablet into the hidden panel and started to work.

"You have sixty seconds, Mr. Rollock," Hakan's voice said over the intercom again. "Come now, it is not that hard a decision to make. Three lives, or the Golden Scepter."

Chauncy wanted to say something smart but he couldn't think of the words. What *did* one say to a man like Hakan?

A surge of power went through the elevator, turning the lights and buttons on. Erick placed the tablet into the panel and turned around with a satisfied smile. He punched the button for the lab and the elevator started its swift descent.

"Portable backup power?" Jake asked, his tone that of one professional addressing another.

"*Ja,*" Erick said, his satisfied smile twisting slightly. "This is not the first time I have been threatened by terrorists or corporate thieves. Our path through the lab is clear. Agents will be waiting to escort me out of the building and to my private auto."

Chauncy felt his eyebrows lifting but Jake beat him to it. "Agents? You mean GSG-9? Like the team that is currently trying to kill us?"

Erick pursed his lips. "They are not GSG-9, but you raise a good point. We will have to find an alternate means of leaving."

"Why are we going to your lab?" Jake persisted. "Won't Hakan be able to follow you?"

Erick shook his head emphatically as the elevator reached the bottom and the doors opened. He grabbed his briefcase and tablet and motioned for them to follow him. Chauncy stepped out, trepidation running through him. The long corridor was eerily lit by red emergency lighting with only the light from the elevator spilling out. It looked like a long, dark hallway to his death. Erick pulled a flashlight from the wall and pointed it at the same little cart they'd taken earlier. "Get on," he ordered, handing the light to Jake. "I must secure the elevator."

Jake and Chauncy hurried to get onto the vehicle. They'd just settled down when the light from the elevator suddenly went dark. Chauncy felt his heart trying to escape his throat. "Erick?" he called, his voice echoing strangely in the corridor.

"I locked down the elevator," Erick said, his voice coming closer. "It will not move without my direct intervention." He appeared suddenly in the glow from the flashlight and got into the driver's seat. "Hold on."

They drove forward and it felt almost like the first trip. Except this time, of course, they were on the run from a homicidal genius.

And the corridor was lit by blood-red lights. The symbolism was not lost on Chauncy.

Erick came to a stop about halfway down the corridor and opened another of the ubiquitous hidden panels. Chauncy felt like a sitting duck despite being in a small hallway. He felt the hair on his neck stand straight up and turned around, half-expecting Hakan to be hot on their heels. There was no Hakan, but he was in time to see an enormous concrete block slowly lower itself to the floor.

"Security measures?" he asked.

"Just one of many," Erick said. "My lab is worth more than the GDP of many smaller nations. I take security very seriously. So does the *real* GSG-9. There are three entrances to the lab and I have already closed this one."

They rode for several more moments before the cart took a sharp turn instead of stopping at the entrance they'd passed through earlier. The cart stopped and Erick got out again and repeated the process, with another enormous concrete barrier lowering itself into place. The measure was repeated once more a few minutes later, but this time they were on the exterior of the barrier. This corridor was also significantly larger than the others.

"Cargo path?" Jake asked.

"*Sehr gut!*" Erick said. "This is the corridor which brings the raw materials for the machines, new machines, or the things which we are scanning. It is large enough for my future expansion into nuclear turbine designs. It is also harder to secure, because of its size, but not impossible."

They continued on and Chauncy noticed that the ground was now sloping upward. They were heading for the surface, where Hakan was. "Can't we just stay safe and sound in the lab until this blows over?" he asked.

Erick shook his head. "They have either bribed a GSG-9 team, which seems unlikely, or they have imitated one well enough to trick one of the best counterterrorist teams in the world. We could stay in the lab, for months if we had to, but I would not want to do that. I need to get in touch with my private GSG-9 contact and tell him what has been done, and I no longer trust any of the communications in my building at the moment."

"Besides, don't you need me to get a message to your family?" Jake asked.

Chauncy nodded. Part of him still wanted to just bunker down and weather the storm, but he couldn't argue the points being made. He needed that message to get to Anita.

They came to a stop in front of gigantic steel doors that filled the entire corridor. Erick turned and parked the small cart in an alcove to the side, which also had a door in it. He moved slowly and carefully, holding his tablet in front of him like a sword. He put his finger to his mouth to signify silence and then proceeded to open the door. There were no surprises waiting for them on the other side. In fact, there were no surprises waiting for them as they continued to move stealthily along the outer wall of the loading/unloading room, which was even bigger than the lab. Huge cranes were attached to the ceiling, forklifts and various other heavy equipment were lined up in almost OCD order, and all things told it was a very impressive show of industry.

It was kind of hard to focus on that show while expecting a murderer to jump out from behind every object. The room was open on the far end to the outside world and light was spilling in, but it was obvious that the sun was not meant to be the only source of light. Every piece of equipment was thrown in sharp contrast with deep shadows plaguing most of the room. Chauncy spent the entire trip twitching like a hyperactive puppy, jumping at every creaking sound and staring at every shadow.

He was a nervous wreck by the time he made it into the seat of a strange-looking utility truck on the far side of the bay. He didn't notice the make or year of the vehicle and at the moment he really didn't care. Erick drove the vehicle carefully out of the bay, out into the yard, and then onto the streets. Chauncy looked in the side mirror and saw the Future Engineering Technology skyscraper begin to recede into the background.

The briefcase weighed heavier upon his lap as he clutched it closer. "I don't like this," he said quietly, staring at the large buildings surrounding them. He felt just as claustrophobic as when they'd been in the corridors. "We got away too easily."

A hole appeared in the hood a split second before the *crack* of a high-powered rifle reached his ears. Distantly, he was aware that he was suddenly screaming his lungs out as Erick grabbed him and shoved his head down. Another *crack* rang through his ears as the engine revved for all its worth. Chauncy had a hard time keeping his lunch as Erick swerved the car in and out of traffic. Jake was shouting something, Erick was shouting something back, horns were honking and everything in the universe was erupting into chaos.

The back of the car rocked suddenly as two shots pounded into it. Erick jerked the car into a new direction and Chauncy peeked up over the dashboard. A bus was bearing down on him and he immediately ducked back down, gripping the briefcase so hard his fingers hurt. Half a dozen more shots rang out, each impact trying to tear the car apart. The car swerved suddenly and the sunlight was abruptly darkened. Chauncy raised himself a few inches again and looked out the window. Erick had taken them down a very tight alleyway that was leading them in various angles away from their original vector.

"How are we still moving?" Jake asked from the back.

"This is a hybrid mid-engine design of my own making," Erick responded, and Chauncy saw a grim smile on his face. "One of the very few non-two-seater mid-engines in existence. The shooter would have had to target the middle of the vehicle, not the front or back like most other cars."

They made it to the private airport without any further discussion or attacks. Erick pointed to one of the various planes sitting in the hangar and directed Jake to it. "That is your plane. Try not to use it for illegal purposes before you return it to me."

Jake grinned, but there was a hardness around his eyes. Chauncy could tell he was still shaking from the sniper attack. Who wouldn't be?

"And where are you going? To see your Russian friend?" Jake asked. When Erick nodded in the affirmative, Jake's smile widened. "And how exactly are you planning to get the scepter through customs?"

Erick and Chauncy exchanged startled glances. Neither of them had thought that far ahead. "I am not sure," Erick said slowly. "I have traveled to Russia many times in the past. I can claim this is part of one of my products."

"And trust the Russians to leave it alone?" Jake asked with a sarcastic chuckle. "Here. Try this instead." He dug through his wallet and handed a business card to Erick.

Erick held the card up with a frown. "Alina Ivanovna Grekov.

Let me guess: she's a smuggler."

"No, she's a perfectly legitimate customs officer in Moscow...who happens to work for me on occasion. I'll give her a call and tell her to expect you."

Erick and Jake discussed the details in low tones for a few minutes. It was perfectly obvious that Erick did not like this idea and it was equally obvious that they didn't have many choices. When they finished their discussion, Jake turned to Chauncy and held out his hand.

Chauncy gripped the proffered hand in a tight handshake. "Thanks, Jake," he said, a lump mysteriously appearing in his throat. "Be safe, okay?"

"Hey, 'Safe' is my middle name," Jake said with a cocky smile.

"And 'Not' is your first," Chauncy retorted.

"I'm more worried about you and that scepter. Try not to blow up with it. Don't worry; I'll make sure the message gets to your family. And I'll charge you later."

They bade each other farewell and Chauncy climbed aboard Erick's private plane. He wondered if he would ever see Jake Thrasher again. He hoped so.

***

Hakan hunched down in the backseat of his car and rubbed his eyes. Everything had been going perfectly: flush out the target with threats from a phony GSG-9 team and disable their vehicle with well-placed sniper shots. He'd correctly called every step of the operation, right down to which of the loading bay doors Erick Hausen would escape from. His rooftop had been perfectly situated to shoot the engine out regardless of which streets Erick took for up to two miles. There was no way the plan could have failed.

And yet it had failed completely. His duplicate GSG-9 team was now in custody, taken down and arrested by the *real* team that had been on the mission. He'd half-expected that, really. The GSG-9 had a sterling reputation. That wasn't too bad a loss, although he wished it had gone otherwise.

But losing Jake and Chauncy, and more importantly the Golden Scepter, all because the vehicle didn't have a standard engine placement? That was the only explanation. It couldn't have been an electric car; he'd shot in all the right spots for a battery pack. It had to have been a mid-engine. Mid-engine vehicles were exclusively sports cars or old buses. How could he possibly have known that? And shooting out tires from a rooftop was tricky and might have caused an accident. An accident might have damaged the scepter and bad things would have happened.

He was rationalizing, he knew. But he better come up with an excuse, and fast, because this was now his third failure. First in the desert, then in Ankara, and now in Hamburg. But he wasn't going to wait for the Great Exalted One to call him. Hakan picked up the phone and dialed the number. The voice on the other end already knew the results. "You are to leave Germany at once and come to my sanctuary, do you understand?"

Hakan's whole body felt numb. "Yes, Exalted One.'

Chapter Sixteen

Erick Hausen's corporate jet streaked across the sky toward Russia. Chauncy stared out the window at the landscape below and tried to ignore what had happened in Hamburg. No matter what mental gymnastics he tried to pull he couldn't tear his thoughts away from the shooting and, more importantly, his big failure.

He had gone to Erick for answers. He'd been absolutely convinced that Erick would be able to decipher the mystery of the Golden Scepter, even if he hadn't said so to Jake. And while there had indeed been some answers, now there were even more questions. The most troubling question: how on earth could ancients have put something that looked like quantum physics in the scepter? Had Erick's computers made a mistake? After all, computers were only as perfect as their programmers. Chauncy fervently hoped that it was a mistake.

The landscape changed beneath him from land to water as they passed over the Baltic Sea; it changed back to land but he barely noticed the difference. They were descending into Moscow before he even realized it. The giant spoke-and-wheel design of the city was apparent even from their angle of approach and he took a moment to gaze out at the city. He knew next to nothing about Moscow. His studies of antiquities rarely dealt with Russia, or to be honest, most of Europe. He was considered an expert in the Yucatan and parts of South America, and the ancient history of the Mediterranean and Middle East. Those places were about as different as it was possible to be from Russia and Moscow. It was kind of exciting to be visiting the home of the Kremlin and St. Peter's Basilica. He sincerely doubted he'd get a chance to see either of those locations. Not with Hakan and his Divine Flame after him.

They landed safely at the Vnukovo International Airport, disembarked and went immediately to customs. As they approached the security and screening area, a well-dressed woman smiled and approached them. She bowed her head slightly at both of them before speaking. "Erick Hausen?" she said, her accent barely noticeable.

Erick nodded, a guarded look on his face. Chauncy felt the same. Just because they were expected didn't mean that this was their contact. "I am," Erick affirmed. "And you are?"

"Alina Grekov," she said, waving her hand toward a private screening room to the side. "I believe we have a mutual business associate. Will you come with me, please?"

As they entered the private screening room, Chauncy was filled with trepidation. But nobody jumped out of a closet to shoot them or steal the briefcase. Alina didn't even look inside the briefcase; she simply accepted their passports, smiled at them, and waved them on their way. They made it out of the customs area and safely into a taxi before Chauncy could breathe again.

"That was rather amusing," the German said, a smile on his face. "I never thought it would be helpful to know someone on both sides of the law."

Chauncy instinctively reached for his fake passport. It was the only way he was able to move about, now that he was officially dead. "I know what you mean," he answered quietly. "Never thought I'd need Jake's services again."

"One day you will have to tell me how you met him," Erick said, still smiling as he looked out the window. "It is twenty-six kilometers to the D. V. Skobeltsyn Institute of Nuclear Physics. That means it will be thirty minutes or so. I suggest you try and relax for a while."

Chauncy did anything *but* relax as they approached Moscow from the southwest. He expected a sniper on every building or a bomb on every road but they made it safely to the institute. At first it looked like a giant *Star Wars* X-Wing spaceship eternally trying to fly out of the earth. As they got closer the X-Wing resolved itself into the multi-tiered, neo-classic towers that Erick informed him had been built in 1953.

Chauncy paid the fare out of the slush fund he'd received from Jake's sale of the sword, while Erick retrieved their other luggage from the trunk. Chauncy slung the backpack over his shoulder and kept a tight grip on the briefcase while walking up the stone steps behind Erick. There were few people around and the long hallway they walked through appeared to be deserted except for them.

Their steps echoed off the walls as Chauncy looked around at the furnishings. They arrived at a wooden door that had Alexander Yubarov's name embossed on a plaque. Erick hesitated for a moment before knocking loudly on the door.

A burst of Russian that sounded like swearing came from within the room and Erick smiled as he heard the translation. He said something quietly into his translator and a moment later the device spewed out more Russian.

The door opened almost immediately to reveal a very rotund man. His bulbous nose was almost as large as his enormous scowl, and the tuft of white hair on top only made the whole expression more comical. The man's scowl deepened for a moment before shock replaced his anger. "Erick *Hausen*?" the Russian demanded, his accent significantly thicker than his hair.

Erick grinned maliciously. "Good to see you too, old man. Can we speak in private in your office?"

Alexander's scowled deepened. "You are only a month younger than me, Erick," he rumbled. He turned around and shambled over to sit at his desk and Chauncy walked in behind him. The office was not large and the wide wooden desk took up most of the floor space that wasn't claimed by the bookshelves.

Alexander dropped his considerable mass into his chair and peered very closely at Chauncy.

"Chauncy Rollock. Protégé of our late friend René. I last saw you during René's final Mind Game in Quito. I must say that I am surprised. The last time I saw you, in Ecuador, you were alive. How is it that you stand before me now, and you are dead?"

"He is alive and breathing, as you can plainly see." Erick said.

"Did you stick him in one of your ungodly machines and bring him back to life?" Alexander asked, his tone riding the divider line between mocking and jovial.

"I did no such thing," Erick said with a laugh. "Although I wish I had a machine like that."

Alexander folded his hands on top of his desk. "All of the news sites seem to agree that Chauncy is dead. Since ghosts do not exist, you must explain."

Erick gestured for Chauncy to speak, and so Chauncy told Alexander the whole story. Alexander was quiet the entire time, listening with rapt attention, and when Chauncy finally finished the physicist shook his head slowly. "Any man that accepts his official death without contesting it, and then travels through Iraq, Turkey, Germany and now to Russia, must have something very important to hide. You realize, Erick, that this would have made an excellent Mind Game."

"Yes it would. Chauncy beat us to it."

"The physical object holds little interest for me at the moment," Alexander said, glancing at the briefcase Chauncy carried. "I am more intrigued by the data. I assume that you did not travel all of this way without bringing me some data, Erick."

Erick reached into his coat and brought out a small, armored flash drive. "I would not think of visiting you without bringing data to distract you. This is the information dump from my computers. I erased every trace of it before we left."

Alexander took the flash drive and studied Erick. "It just goes to show you that I was right, all those years ago at the University of France. You should have joined me in studying the physics of our universe. I guess you were not smart enough to make the grade."

Erick's eyes flashed but he merely shrugged. "We all have our own talents, Alex. I do not think I would be happy if I was forgotten and stuck in a musty, tiny office."

Alexander snorted as he went to his desk and plugged the flash drive into his computer. Everything else in the world ceased to exist as the physicist began to visually devour the intricate formulas and reports that were contained in Erick's information. An ancient and majestic clock stood in the corner and loudly counted out the seconds and minutes that passed.

Chauncy and Erick sat down in chairs without a word and Chauncy took the opportunity to look around the office. A stylized portrait of Alexander Yubarov was behind the desk, and considering the amount of hair showing in the painting it had obviously been commissioned many years ago. Several awards and certificates lined the walls but they were in Russian so Chauncy was unable to decipher them. The most outstanding feature of the office had to be the bookshelves. They took up every inch of wall space that was within easy reach, and they were absolutely packed with books. No dust covered any of them, but Chauncy didn't know if that was because of rigorous cleanliness or because the books were often used.

The tops of the bookcases were devoted to the non-paper awards, and there were many of them. Several of them looked like models of atoms, one or two were star-shaped, but most were a variation of a cylinder or triangle of some kind. Chauncy felt his half-smile growing into a full one as he looked around. Erick Hausen's genius was displayed for all the world to see by a giant skyscraper, but his real genius was hidden away in a lab filled with teams of workers and tons of incredible technology. Alexander Yubarov's genius was displayed in awards and plaques and citations above the many books in his tiny office, several of which even bore Yubarov's name as the author. They were both SSOSA members and yet their methods and decorating touches could not have been more different.

His ruminations were interrupted by a startled Russian phrase that escaped Alexander's lips. Erick and Chauncy both jumped. "This cannot be so," Alexander exclaimed in English.

"What is it?" Erick asked eagerly as he stood up and leaned on the desk. "What do you see?"

Alexander was still staring at the data on the screen, his eyes wide and his jaw slackened. He finally focused his eyes on Chauncy and stood up. He walked over to Chauncy very deliberately. "Do you believe in God, Chauncy?" he asked.

"I'm a Biblical archaeologist. Of course I believe in God."

"That is good. When you get a chance, I suggest that you get on your knees and thank him very much."

Chauncy shrunk back from the intensity of Alexander's expression. "Why?"

"You say you attempted to open the scepter at the dig site, am I right?"

Chauncy nodded.

"Then you should be thanking your God that your attempt did not succeed."

"Why?" Chauncy asked, slowly pushing the briefcase away from his chest and holding it at arm's length. "What's the problem? What is the scepter?"

Alexander spoke very slowly and methodically as he answered. "If you had opened the scepter you and your tent would have been instantly vaporized, and the desert sand you stood upon would

111

have been turned into molten glass."

Chauncy tried to sink even more into the chair while simultaneously trying to make his arms longer so they'd hold the briefcase farther away.

"Quit trying to frighten him and tell us what you found, Alex."

"I am not 'trying' to frighten him," Alexander said as he stood up to his full height. "That scepter contains something that is far stronger and more powerful than nuclear energy!"

Chapter Seventeen

The plane ride had been without incident, mostly because Anita spent half of it sleeping. She woke up in spurts and alternated between staring out the window and staring at her son, who was mostly playing on his tablet in the seat facing her. Every now and then she'd get up and go to the restroom or get a drink from the steward, but her waking hours were mostly spent staring at nothing. Adrenaline overload fatigued her body and she was asleep when they stopped to refuel in Paris. She was a little sad that she'd missed seeing the Eiffel Tower and the City of Lights, but it was hard to get too worked up about such minor things when your life was in danger.

They landed in a tiny town in Turkey that she'd actually heard of. It was the town she where she'd sent mail to Chauncy. Her throat tightened a little but she swallowed past it. Either her husband was really dead and she'd just have to deal with it, or her denial was reality and he was alive. There was no point in getting all choked up about something that she didn't have full data about. It still amazed her, sometimes, how her mind would shift into clinical, medical mode at the strangest times. Other people might be sobbing messes in similar circumstances but she was determined to find facts before investing emotional energy. She didn't know if that made her strong or strange and she didn't care.

Dr. Mayal procured two vehicles, late-model Land Rovers, and had supplies packed into one of them while sitting in the other with Anita and Troy. She asked him the reasoning behind this and he smiled sadly.

"One does not travel into the desert without being prepared, Anita. If your car breaks down there is no, what do you Americans call it, no Seven-Eleven down the street to walk to and get water or food. There are no firemen or police to come rescue you at a moment's notice. It might take days for your saviors to come. Hence: food, water, extra clothing and a couple of tents. Just in case."

He rambled on for a couple more sentences, reminiscing about how the desert was a harsh mistress. Anita smiled to herself. He was chatty because he was nervous. She couldn't blame him. They were heading out into the desert to challenge Turkish authority over his dig. She had no real doubts about his ability to talk them onto the site, though. She had faith.

Dr. Mayal sat in the front with the driver while she sat in the back seat with her son. The daylight was slowly growing as the sun rose on the eastern horizon and she looked around at their surroundings. It wasn't really all that different from Wyoming, just at the opposite end of the temperature and sandiness scales. The mountains were harsh yet beautiful, sharp and jagged ranges cutting up into the reddish haze of the sunrise. It was a beautiful land if one appreciated it. It reminded her of an Ansel Adams photograph that she and Chauncy had over their fireplace. Or, *used* to have before the house burned down.

She slept again for a while but awakened when the vehicle came to a stop. She peered over the front seat to look out the windshield and saw a single military vehicle on the road and a dilapidated building.

"Where are we?" she asked.

Dr. Mayal pointed at the small inspection booth up ahead. "We should be entering Iraq."

Anita was slightly confused. "I thought the dig was in Turkey?"

"The dig is in Iraq," Dr. Mayal corrected her. "But as you can see it is very close to the Turkish border. But do not worry, this border crossing is not too difficult. The challenge will be gaining access to the dig. And it will be especially challenging and interesting when they see a blonde-haired, blue-eyed American woman with her son riding with me."

"I'm sorry if our presence will cause any hardships," Anita responded.

Dr. Mayal waved his hand in disdain. "No, no, having you two with me will augment the reason we are here. Please get your passports ready."

As she watched, two armed men got out of the booth and approached. Mayal rolled down his window and beckoned the men over, speaking in Turkish. An entirely civil argument began and

Anita listened, her ears trying to decipher the foreign words. She couldn't understand what was being said but she had a distinct impression that Faruk was winning the argument handily, especially after he showed some identification. The armed guard doing all of the speaking looked uncomfortable and out of sorts, and before long his face looked like somebody was pinching it. After another bout of conversation he nodded sharply and jogged back to his vehicle, beckoning his comrade to join him.

Mayal looked over his shoulder at her, a satisfied, almost gloating smile on his face. "They did not stand a chance," he said. "They do not even agree with locking me out of my own dig site. I knew I should have just come here in the first place instead of going through official channels."

"Yes, but then I wouldn't be here," Anita said.

Dr. Mayal's smile faded, replaced by a solemn look. "You are absolutely correct. Let us find some answers together. Perhaps we may even find justice."

They drove onward and before very long they approached the campsite. It was on a small hillock that overlooked the excavation zone. Anita had seen enough of her husband's digs to have an idea of what she was looking at. The line of ancient buildings that were still partially buried in the sand were laid out symmetrically, which implied an official function. These were not built haphazardly by civilians just trying to carve out a meager living wherever they could build a hut; these were built by a chieftain, noble or military mind. She gazed out at the buildings for several long moments as the car came to a stop in the middle of the campsite.

Dr. Mayal looked over his shoulder again. "The bodies have already been recovered, or what was left of them."

Dr. Mayal got out of the car and Anita and Troy followed suit. The heat reflecting from the sand made her wince and she immediately reached back into the car for her water bottle and sunglasses. She walked slowly among the burned remains of the campsite, her eyes going over everything with a clinical precision. The tent poles still stood where they had been placed, but all that remained of the fabrics had been blown away by the desert winds.

She would have recognized the largest area staked out by poles, even if the burnt kitchen appliances and benches hadn't been there to cement the identification. This was the mess hall, where the fire had officially started.

Anita walked slowly over to the appliances and shook her head.

"It wasn't an accident," Troy said behind her, making her jump. She turned to her son, impressed.

"What makes you say that?" she asked.

Troy pointed to the appliances. "The report said a windstorm knocked over a malfunctioning stove. That stove is still upright. I think it would take an F5 tornado to move that stove anyway. What is it, solid iron?"

She smiled sadly, filled once more with pride in her son. "It looks it," she affirmed quietly. "And you are right. This was no accident."

Dr. Mayal was on his satellite phone. There was a concerned expression on his face as he listened to the person talking. When he was done he walked over, his face set into stone. "You are extremely observant, Troy," he said with a nod. "You do your father proud. I have to agree; this was no accident."

Anita was going to say something to Dr. Mayal but she noticed his facial expression. "What's the matter?"

He turned to Anita. "That was my attorney. We must return to Ankara,"

"But why?"

"He just informed me the authorities are trying to shut down my museum, and if I'm not there personally they just might succeed."

"What's the problem?"

Dr. Mayal gestured at the site with an expression of great disgust. "They say I am liable for this disaster. Your husband was not the only one who died here. There were at least six other bodies found in the ruins."

Anita's indignation disappeared. Mayal had spent millions of dollars building his museum; it was his life's aspiration. "It's happening isn't it? They want to destroy both of us. The cult is attacking us from all sides."

Dr. Mayal sadly nodded as he looked out at the depressing scenery. "You are very perceptive. Now you see why I suggested we work together. Just when we came here to get answers they pull this trick to get us away from here."

"Can we have just fifteen more minutes?" she pleaded. "I'd to look around and before going with you."

Dr. Mayal looked at his watch. "I suppose even half-an-hour would not make that much a difference. Thank you, Anita. I have spent millions of dollars and decades of my life on that museum. I cannot let political jackals take it from me for any reason."

"I understand, and thank you." Anita nodded and then walked slowly toward the rest of the campsite. Somewhere in all of this debris she was supposed to find evidence that her husband was still alive. They'd already proven that the fire was not an accident caused by a windstorm, but now she had to try and find evidence that her husband had made it out alive.

"We're going to be fine, Mom," Troy said with a truly genuine smile. "We'll look around, see what we can see, and then head to Ankara. It'll be fine."

Anita slowly panned the area looking for a specific tent. "Which one was Chauncy's, tent, Faruk?"

Dr. Mayal shrugged his shoulders. "I only visited the dig once. If memory serves..." Dr. Mayal walked over to a tent that was charred. "It may have been this one."

Anita and Troy slowly approached the burnt out tent. Dr. Mayal wisely kept his distance. Not wanting to meddle or influence with his opinion and to leave them to their musings, he took his satellite phone out again and dialed his attorney to continue the conversation.

Anita and Troy searched as quickly as they could through the remains of tent cloth and burned furniture.

Troy's sifted through blackened debris and suddenly pulled out a half burnt photograph. "Mom, look, it's a picture of you and Dad."

Anita wasted no time in taking the photograph out of her son's hands. "This was definitely Chauncy's tent."

Troy gazed about his surroundings. "Mom, even if the fire started in the kitchen, it doesn't look like the flames could have jumped over here to Dad's tent. And even if they did, he would've had enough time to flee. Something doesn't look right here."

Anita nodded as she also gazed about. "He didn't die in the fire," she said. "I don't know if he's still alive out there, but he did *not* die here."

117

She walked back to the Land Rover and told Dr. Mayal the news.

"It is as I expected," he said and then made a fist and gritted his teeth. "I swear Hakan will pay for his mistakes."

"How do you plan on arresting him?"

Dr. Mayal raised his satellite phone and gave her a weak smile. "I am ahead of you Anita. My attorney has already issued a bulletin to the Turkish police and Interpol to be on the watch out for that jackal!"

Anita sighed with relief. "Thank you."

"When we get back to Ankara," Dr. Mayal continued, "you and Troy will enjoy fine hospitality at my house while I settle my legal issues with the museum. I want you to not trouble yourself or be worried about these events for a time, at least. Once I get the mess at my museum sorted out, we can turn our attention to plans of justice. For both of us."

Anita climbed into the Land Rover and leaned back with a smile. The weight of the world had been lifted from her shoulders and she felt better than she had in a very long time. There was a good chance Chauncy was alive. And that was all she needed: a fighting chance.

Chapter Eighteen

Meteora, Greece

The glowing embers exploded in a shower of sparks as the iron poker rustled through the dying fire. Another thrust of the poker and a small flame sprung forth and grew, bringing light and warmth to the large room once again. Satisfied with the results, the ninety-nine-year-old man stood and returned to the large window.

The view was spectacular from atop the granite spires that were a major geographical feature of Meteora. The old man reflected on the many religious thoughts he'd had while looking out these windows. The Greek Orthodox Church had built this monastery in the 1500s and now he was proud to call it home.

Since Julius Arcosanti had cleansed it of any remnants of the Greek Orthodox teachings this was now *his* monastery, and *his* teachings that would bring light to the surrounding darkness. The old man smiled as he sought out his chair and wrapped a blanket around him. It was the middle of summer, but atop the enormous spires it seemed to the man that winter held a near-permanent grip. He needed more warmth now than he did when he was younger, but he did not mind his advancing age. With age came wisdom, but only if you applied your mind to what you've learned. He looked around at the rows of bookcases that surrounded him and smiled with self-satisfaction. He'd spent his entire life trying to apply his mind and he was not going to let a little thing like old age stop him.

It was somehow fitting that the books his father and brother had tried to hide from him were now out in the open, ready for any of his disciples to delve into. The knowledge that his family deemed dangerous to their way of life was now front and center to Julius' way of life. He'd vowed decades earlier that the truth would never stay hidden as long as he had breath in his lungs

A loud knock echoed from the heavy door at the end of the library. "Enter," Julius said, his voice still as strong as his mind.

The young man who appeared was wearing the monk-like

traditional garb of the monastery: a tan robe and leather sandals. "Teacher?" he asked, his voice quavering only slightly. He was obviously still in awe of the Teacher.

"You may speak, Disciple James," Julius answered, turning his head to view the young learner.

"I have news from the archaeological dig that you instructed us to watch," the disciple said. "A fire has consumed the workers, killing all."

Julius' hands involuntarily clenched into fists. His arthritis made the gesture painful, but he ignored the pain. "Including Chauncy Rollock and Hakan Ramush?"

"Yes, they are listed as dead, Teacher. Here is the newspaper report. I retrieved it from the village this morning."

Disciple James brought the newspaper to Julius, who snatched it away and read through the report swiftly. It did not matter to him that the arduous journey to the village might have exhausted his disciple. The report in the newspaper was more important at the moment. His brows were furrowed not with age but with a great disquieting thought.

Julius picked up another newspaper he kept nearby and leafed through the pages until coming to a picture of a specific event. It was exactly as he had feared. His frown deepened and he stood with sudden energy. He tossed both newspapers into the fireplace. The paper ignited immediately, casting a harsh light upon his face as he watched them burn.

"What is the matter, Teacher?" the disciple asked as he stepped closer. "What is bothering you?"

"It is perhaps better that you do not understand," Julius said quietly.

The disciple stepped even closer. "I came here seeking enlightenment and understanding. I came here because I truly believe you were the one to provide that for me. I would like to understand what this problem is."

Julius turned slowly, a thick sadness deepening the lines on his face. "A great calamity is coming, a calamity that only God himself can stop," he said, his voice booming.

"I do not understand, Teacher."

"The Golden Scepter has been unearthed."

"What is the Golden Scepter?"

Julius was about to berate him but a thought came to him. He furrowed his brow. "You have been a devout student for many years, Disciple James. I think you are ready to hear of this. Of course you are aware of my vast collection of books."

Disciple James smiled. "Hence the reason I have come to Meteora, to be instructed by your wisdom of the ancient writings."

Julius looked at James with a challenging stare. "Name some of the books you have at your disposal, Disciple James."

"Well, Teacher...we have the Samaritan Pentateuch, the Greek Septuagint, the *Textus Receptus* and the Alexandrian Codex."

"And what have you gleaned from these books?"

"The truth about God, Teacher, and not the lies the modern churches are teaching mankind today."

Julius smiled, pleased. "It is this truth that got me excommunicated from the churches, is it not? And yet they could not stop me from teaching. It was fear of excommunication, fear of a loss of his lifestyle, that prevented my father from doing what was right. Ah, but the rest of his books were on display. Did you know that people from distant lands would visit his house to look at his history books?"

"I did not know that, Teacher."

Julius continued as if his student hadn't spoken. "But my father's fear drove him to hide the Pentateuch and the others. The truth does not deserve to be hidden in secret vaults, Disciple James."

"No, Teacher, it does not," James said, smiling. "That is why we disciples come up to your monastery to become monks, so we can get taught by you, the great master."

Julius waved away the compliment. "But there are other books, Disciple James, books that you and the other disciples do not yet have access to. I have in my vast collection of books ancient knowledge, knowledge so powerful that in the wrong hands...would mean a great calamity."

"Hence that is why you speak of this Golden Scepter."

"You are perceptive, Disciple. One of my books contains information about a dangerous cult called *Flamus Divinus*. This book contains prophecy that says the Golden Scepter would be unearthed in the Last Days."

This time, it was Disciple James' eyebrows that shot up. "But

Teacher, according to the Bible, *these* are the Last Days."

"Yes," Julius Arcosanti agreed, his voice rising. "The Golden Scepter has been found. A great power has been unleashed!"

Chapter Nineteen

Hakan Ramush closed the outer door behind him and tried to keep his head high as he walked down the corridor toward The Sanctuary. This room was several stories beneath an ancient building on the streets of Ankara, Turkey. It was to be used for very special occasions only and the security and privacy involved in getting within was tedious. The muted lighting came from craftily concealed bulbs lining the ground and ceiling, but it was still perpetually dim.

He exited the corridor and stood in the single large room. It was cylindrical in shape with a domed ceiling. The left and right sides of the cylinder were accented with carved niches. Each niche had a statue of a different Babylonian deity and the lighting within accentuated the violent poses they held. Some of them were nonhuman, but those that depicted humans had fierce expressions and raised weapons. Their resplendent gold seemed to glow in stark contrast with the polished black marble that lined most surfaces of the room. If the idols came suddenly to life, Hakan reflected, they would kill anything in their path.

Most of the room was encased in darkness, but Hakan knew from past visits that there was a golden throne directly ahead. There were exactly six steps leading up to the raised dais on which the throne sat. The exact center of the floor was a circle covered in various sacred symbols. A bright spotlight from above made it look like a circle of pure energy. Hakan swallowed, a sudden flutter coming to his stomach. He stepped into the light and kneeled slowly, bowing his head almost to the floor. The light was so bright he could still see it with his eyes closed.

"I have arrived as summoned, Exalted One," he said, his voice wavering. He cursed himself for his weakness.

"Do you know why you are here?" the booming voice of the Exalted One asked from the throne. Hakan jerked involuntarily and cursed himself again.

"I am here because I was summoned," Hakan said. He would

not admit to his guilt and his failures so quickly, not even to the Exalted One.

He heard the rustling of cloth as the Exalted One stood. The sound of metal scraping metal rang clearly in the room and was swiftly followed by deliberate footsteps. He tensed as something icy cold and sharp dug slightly into his chin and forced his head to rise slightly. He squeezed his eyes shut and clenched his jaw.

"Open your eyes," the Exalted One ordered. Once he had done so, the Exalted One continued. "Do you know what this is?"

Hakan stared at the golden sword and felt his heart skip a beat. It was an Arabian sword, at least six hundred years old, significantly longer and heavier than the scimitar design that was more popular in this part of the world. "It is the Sword of Justice," he said, licking his dry lips and trying to force moisture into his mouth. "It was used to execute the condemned."

"Correction: it *is* used to execute the condemned," the Exalted One said. "Do you know why you are here?"

Hakan lowered his head again. "I am here because I have failed," he said in a rush of exhaled breath. He had known he was to be executed and had told himself he would face it with dignity. He did not feel dignified or bold. He felt cold and lost, like a child abandoned. "I lost the Golden Scepter and have failed to retrieve it."

"What you have done deserves death," the Exalted One said loudly, his words reverberating through the room to sound even stronger than they were. "You shall lose your head as I have lost my Scepter. Your blood will be easy to clean off of this cold stone."

"Please, forgive me," Hakan begged. "I can still be of use to you."

"And why should I forgive you? You had a final chance and yet you failed."

"Because forgiveness is a path to Allah; it is written."

Hakan winced as he felt the sharp, cold metal come to rest heavily on the back of his neck. "You seek to appeal to my piety, Hakan? Yet you know I am not a practicing Muslim."

A surge of hope flooded through Hakan. "Then I appeal to your sovereignty. Allow me to regain your confidence and it will prove that your first confidence was not misplaced. My failings were not due to negligence. Our foes are intelligent and powerful."

The weight of the sword increased and Hakan clenched his fists as the weapon dug into his skin. He felt a small trickle of blood flow down both sides of his neck. The sword abruptly lifted and he squeezed his eyes shut, envisioning the golden blade sweeping downward and removing him from this world.

The blow never came. "You have one more chance to regain my confidence," the Exalted One said, his voice sounding far away. "Arise, Hakan, and prove your worth!"

Hakan slowly got to his feet, his entire body shaking. He bowed his head low toward the man seated in the throne. The lights came on slowly to reveal the face of the Exalted One: Dr. Faruk Mayal.

"Chauncy Rollock is more resourceful than I might have guessed," Dr. Mayal said after Hakan was standing. "His wife is intelligent and resourceful as well, and their son shows every sign of following in their footsteps. He may be an archaeologist, but with Jake Thrasher and Erick Hausen...I do not think we could have found more worthy adversaries. Your assessment is correct, Hakan."

Hakan's heart soared. He'd done as well as could be expected! They'd had no idea of the extant of Chauncy's intelligence and cunning. He didn't dare point that out, however, lest Dr. Mayal lose his merciful streak.

"Chauncy is no longer in Germany," Hakan stated. "I do not know where he has gone. He has to surface eventually, however. We *need* him to surface. We must have the Golden Scepter."

"The Golden Scepter shall return to us. It has been prophesied," Dr. Mayal said, a wicked grin coming to his face. "The Power of the Divine Flame is stronger than the hearts of men. To quote Alexander the Great, '*there is nothing impossible to him that will try.*' I already see the power at work, Hakan. For centuries the scepter has surfaced only to be hidden again and again. We will not allow it to be hidden away this time. We have an obstacle, yes, but we have courage as well. The Quran instructs us in chapter 4 verse 104: '*Do not relent in pursuing the enemy*'. The best way to make a fish surface is to dynamite the pond. Chauncy will show himself if his family is in danger."

"Do we kill them?" Hakan asked. "I do not like killing those that might still be useful."

"You *do* have some worth left in you," Dr. Mayal said mockingly. "No, we will not be killing Anita and Troy. Instead, I have two assignments for you. First, you will kidnap them and take them somewhere far away. We have thousands of Embers all across the world, and I will leave the choice to your discretion. With his family kidnapped, I will plaster the media with tales of this heinous crime and the news is sure to reach Chauncy. It will break him."

"And what is your second request, Oh Exalted One?"

The supreme leader of the Divine Flame stood and pointed the sword at Hakan. "You will travel to Meteora and burn down Julius Arcosanti's monastery."

"The Keeper of Knowledge."

"Exactly. My nemesis will pay for his past sins. That self-righteous, pompous prophet attempted to keep divine knowledge from me. However, do not kill Julius. Burn his precious books to ashes, but keep him alive so that he can witness our rise to power."

"I will not fail," Hakan said.

Dr. Mayal pointedly ran a finger along the edge of the golden sword. "You know the outcome if you do fail, Hakan."

Hakan rose from his prostrated position, taking a deep breath. "I will not fail," he repeated.

"So be it!" Dr. Mayal slowly shifted the sword around and held it high above his head. "'I am the Lion of the Desert,'" he quoted the old prophecy, his voice growing stronger with each syllable. "'I shall shock my prey with a mighty roar. The gazelle that is hiding in the tall grass will be flushed out for my feasting!'"

Chapter Twenty

Even as a child, Faruk Mayal was viewed as different from other children. His parents and relatives noticed the difference soon enough. The moment he learned to talk, he was constantly asking questions, a rather normal thing among youngsters, but with Faruk it was a chronic habit. Everything and every detail was questioned and if the answer was not satisfactory he would badger the one doling out the answers until he felt he had received a suitable response.

As he continued to grow and mature, his questions became deeper. Although he grew up in a Muslim household and had read the entire Koran, Faruk was unsatisfied with his religion, so began searching other writings and ideas to find the answers to his questions about the meaning of life.

Faruk became a consummate reader. He read the works of the Greek philosophers and the entire Holy Bible by the time he was sixteen. He then plunged headlong into reading the biographies of the great men of history such as Napoleon Bonaparte and Alexander the Great.

Still hungry for knowledge and guidance, he continued his spiritual journey by reading about the Hindu religion. He was greatly influenced by an allegorical novel entitled *'Siddhartha'* written by the German author Hermann Hesse, about the spiritual journey of a young boy from India. The story is set in Nepal during the time of Gautama Buddha about the fourth century B.C. Siddhartha and his companion Govinda set out in search of enlightenment and Nirvana while living as ascetics. Faruk added to his knowledge of Hindu faith and philosophy by reading the Bhagavad-Gita, the most sacred of the Hindu scriptures.

Filled with various ideals and concepts and fueled by the fact that he was considered a genius by his schoolteachers, Faruk envisioned that he would one day be a great man. He would often relate this opinion to his friends, teachers and family. Some scoffed and ridiculed him while others simply shook their heads in dismay.

His parents tolerated such talk from Faruk until the day he turned eighteen, when he made the formal announcement that he was going to quit school and go on a spiritual journey of his own, just like Siddhartha. His father became furious and threatened to beat him. And just like Siddhartha, Faruk disobeyed his father's wishes and protested by standing rigid on the sidewalk in front of their home in Ankara for fifteen hours without food or water. When his father saw the strong determination in his son he acquiesced and let him go.

With only a backpack stuffed with extra clothing and necessities, Faruk left home and walked for many miles toward Jerusalem. Hitching rides and sleeping in dark alleys and begging for food, he eventually made it to his destination. He then wandered through the Judean deserts and frequented the abandoned ruins of the Bible lands.

Faruk truly became a victim of the Messiah complex as he claimed to see supernatural visions and heard voices in his head. During one hot summer night near Masada, he dreamt he should return home and continue his studies to reach his goal.

He came to the realization that all great men need to be educated to reach their destination. His parents were thrilled when he returned home. They permitted him to inhabit his former bedroom, thinking that what he had gone through had been a temporary phase.

His friends and family noticed a change in his demeanor. He had become a strict vegetarian and lost interest in the opposite sex. Not that he had been known as a Casanova prior to his departure to Jerusalem, but he now openly declared his dislike for romantic emotions, saying they were a distraction rather than a help in reaching his goals. He cited examples how some of his friends had left school and married due to unplanned pregnancies.

At the university, Faruk's major was history and Middle Eastern archaeology. After graduation he started his own archaeological company and led many expeditions into the field to uncover long-abandoned, ancient cities. As the years passed, Faruk became restless and bored with his job. His dream of becoming a messiah was slipping through his fingers. He wanted direction in his life; he wanted to hear from God himself if he indeed was the chosen one.

When he was thirty-five years old he sold his shares of the archaeological company and disappeared again. This time he was gone for two years. When he returned to his hometown, his family noticed an even more drastic change in his personality. There was a fire in his eyes and enthusiasm that no one could deny. He had found something of great importance, but Faruk was not yelling about it or preaching it from the rooftops.

His aged father was furious and his mother simply cried when rumor began to circulate that Mayal had started his own religion. They could not understand why he had chosen to leave the Muslim faith and start a new one.

Mayal refused to publicly acknowledge the rumors while he privately occupied himself with hand-picking members from around the globe for his new church. Some were poor students in other lands who wanted to see changes in their governments; others were rich magnates and businessmen who were soured by current policies.

Another major change in Faruk was the fact that he no longer lived as an ascetic. He dressed more professionally, drove a nice car and hobnobbed with the rich and famous. He made a public announcement that he planned to build a large museum. Once he found prime real estate for his building he secured loans and donations to construct it. He started a new archaeological outfit and hired men to dig for artifacts. Some of the relics were sold to acquire more funds and some were to be housed in the new museum.

One thing was certain: Faruk was full of great energy and zeal. He had a master plan in mind. The time was coming when he would show the world he had found a power, a power greater than nuclear energy!

Chapter Twenty-One

"You must be joking," Chauncy said, standing up quickly. He placed the briefcase on the seat he'd just vacated and moved several steps away. "How can there be something more powerful than nuclear energy in this ancient relic? You must have read the calculations wrong. Or maybe the computers made a mistake."

"My computers did not make a mistake," Erick said quickly. He had also moved several steps away from the scepter. It was almost a repeat of earlier, and it would have been funny if it wasn't so serious. "Three machines working independently of each other do not reproduce the same mistake."

"Erick is correct, for once," Alexander said stiffly. "And I did *not* read the calculations wrong. Do you not see the many awards I have received for my work?"

Chauncy tore his gaze away from the briefcase and made an apologetic smile at Alexander. "I'm sorry, I didn't mean it that way. This is just...this is too strange. Forgive me."

Alexander puffed out his chest and continued to look appalled, but he only did so for a moment. "I accept your apology," he said. He walked to his desk and pulled out a piece of paper and some scissors. He chopped away at the paper for a minute before holding up a five-pointed star shape. "What do you see here?"

Erick looked vaguely amused. "It is a paper star, Alex." He started to laugh but the increasing seriousness of Alexander's expression killed the joke.

"You see the star as well, correct Chauncy? Good." He then reached over and held up the paper from which the star had been cut. "What would we call this then?"

"The anti-star," Erick said, snapping his fingers. "You are talking about antimatter, correct?"

Chauncy cleared his throat. "Excuse me? Antimatter? Isn't that strictly in the realm of science fiction? This isn't science fiction, Alexander."

Alexander's lips might have twitched into a smile but it was hard to tell. "Antimatter was theorized in 1928 by the British scientist Paul Dirac. He was working on quantum mechanics but his equations kept coming up with strange results. The only way his results could be true was if there were a particle that had the same mass as an electron, but with a positive charge instead. It was not until years later when Carl Anderson actually observed positrons that the theory of antimatter was proven."

"Are you absolutely sure that is what the calculations are telling you?" Erick interrupted. "That there is antimatter in the scepter?"

"Yes, as sure as I am that Chauncy is standing here in front of us instead of being dead."

"So why did the computers show an explosion?" Chauncy asked.

"For every action there is a reaction, every positive has a negative, Yin and Yang, up and down," Alexander held up the pieces of paper, "star and anti-star. One gram of antimatter annihilating one gram of matter is basically three times as powerful as the nuclear bomb dropped on Hiroshima."

Chauncy took another step back from the briefcase. "Good grief, no wonder you asked if I believed in God! But how on earth does the scepter contain antimatter?" he asked, feeling exasperated. This wasn't making any sense. "You just said antimatter reacts violently with matter. Am I missing something, or is the scepter not actually matter?"

Alexander laughed, his whole body shaking with the sound. "You have missed nothing, Chauncy my lad. The scepter is indeed matter."

"Are you suggesting the scepter is an antimatter trap?" Erick asked suddenly. "The kind used in particle accelerators?"

"Don't particle accelerators use really powerful magnets?" Chauncy asked.

"Yes, that is part of the process," Erick said. "They also use ionizing radiation in the traps to keep the antimatter atoms cool. It is rather like keeping angry hornets in a jar: you keep the inside of the jar cold and it calms them down. Is that what the scepter is?"

"That is my current theory," Alexander said. "But it is still quite improbable."

"So would either of you like to explain to me how men living thousands of years ago built an antimatter trap?" Chauncy asked. "They sure as heck didn't have particle accelerators to help them."

"Is it not obvious?" Alexander asked, grinning. "It is a hoax! Somebody recently placed the scepter at the dig site to make it look like an artifact from long ago."

"Of course," Erick said. "It is a joke on Doctor Mayal. He would take the scepter to his museum and claim it was a powerful artifact, and everyone would laugh at him when it was proven otherwise."

"I hate to burst your bubbles, guys, but that's not possible," Chauncy said firmly. "I oversaw the entire dig operation, from start to finish. I was the first and only person to enter that storage bin, and it had not been disturbed for centuries before I got there."

"There must have been a way, a secret tunnel perhaps."

Chauncy shook his head. "There were no tunnels that I saw. And why would somebody go to all of this trouble? I was ushered in to the dig site very secretly, as were the workers, and we were not allowed to leave. There is very little chance that somebody could have come in during that time to place the scepter for us to find. Again, the room looked undisturbed. Besides, what's the point of going to all that trouble just to hide a bomb for us to find?"

Alexander looked startled. "Bomb? No, Chauncy, you are sadly mistaken. The scepter is not a bomb."

Erick sighed and rubbed his head. "Alex, you are not making any sense. You just said the scepter contains antimatter. You saw the same video we did. Once the rings were opened it obviously released the antimatter and exploded."

"I said it contains antimatter particles but I never said it was a bomb," Alexander said adamantly. "Are both of you so blind that you did not see the details in the video? Come, look!"

They all went around the desk and looked at his monitor. He brought up the video and played it in slow motion. The rings fell into proper place and a bright light appeared, just as before. But now that it was played in slow motion it was as plain as day: the scepter was still intact. It had not exploded. The light was coming out of the end of the scepter but was not destroying it in the process.

"See?" Alexander said, pointing at the screen like it was the answer to everything. "If you had retrieved the entire intact scepter you would have seen its real purpose. I firmly believe that the missing part of the scepter is a regulator that will align the antimatter in a stream coming out the end."

Chauncy leaned against the desk. "Like a lightning bolt," he said quietly.

"Exactly like a lightning bolt," Alexander affirmed. "A highly destructive bolt of energy that can decimate anything in its path. *That* is what the scepter is: a directional weapon of mass destruction."

Chauncy shook his head. "This can't be right. This is getting more like science fiction, not reality."

"Many things we use on a daily basis were once science fiction," Erick said. He was still staring at the screen. "I help bring many more to the market. That is why I agree with Alex. This is a modern device, designed to look like an ancient one."

He didn't have the energy to shake his head anymore. "And I'm convinced that it is the genuine article. The symbols on the scepter are not widely known; even *I* had a hard time recognizing them. Only somebody with extreme knowledge of the Babylonians, and even cultures before them, could have made the scepter look like this. Why? Why would somebody go to that much trouble just to hide something as a hoax? Keep in mind, gentlemen, that this is a *working* hoax. It really has antimatter particles in it, otherwise Erick's computers wouldn't have shown us this data. That makes the scepter beyond valuable. You don't just bury something like that."

"It is possible that it was designed in modern times by somebody who suddenly got a conscience," Erick said. "He realized the horrors that could be done with the weapon and then hid it."

"In the back of an ancient grain storage bin that would eventually be excavated?" Chauncy asked with a snort. "Yeah, right. You'd do better to dump it off at the Mariana Trench. No, this scepter is real, whether you believe it or not. That means that ancient man built a working antimatter weapon."

The three men were silent for many minutes as they stared at the video frame of the scepter delivering its deadly payload.

"We need to speak to an expert on ancient technology," Erick said finally. "Unless you are volunteering, Chauncy?"

"I am an expert in ancient cultures, languages and customs," he said. "My knowledge of their technology is not extensive. Not *this* extensive, that's for sure. I have no idea how the Babylonians could have accomplished this."

Erick looked at Alexander with a knowing grin. "So we need an expert on ancient technology."

Alexander laughed. "I would not call him an 'expert,' although he would disagree. What are you trying to do, have a SOSSA class reunion?"

"Milos Karakoles," Chauncy said, his laugh equaling Alexander's. "Of course. He's a history buff, isn't he? And he's the only SOSSA member not here. Where is he, anyway?"

"He lives in a villa in Greece these days," Erick said. He gestured to the keyboard. "May I send him a message? Coded, of course?"

Alexander stepped back. "Be my guest. I think that between three SOSSA members and Chauncy here, we may finally figure out just what this Golden Scepter really is and what it was made for."

Chauncy looked back at the briefcase. Right now it seemed like a brooding metal animal, crouched and ready to spring. "Hopefully before it, or somebody searching for it, kills us."

Chapter Twenty-Two

Anita looked away from the skyline and smiled at her son. He hadn't left the confines of Wyoming since the visit to Cancun and now he was in one of the most exotic locations in the world. Anita knew a little about the history of Turkey and the Ottoman Empire before it. The gaps in her knowledge were quickly being filled in by the architecture and the city before them, as well as by the words of their helpful chauffeur. Mayal had put his chauffeur completely at their disposal when he'd left to take care of business at his museum. "Explore the city," he'd said with a smile. "There is a lot to soak in, especially for those who truly care about history. Someday you will have to visit my museum."

So they'd spent the day being driven around Ankara and its outskirts, taken to all of the best spots. Their driver, who revealed his name as Tanju, spent only a small portion of the day taking them to the 'tourist spots,' as he'd called them. The rest of the day they'd visited the real historical sites, becoming engrossed in the history of the city. They'd eaten twice at completely authentic 'hole in the wall' eateries, as Chauncy would have called them, and she found herself dutifully impressed by the cuisine.

Between historical sites, she spent the time calmly and quietly talking to Troy about his father. Now that they both knew he *had* to be alive they could discuss him without grief. Troy was curious as to how they'd met, a question he'd never asked before. So she told him the story of Chauncy's trip to Egypt and the highly illegal photo he'd taken atop the Grand Pyramid. She had noticed him before that, of course, in their shared meteorology class at the university. But that picture showed he was daring and adventurous and they'd fallen in love rather quickly.

It helped her to talk about the early days. Like all married couples they'd had their ups and downs, and it helped to remember the reasons they'd fallen in love in the first place. It helped keep the love alive and kept her hopes alive. Chauncy had survived Egypt, he'd survived Mexican cartels...he would survive this as well.

As the sun started to head toward the horizon she realized that she wanted to go shopping. She had yet to visit one of the many marketplaces she'd seen throughout the day and she really wanted to correct that oversight. What better way to become engrossed in a local culture than to shop their shops? Tanju was not as enthusiastic about the idea as she was and neither was Troy. But she insisted, so Tanju drove them to one of the larger local bazaars. He started to accompany them but Anita wanted to do this with just her son. Tanju argued about that for nearly five minutes, warning her about the many ways that she might be taken advantage of. She acknowledged the warnings but just as firmly ordered him to stay with the car.

The shops were all filled with bright merchandise, from local clothing to indigenous food. The noise level was something she hadn't expected as every merchant called out for customers and haggling took place at increased volumes. She wandered the tight maze between the booths. She and Troy were wearing local clothes, provided by Mayal, but they still stood out in the crowd and she could feel all eyes upon her. She did not feel unsafe, however, and Troy seemed to like the attention.

At the moment, shopping was the only thing to do to waste time until Dr. Mayal tended to his legal woes. He had promised her that when he was done, they would embark on a fact-finding mission.

She turned aside to one of the booths, attracted to the bright reams of cloth that were on display. The owner was a tiny little woman, as ancient as the city around her. "Do you speak English?" Anita asked.

"I speak," the woman responded, her nearly-closed eyes lighting up at the prospect of a sale. "What you want?"

The two women talked for a few minutes, Anita asking questions and the shop owner responding with even more questions. Before long the owner disappeared into the back of her booth, promising that she had something special. The booth owner re-appeared suddenly with a roll of cloth that was absolutely gorgeous. Anita started to pull out her money, but something distracted her.

About a half block away there was an increasing commotion as a man pushed his way through the crowds. He wasn't a Turk; in fact, he stood out from the crowd just because of that. He was a tall, thin Caucasian man wearing Western garb who appeared to be in his sixties. He was saying something but due to the noise in the market it was incomprehensible to her. He was making his way straight toward her, and even at this distance she could tell that he was shouting at her. That was worrisome. Nobody should know where she was.

She was opening her mouth to warn Troy when a strong arm snaked around her neck and lifted her bodily off the ground. She gasped for breath, panic flooding into her. A moment of clarity struck and she twisted her body, long-forgotten self-defense measures coming into her mind. She threw her elbows behind her and struck flesh and bone. The pressure on her throat eased just long enough for her to draw a breath.

The world tilted as she fell to the ground. She pushed herself up to a kneeling position, adrenaline coursing through her veins. Her attacker was nowhere to be seen, but the older Caucasian appeared suddenly.

"Anita, grab my hand," the man said in perfect English.

"Who are you?" she demanded, her adrenaline surging as attack possibilities occurred to her.

"Jake Thrasher," he answered. "We need to go or they'll be back to get you too!"

The name was ringing bells but she couldn't quite place it. "Why should I trust you?" she asked. The name still sounded familiar, but this was no time to go blindly trusting people.

"Chauncy sent me. He told me to tell you this: 'listen to him, my little Xochitl.'"

Chauncy's private name for her. Her vision darkened as emotions swirled through her. She'd suspected Chauncy was still alive, but to actually hear it was something else. "Chauncy's alive? Where is he?" she asked eagerly.

Jake firmly pushed her away from the growing crowd. "Later. They're probably already coming back."

The phrase 'coming back' suddenly kicked cobwebs loose in her brain. She turned frantically around, her eyes sweeping the marketplace and telling her what her brain already knew: Troy was gone.

"Where's my boy?" she demanded, panic choking her as effectively as her assailant. "Where's Troy?"

Jake grabbed her shoulders. "I can explain that later, Anita, we need to *move!*"

Every instinct in her body wanted her to rush around the marketplace looking for her son. Logic, reality, and medical training for a crisis proved more powerful. There was no way she could search the entire place quickly enough to locate Troy. Her throat tightened as she took shuddering breaths, but she knew that her mind wasn't lying to her. She suddenly remembered where she'd heard the name: Jake Thrasher was the man who'd helped Chauncy climb the pyramid in Egypt. He was the reason they were married. She had to trust him for now.

She followed Jake swiftly from the scene, a huge part of her feeling guilty and helpless. She felt like she was abandoning her son. No amount of logic could erase that feeling, not right now. Jake hopped into a small car and she followed suit. "I need to call Dr. Mayal," she said distantly, her hands fumbling through her purse. "He needs to know about Chauncy and maybe he can help find Troy."

"No," Jake said emphatically as he started up the car. "Dr. Mayal is the problem, Anita."

Without warning, Jake grabbed her cellphone, turned it off and gave it back to her. "What in the world are you doing?" Anita demanded.

"Your phone can be traced, Anita, and that's the last thing we need right now."

"You'd better explain yourself quickly," she said, a fire burning in her eyes.

Jake looked at her and his usual joking attitude died. He explained how Dr. Mayal was behind Hakan's attempts to kill Chauncy and behind this latest kidnapping. He had to pause frequently as they moved in and out of traffic, and he checked the rearview mirrors every couple of seconds. He told her how he'd rescued Chauncy and the trip to Erick Hausen. He explained as best he could about the Golden Scepter and how the Divine Flame cult wanted it more than anything else. She was rather quiet when he finished his explanation.

"And you're absolutely certain Dr. Mayal is behind all of

this?" she asked incredulously.

"It's kind of hard to argue with the video evidence I got," Jake said. "I still have operatives and spies all over this city. Amazing what a little money in the right palms can do for your worldview."

She closed her eyes and leaned back in the seat. Her body still ached as she thought of her son. "You really think they won't hurt him?"

Jake fidgeted in his seat. "I can't guarantee that they won't *hurt* him, but they definitely won't kill him. It's obviously a ploy to flush Chauncy out. If they kill Troy they'd just drive him deeper into hiding."

"They'd drive *me* into killing *them*," she said hotly, her eyes snapping open. "Dr. Mayal is such a weasel! No wonder he was always asking if Chauncy had contacted me. Why doesn't Chauncy just give them the Golden Scepter?"

Jake shrugged. "You married him, you'd understand it better. They tried to kill him for it. He's determined to figure out how it works and what he can do to keep it from them."

She looked out the window at the city. "He's very stubborn," she said softly. She missed him terribly and wished he was with her right now. "What's the plan?"

"We're going to my headquarters in San Diego; nobody will find you there. Then I'm going to get in touch with Chauncy, tell him to give up the scepter so you can get Troy back. I get my paycheck and everybody lives happily ever after. Well, except Chauncy. He seems to love trouble."

Anita didn't smile. She was sick with worry about her son.

Chapter Twenty-Three

Baja California, Mexico

The view of the ocean was almost serene enough to take Geraldo Esperanto's mind off of his Jeep. Almost. It was about two seconds away from collapsing into a pile of bolts and rusty metal. He took his foot off the accelerator and let the Jeep coast slowly down the slight decline. It wasn't fair, really. His *madre* had always told him he was too pretty to be poor. He took a moment to admire his striking *Yaqui* Indian good looks in the rearview mirror: jet-black hair combed into a ponytail, high cheekbones and bronzed skin. His clothing was well-pressed and he knew his mannerisms were exquisite.

But his *madre* had been wrong. Being beautiful had not brought Geraldo money. It had brought him an excellent fiancée, it was true, but the pesos had not followed. His Jeep was more than enough evidence of that; he didn't have enough funds to get a new one, and not enough funds to get this one repaired. The journey to his *Mision de Alcala* was slow and tedious because he could not push the vehicle to its true potential. He would get there eventually, he knew, so he returned his gaze to the Pacific Ocean visible on the horizon.

He was so engrossed in trying to forget his problems that he nearly crashed into the abandoned mission that was his home. Not that it would have been that big of a crash since he was barely going five kilometers an hour. He shut off the coughing engine and listened to it sputter its way to silence. One of these days it would sputter for the last time. He looked up at the mission and felt more depressed than ever. As far as he was concerned, this once-proud symbol of Catholicism was supposed to be his center of ruling. Sure, it was in far better shape than when he'd found it three years ago. Back then it had been defaced, covered in graffiti and practically hidden by weeds. Now it was cleaner but there were still cracks to patch and a hundred other little things that needed to be done.

He took the groceries from the back of the Jeep and walked up to the door. A large black dog started barking at him ferociously. "Shut up, you stupid mutt," he said. "Don't you recognize me?"

The dog continued to bark at him and Geraldo rolled his eyes. Yeah, this was going to be a great day. He pushed the door open with his feet and yelled to get his friend's attention. His shout went unanswered and he swore. Continuing to grumble, he made his way through the courtyard and came to the old administrative building. He kicked this door as well, his way of knocking because his hands were full. He was positive that the loud roaring of the generator was going to make him deaf, and right now it was preventing his friend from hearing him.

A moment later, however, a chubby man about the same age as Geraldo opened the door. "Sorry, didn't hear you," Marcos Campana said as he took one of the grocery bags.

"I don't doubt it," Geraldo said disgustedly. "That generator is a pain in the butt. I wish we could get rid of it."

"You know it's the only way to get electricity way out here," Marcos chided him.

They put the groceries away and Geraldo collapsed onto an old couch next to the computer desk. Marcos got back on the computer. "I'm getting sick of this way of life," Geraldo complained.

"You are living the life of a messiah," Marcos interjected. "You and I are Embers of Mexico."

"We're dying Embers, Marcos, I am living the life of a miserable poor man," Geraldo retorted. "We gave all of our money to the church to help build the organization." He pulled out a can of beer, opened it and took a long swig. When he was finished he looked at Marcos. "What I want to know is when is *my* time going to come? I have been toiling in this old-crumbling heap of a church for three years now. I'm even in danger of losing Perla."

Marcos laughed. "Well, no respectable woman wants to live so far from the city in a despicable dump like this one."

Another swallow of beer and Geraldo pointed at Marcos. "That's what I am saying. Where are the riches and glory that were supposed to be showered upon me, huh?"

"We must be patient. All good things come when we are patient," Marcos reminded him.

"Oh, please," Geraldo threw the empty beer can in the trash can. "I am patient, I just don't like waiting." He stared out the window as something caught his attention. "Did you hear that?" he whispered.

"Yeah, it's the generator."

Geraldo slowly walked over to the door. "No, I hear that stupid dog barking. Something is wrong."

They looked at each other and then lunged for a wooden box that was located in the corner of the room where they produced two long knives.

"I hope it's not thieves again," Marcos said with a tremble in his voice as he grasped his knife.

"Come on." Geraldo opened the squeaky door and then they sprinted across the open courtyard, past the noisy generator to the rear church door.

The two men ran into the church and then rushed to the front double doors at the entryway. Geraldo, being more athletic than Marcos, was way ahead as he jumped over the broken wooden pews. When they reached the doors, they were panting heavily as they peered out of the holes in the wooden door.

"It's a truck with a camper," Geraldo said.

"Think it's a drug dealer looking for a place to roost?"

Geraldo looked down at his weapon. "If it's a drug dealer then these stupid knives aren't any match for an AK-47," he said ruefully.

Geraldo looked outside again. "I only see the silhouette of one man. Maybe he is alone or maybe he has an army of guys in the camper."

"We're doomed, they'll surround the place!"

Geraldo suddenly laughed. "Well, well, it looks like we have a dignitary visiting us."

Marcos got up enough nerve to look outside. He laughed when he spotted the large, portly man. "It's the Great One. I wonder what he wants with us. He's second-in-command...we're rats to him."

"Why don't we find out?" Geraldo asked as he opened the door.

Their dog, *Pendejo*, was barking furiously at Hakan. The Great One said something loudly in a different language and the dog

145

backed off, baring its teeth but no longer barking.

Geraldo stopped a few yards away from Hakan and bowed his head low. "What brings you to my palatial estate, Oh Great One?" he asked in English.

"I have excellent news and a job for you," Hakan answered in Spanish. "May I come in to explain it?"

Geraldo's waved his hand at the church. "What's ours is yours, Great One."

After the three men assembled in what passed for the administrative part of the complex, Hakan took the lead in talking. "I will be as brief as possible. First I have to tell you the good news. We found the scepter."

Marcos and Geraldo looked at each other in amazement. "Why weren't we informed on the website?" Geraldo asked.

"Because we have a serious problem. The scepter is in the hands of an American archaeologist. The Exalted One will not make the find known to all the Embers until we actually have it in our hands."

Geraldo was still in shock about the good news. He leaned back in his chair with an expression of wonderment in his eyes. "This is awesome, it was all true. Every word we were told was true. The real power will come!"

"Before the real power can come, I need your help," Hakan said, raising his voice so they would listen. "I trust no one else but you and your friend. You see, we need to get the archaeologist's attention. He is holding the scepter hostage and he won't resurface unless we force him. That's why I have his son in my truck."

"What?" Geraldo sat up. "You want us to keep him...here?"

"Yes. I want you to keep him under lock and key until you receive further orders. You are to do as I say. When the scepter is returned then you can release him."

"Why should we take orders from you?" Geraldo asked in a defiant manner.

Marcos looked at his friend, mortified. "Is that how you speak to the Great One?"

Geraldo raised his hand in his defense. "I've already made tons of sacrifices, I just want to know what's in it for me. Kidnapping is serious business."

"Do my bidding and you will become the Grand Ember of Mexico."

Geraldo's eyes widened slightly. "That's nice, but we have no money and we can't afford to feed another mouth."

"Those days are over Ember," Hakan said as he opened his briefcase and pulled out large stacks of money. The young men's eyes widened with wonder. "Here is ten thousand dollars. If you do the job right, another ten thousand will come."

"How did you get the boy and the money past the Mexican authorities?" Geraldo asked, staring at the money like a starving man stared at a free meal.

"It is amazing what the power of a bribe will get you here in Mexico," Hakan said with a chuckle.

The young men trembled with excitement as they touched the money. It was intoxicating and mesmerizing and obviously too grand for them to ignore.

"And all we have to do to get twenty thousand dollars is hold the boy until told otherwise?"

"Yes, and that sum does not include whatever the Exalted One promised you. The scepter is unearthed, Embers! It is only a matter of time until we will have the ultimate power in our hands. Play this right and good things will happen to the two of you."

There was no need to wait for an answer. The expressions on the two young men spoke volumes.

Hakan smiled. "Now if you do not mind, I would like to introduce you to the boy. But we must hurry, I have another appointment in Greece."

Chapter Twenty-Four

"The Pacific Ocean is about an hour's walk from here," Geraldo advised as he led Troy to the church. "See those mountains over there? They are full of snakes and hungry coyotes. North and south of us is nothing but hot desert. You'd last ten minutes."

"Where am I?" Troy asked.

Before Geraldo could respond the dog came out of the mission barking at Troy.

Geraldo laughed. "Hey, *Pendejo*, don't eat our guest."

"I don't think he likes him," Marcos wryly commented.

"I don't like dogs," Troy said. "Get him away from me."

"Do not worry, *Pendejo* is all bark," Geraldo laughed. "But don't come out here alone. *Pendejo. Vámonos!*"

The dog barked for a few more seconds before skittering off somewhere else to do something equally annoying. Geraldo tensed as another vehicle came racing up to the church. He relaxed when he recognized the car. A pretty, nineteen year old Hispanic woman with large brown eyes emerged from the rear seat. In the front seat were Perla's two brothers, Pablo and Enrique, who also climbed out of the car.

Perla quickly ran to embrace Geraldo. "Geraldo, it's good to see you." Still clutching Geraldo, she looked at Troy. "Who are you?"

Geraldo explained the situation as quickly and concisely as possible. Perla looked apprehensive. "I don't like taking little kids from their parents."

"It's really just an exchange," Geraldo said earnestly. "Once Chauncy gives us the Golden Scepter, he gets his kid back. Simple."

"It doesn't seem that simple to me," she said, drawing back. "It's still kidnapping. What if the authorities find out?"

"There's no way they can. Besides, you deserve the best, my Perla, think about it. Twenty-thousand *American* dollars."

Her smile came back tentatively. "As long as we don't mistreat him. Look at those big blue eyes."

"Yeah, he's a gem no doubt," he responded sarcastically. He leaned over and looked at Troy. "Cooperate and we'll treat you nice. Perla is an excellent cook and we'll feed you well. If you try to escape, things won't look so good for you. Got it?"

Troy stood defiantly but nodded in agreement. Perla stepped forward and took his hand. "I will look after him," she said, giving Geraldo a look that meant she wouldn't accept an argument. She smiled at Troy and switched to English. "What is your name, young man?"

"Troy."

Perla tried to say the name, but she rolled the R's, like any Hispanic would. "Trrroy?"

"Just Troy. One R."

She smiled and said it again, right this time. "Will you come with me, Troy? I will make you some enchiladas."

Troy perked up at the mention of food. He hadn't eaten in hours. Perla led the way into the kitchen. Troy followed her and sat down on a bench that faced the large oven.

"I like your pants," she said, trying to make him feel at ease. "They have a lot of pockets!"

"My mom got them for me," he said, suddenly apprehensive. "I like to keep stuff in them."

"Well, they look good for that. Do you like chicken?"

He responded in the affirmative and she went about getting the food. "This is a pretty place," he said, looking around. "Where is it?"

Perla smiled at him. "We are in Baja, Mexico. Have you ever been to Mexico?"

"I've been to Cancun," Troy said, beaming. "But I meant this building. It looks Spanish. Is it a mission?"

"You are quite smart. Yes, it was abandoned over a hundred years ago. My Geraldo found it and fixed it up."

Troy looked around. The place sure didn't look fixed up. It looked like a dump. Perla caught his glance and the expression on his face and laughed. "Oh yes, he cleaned it up. You should have seen what it looked like before."

"What's it called?"

"You are a curious one. I believe it was called *Mision de Alcala* before. Nowadays Geraldo calls it the *Ecclesia Flamus Divinus de Geraldo*. He has such dreams for this place, and for us."

She went back to preparing the chicken enchiladas and Troy permitted himself a small, self-satisfied smile. He surreptitiously looked through the window behind him. Geraldo and Marcos were still outside, apparently arguing about something. Perla was busy with the food preparation. He probably wouldn't get a better chance than this. He reached deep into his bottom cargo pocket and pulled out the small smartphone his mother had convinced his father to get him last month. Hakan had frisked him quickly but had missed it. He glanced up again to make sure Perla was preoccupied with the food and then flipped on his phone.

There was no cell service out here. Big surprise, that. There was, however, an unsecured WiFi access point with an extremely strong signal, which meant it was in the mission. Troy snorted; these men really *were* amateurs. He connected to the network, got internet access, and pulled up his email. He started to type out a short message.

"Troy!" Geraldo shouted.

Troy pressed send and tried to hide his phone, his heart pounding so hard it hurt. Geraldo rushed over and grabbed him, forcibly wrenching his hands apart and taking the cellphone. His face turned red and he slapped Troy so hard the boy fell off the bench.

"Geraldo, stop!" Perla said.

"Don't tell me what to do, woman! This little rat was using a cellphone. What did you send? Huh?"

Troy rubbed his face and didn't answer. Geraldo stepped forward to kick him but Perla held him back. "You can't torture him," she spat. "They will never accept a trade if you harm their son. Think of the twenty thousand, Geraldo, and look at his phone. Maybe he didn't send a message."

Geraldo looked at the phone, still breathing heavily from his fury. After a moment his face cleared a little. "It's worse than I'd like, but not as bad as I feared. '*Mission de Al*' is all he got off. Why did you tell him the name anyway, Perla?"

"I was trying to keep him calm. He'd just been kidnapped."

151

Geraldo glared at Troy. "No, he is smart. You don't get chicken enchiladas for dinner, kid." He dragged Troy none-too-gently along the floor to the wine cellar and tossed him inside. "A little hunger and darkness will teach you not to try anything around the Divine Flame."

Geraldo was still fuming as he walked down the hallway. He spotted Marcos and noticed the nervous expression on his friend's face.

"What's the matter with you?" Geraldo angrily asked.

"I think we better tell the Great One the kid emailed a message."

Geraldo raised his hands in the air. "Are you insane? Then we'll look like incompetent idiots. Didn't you hear him say he was going to recommend *me* as Grand Ember for Mexico?"

"Yeah, but the message—"

Geraldo interrupted him as he turned away. "I said not to worry. There's no way anyone could translate that message anyway."

Filled with fear of doing something wrong against the Divine Flame, Marcos Campana closed his bedroom door and started typing a message to Hakan.

Chapter Twenty-Five

The journey from Mexico to Meteora had been mostly without incident for Hakan, even if it was convoluted and involved a lot of flying and driving. He was tired but ecstatic. He had already called Dr. Mayal and notified him of his success in securing Troy. As for Anita and Jake, Dr. Mayal advised Hakan that they too would eventually be captured.

He tenderly touched the cut on his neck where Dr. Mayal had placed the sword. It was still sore. It was amazing how quickly things changed in life. A few days ago he was so close to getting his head chopped off, but now things were looking better.

The giant granite spires looked like claws reaching up from the earth, trying to snatch the sky and eat it for lunch. Atop those spires were monasteries that were built many centuries ago. Hakan didn't really know all that much about them; they were secondary to his mission here. He knew about the architecture of his target monastery and that was about as much research as he'd done.

The monasteries were difficult to approach since they were built on sheer granite ascents. Most were only accessible via rope bridges that connected to other granite spires, or reached by crude elevators operated by a hand pulley. Julius Arcosanti's monastery was the former type. Hakan had come prepared for any eventuality on this difficult terrain. He had a collection of vertical-ascent climbing gear as well as a wingsuit in case of emergency.

The morning came bright and early and Hakan ascended the steps that would eventually lead him to the monastery. His royal robes, long, flowing and purple with stylized golden flames sewn on the cloth, shone brilliantly in the sunlight. He kept his head held high as he walked across the bridge, his weight causing it to sway slightly. A monk acting as a guard approached him to inquire the purpose of his visit. He pushed him aside with ease knowing the monk carried no weapon for self-defense.

He walked a few steps onto the courtyard and pushed the large wooden doors open to the foyer. Several men dressed in brown robes rushed to him and berated him for his lack of decorum. They were as easy to move as the first monk had been, his arrogant stride unhindered by their monkish reflexes.

Julius Arcosanti met him in the large foyer. "Why do you come before me with haughtiness?" Julius asked.

"I am Hakan Ramush, Great One of the Divine Flame."

"I know exactly who you are. You are not a great one by any stretch of the imagination, you are but a minion and a slave to a darker force."

"I have come to teach you truth, Julius Arcosanti."

"You wish to bring *me* truth?" Julius asked, his tone dripping with sarcasm. "Pray, enlighten me."

"The Divine Flame has tested your worthiness, and you have been found lacking."

"The Divine Flame is a blasphemous cult that will soon be destroyed by the Almighty."

Hakan shook his head. "No, the Almighty has already revealed the scepter to us and we are now ascending to power. You, on the other hand, failed to share this knowledge with us. You kept the knowledge locked away from us."

"This knowledge was not meant to be in the hands of infidels."

"*You* are the infidel, hence why I have come to teach you truth," Hakan said. He reached into his robe and pulled out a small metal sphere. He twisted the device and rolled it almost casually at a nearby wooden wall. The sphere erupted in a small explosion and flames leapt up the wall.

"This is the price you shall pay," Hakan said, raising his voice. "The Divine Flame shall burn your books to the ground, just like we did at Alexandria. You denied us *one,* we deny you *all.*"

Hakan swung around and exited the building. Once he was out in the courtyard he aimed his handgun at any of the monks that tried to extinguish the flames. The blaze grew in intensity and began to spread out from the foyer.

His satellite phone beeped and he took it out of his robe. It was the number of an Ember. "What do you want?" he demanded.

"Great One, we know where Jake Thrasher and Anita Rollock are headed. You must come at once."

Hakan listened to the information and hung up, swearing softly. Now he was faced with a dilemma. Burning down this

154

monastery was his mission. But if he captured Anita and Jake, the monastery wouldn't matter. He ran through the logic and possible scenarios and came up with only one answer. He lobbed one more incendiary grenade at the monastery. The righteous fire of the Divine Flame expanded quickly and that was enough for him. The trip down the steps would take forever, so he simply shed his royal robes and leapt off the spire. He soared to the bottom, his expert wingsuit skills preventing injury, and set off to hunt down Jake and Anita.

Chapter Twenty-Six

Erick looked up from his laptop. "Milos has confirmed our meeting. Our timing is perfect. He was about to leave for New York."

Chauncy, lost in thought, sipped his soda and turned away from the view out of the airplane window. "I don't believe it," he said.

Erick raised his eyebrows. "Why not? I just got the email from him. It is definitely authentic."

Chauncy shook his head, smiling in spite of his mood. "No, not that, sorry. I was talking to Alexander."

Alexander looked insulted. "Do you think I would make this up?"

"No, that's not what I meant. I meant that it seems unbelievable. I know it's true, but...lightning has antimatter in it?"

Alexander's face cleared. "Yes, it does sound extreme. I would bet that is exactly how the scientists felt when they pointed the Fermi telescope at a thunderstorm."

"*Einen Augenblick*," Erick said, frowning as he looked at the equations. "If the antimatter in the scepter were let out, as we have surmised, would it not be destroyed as it came into contact with the air? Air is matter."

Alexander got up from his window seat and moved over to the small table where Erick was seated. "That is a good point," the Russian rumbled as he sat down. "We may have just discovered a flaw in the mechanism. I will have to research this further, see if I can find a workaround."

"The ancients messed up," Erick said, grinning at Chauncy. "Or the hoaxers did."

Chauncy smiled thinly, not feeling up to rising to the bait. Alexander typed away on the laptop for several minutes before making an exclamation. "Brilliant! That is how it could work. I do not have the cap of the scepter so I cannot say for sure, but this might be possible."

"Well, do not just sit there and gloat," Erick said. "Share it with the class."

"It is the same general concept of one of those bubble-making toys. A thin sphere of soap keeps your breath encapsulated from the air. In this case, the antimatter particles can be contained in a magnetic bubble. It would be an extremely excellent engineering accomplishment. Something that definitely could not have been done by ancient man."

Again, Chauncy ignored the jibe. The two SSOSA members exchanged glances and Alexander closed the laptop. "What is bothering you, Chauncy?" Erick asked quietly, hoping to get Chauncy to open up.

Chauncy grimaced and patted the metal briefcase in the seat next to him. "It's just this whole mess. I don't know if Jake made it to my wife and gave her the good news. I don't know when the next attack is coming. Always watching over my shoulder is starting to hurt my neck."

Alexander cleared his throat. "It is hard at first, that is true. Eventually it becomes a second nature and you begin to ease up. It always helps to have friends watching your back for you."

Chauncy set his drink down and stared at Alexander. "What would you know about this? When was the last time a homicidal maniac was hunting you and your family?"

Alexander's face turned bright red and he pursed his lips into a thin line. "I am a Russian nuclear physicist from the Cold War era. There are still jackbooted thugs from various factions who watch me everywhere I go. If this were not Erick's personal plane I very much doubt I would have been allowed to leave the country. As for my family, I was denied the chance of getting married and raising a family by a regime that felt security was more important than anything else. You cannot have something hunted that you were never allowed to have."

Chauncy felt like an idiot. "I'm sorry, I had no idea," he said, his throat dry. "I'm just—"

"Do not worry about it," Alexander interrupted, waving dismissively. His face no longer looked like a tomato, but there was still a hint of the color about his cheeks. "It is a stressful time for you, for all of us. We must work together, pool our resources. We will tackle this as we have every other problem."

Chauncy looked back out the window, wishing he felt the same confidence.

Their plane descended through the thick layer of smog that surrounded Athens and Chauncy felt a rush of nostalgia. Well, first he felt a rush of nausea; he hated to land ever since Thrasher and the 'Red Baron' incident in Egypt. But the nostalgia was because he'd studied in this great city during his junior year abroad, immersing himself in the antiquities of ancient Greece. Come to think of it, that was before Egypt and Thrasher. His failed trip for a doctorate in Abydos had turned his attention away from the Mediterranean antiquities and to the world of the Middle East, the birthplace of mankind. He hadn't had a chance to return to this place since he left. It was larger than he remembered and the airport was definitely newer. Customs was a nerve-wracking experience.

The fake passport from Thrasher had so far withstood scrutiny, but that didn't mean that some eagle-eyed officer wouldn't suddenly notice something off about it. Maybe it was too blue, or not blue enough. Or maybe the stamp was slightly off. There were a million things that could go wrong.

The scepter had been his greatest concern but it turned out to be the least. Milos was already there awaiting them and had supplied the proper papers for the import of an item of antiquity. That meant the officers barely even glanced at the scepter before returning it to Chauncy.

Milos Karakoles greeted the three men outside in the parking lot. Chauncy quickly recognized him from their first encounter in Quito, Ecuador. He was a short, stocky man, in his mid-sixties. He had a very round face with thick eyebrows that formed one continuous brow. He had a thick accent, but his command of the English language was impeccable. It was this command, and his high IQ, that had originally caught the eye of Dr. Sova when they'd all attended the same university in France decades earlier.

Chauncy knew that Milos once had a huge investment company with headquarters in the Twin Towers of the World Trade Center. Despite the huge loss and the close call of the fateful 9/11 attacks, Milos remained upbeat. He'd become a financial consultant instead of rebuilding his company after the disaster, but he was now using his knowledge of ancient antiquities more and more.

"This is quite the problematic little rod, is it not?" Milos asked Chauncy as he pulled the golden scepter from the briefcase. They were seated together in the back seat so they could discuss the relic.

"Yes, it is. I'm beginning to wish I'd never dug it up."

"Ah, but then you would not be involved in history," Milos said, still grinning. With his tablet he took pictures of the scepter from every angle. "And if not you, who? Somebody who would have given over the scepter to the *Flamus Divinus*, that is who! I am glad you unearthed it."

Chauncy opened his mouth to object, but then had to close it. Milos was right. If Hakan had the scepter, with its unfathomable destructive power, there was no telling what would happen. The burning of houses and skyscrapers would be a drop in the bucket compared to the flame that would envelope the world.

"It is rather a coincidence that we meet at this point in time," Milos continued. "I have just finished my new book about historical antiquities and their technological importance."

"Yes," Chauncy said, finally smiling. "And a coincidence that we need that exact information."

"Life is full of coincidences, my friend. Might I say, by the way, that it is good to see you again. I only wish our René could be here."

Chauncy looked out the window. It still hurt, sometimes. "I wish he was here, too."

Milos spent the next few minutes getting up to speed on the scepter and its properties. Erick and Alexander traded turns talking about the simulation and the equations behind it, and Chauncy explained how he'd discovered it and his take on the intricate carvings and symbols.

"Well, what do you think?" Erick asked as he drove through the scenic landscape. "Alex and I are convinced it is a hoax."

"Of course you two would think that; you have never had the proper respect for your ancestors. No, I agree with Chauncy: this scepter is most certainly *not* a hoax."

"What?" Alexander asked, as he turned around from the front seat to look at Milos with disdain. "How can you say that? If this were genuine, it would be equivalent to finding a replica of the space shuttle beneath the Acropolis."

"So?"

"What do you mean, *so?*" Erick demanded. "Quit joking and give us an intelligent answer."

"I am not joking," Milos protested emphatically. "What Chauncy found is not surprising to me."

"Why not?" Chauncy asked, trying to forestall another argument.

Milos typed a few things on his tablet and then showed a picture to Chauncy. "Can you identify this?"

"Of course," Chauncy said, grinning. "It's the Antikythera Mechanism. One of the oldest, if not *the* oldest, complex scientific calculators."

"Exactly," Milos said, his grin getting even bigger. "Over sixteen hundred years before Christopher Columbus sailed to the New World, the Greeks knew not only that the earth was a sphere, but they knew the exact way the solar system was shaped and how it moved. To prove it, they built this incredibly complicated device that could predict eclipses and such. Again, gentlemen, this was almost two thousand years before Columbus. What they taught you in history class is wrong."

"Okay, I will grant you the Antikythera Mechanism," Alexander said begrudgingly. "It is an amazing artifact and many centuries ahead of its time. But building a model of the solar system and building a particle accelerator to capture antimatter are two completely different things."

"Only on a matter of scale, not principle."

"Not so!" Alexander said.

Milos grinned at Alexander. "You think not? What if I showed you proof?"

"Do it, then," Alex said.

Milos tapped on his tablet again. He handed it to the three men to view. "What you see here gentlemen is an old painting circa 672 CE of two warships engaged in a fierce battle. One ship is approaching the enemy ship head on. On the bow of the aggressor ship we see a man holding a tube. You will notice flames coming out of the tube engulfing the opposing ship. That is Greek Fire, and it was the beginning of the use of incendiary weapons during the Byzantine Empire."

"Greek Fire?" Erick exclaimed. "Are you saying that Greek

161

Fire *was* antimatter technology?"

"No, I am not saying that in an absolute sense. Truth be told, nobody knows what it really was. The formula and the method by which it was dispensed was a closely guarded secret, even to this day, nobody knows what it was. Some say it was naphtha or a resin. Anyway, you can search on the Internet for Greek Fire and see videos of people replicating the use of weapons using naphtha. My point is that flame-throwing weaponry was used long before World War I. The history books are wrong."

"So the history books are wrong about fire weaponry," Alexander scoffed. "What does that have to do with this scepter?"

"During my research I came across an interesting story in a book entitled *De Administrando Imperio.* The story goes that a corrupt official was bribed by the enemy to reveal the secrets of the Fire. He was on his way to meet his benefactors in the Hagia Sophia when a flame from heaven devoured him. Some say it was divine punishment from God, which is entirely possible, but there are those who disagree: the *Ecclesia Flamus Divinus* took full credit for protecting the secret of Greek Fire."

"Everywhere we go we keep coming back to *Flamus Divinus*," Chauncy said. "Where did they come from, anyway?"

"I am not entirely certain," Milos said. "I recall seeing mention of them about 500 BCE. They resurfaced approximately 48 BCE and then again during the Byzantine era."

"500 BCE?" Chauncy asked, sitting up straighter. "Now that's interesting. This scepter is from a statue that was erected about then. There has to be a correlation. But what happened to the secret of Greek Fire?"

"There was a rumor that the *Ecclesia Flamus Divinus* had scrolls concerning the Fire that they converted into the codex form. The book was originally written in the Greek language. Tradition has it that the book was housed in the library of Alexandria, which is a very strange coincidence because the scrolls that explained the mystery of the Antikythera Mechanism were also in that library."

Chauncy shook his head. "The loss of the Alexandrian Library is one of the worst tragedies in history."

"How true," Milos agreed. "So much knowledge was destroyed, knowledge that would prove my theory, that the genius of the ancients has been ignored by modern history."

"I wonder why the mechanism wasn't common knowledge in Greece," Chauncy said aloud.

"Think about it," Milos said. "If you could accurately predict the coming of a solar eclipse, would you give up your secret? No, you would make people think you were an oracle or a god."

"It is always about power, Chauncy," Erick said grimly. "Even now, with this scepter. It has always been about having power."

Everyone was silent for a few moments as they pondered Erick's words.

Milos tapped Erik on the shoulder. "Turn here."

"No," Erik protested. "You dufus, you do not even know where you live?"

"Of course I do. But I have decided we are not going home."

"Then where are we going, genius?" Alexander sarcastically asked.

"Have you two already forgotten?" Milos asked. "We are going to Meteora!"

Erik and Alexander both laughed and answered in unison. "Julius Arcosanti!"

"Who's Julius Arcosanti?" Chauncy asked.

"Julius Arcosanti is a Bible mastermind," Milos explained. "A genius in history and ancient religions. We have visited him in the past for information when we played Mind Games. So you see why it was important for you to come and see me? These two dummies would have never figured out we needed to see Julius."

"Well, give him a call, tell him we're on our way. What's so funny?"

"Julius has no modern amenities," Milos said, still chuckling. "The monasteries are towers of solitude and peace. We have to hike up a mountain and go up rope ladders and bridges to get to him."

"So I'm assuming, despite his lack of modern conveniences, that he's still useful in our quest?"

"He has a vast collection of books. Men flock to his monastery every year to be taught by him. If they stay they live like monks."

"It is about a three hour trip from Athens," Erick said. "We will stay at a hotel room in Kalambaka and then go tomorrow morning."

"That sounds like a good plan," Chauncy said as he leaned

163

back in the seat. Ever since he'd unearthed the Golden Scepter his life had been a mess. Events were occurring at breakneck speed and he was having trouble keeping up. He couldn't seem to wrap his mind around all of the new information he was getting. Maybe he would feel better after a good night's rest. The only problem was that he didn't think he'd be sleeping well any time soon.

Chapter Twenty-Seven

The following morning, Chauncy and his three companions prepared for the hike up to Meteora. After a hearty breakfast they packed some snacks and bottled water and drove to the entrance of the famous granite spires in the scenic and beautiful Thessaly Valley.

"From here we walk. I am warning you this is a difficult climb," Milos said to the others.

"How difficult is the hike?" Chauncy asked.

"*Lieber Gott*, it is deceiving," Erick answered. "It starts out as little hills and then becomes vertical mountains."

Alexander grimaced. "I do not think I can join you. You should go on without me."

"Oh, stop being a weakling," Milos chided him. "You are not that much older than the rest of us."

The glare that Alexander gave Milos could have melted iron. "Have you forgotten what the Soviets did to me?"

"I am sorry, I *had* forgotten. What will you do? Surely you cannot stay in the car."

Chauncy came to Alexander's rescue. "We can take it slow. I want all of you up there with me."

They all agreed that the destination was worth taking their time, with high hopes that Julius Arcosanti could shed some light on their troubles. So they began the journey up the steps of Meteora.

For awhile the SSOSA members chatted about mundane things. It wasn't long before the conversation drifted toward previous mind games and challenges they faced. Chauncy enjoy listening to the older men talk about their past, especially because he'd been included in one of those games. He was about to ask a question when Erick spoke up.

"I have an idea. Why not engage our minds to take them off this climb? You are welcome to join us in a mini mind game, Chauncy."

"A good idea, and I have the perfect subject," Milos said, pulling out his tablet. "The significance of the symbols on the scepter."

"You line up the symbols and the antimatter is released," Alexander said with a huff. "There, mind game done."

Erick laughed. "Yes, we know that. But what do the symbols themselves represent? Surely they are not random, so why were they chosen?" He pointed to one of the symbols on the picture, the one at the end of the scepter. "Let us start with this one."

"I am certain I can decipher its meaning before the rest of you," Milos gloated. "I have an extensive knowledge of ancient history."

"It looks like a figure holding a lightning bolt," Alexander said. "If I were to design a weapon of this magnitude, I would make the combination something familiar. What was familiar to the Babylonians?"

"Do not think I will tell you the answer. You must put your own brain to work," Milos said.

Within a short while the three men were arguing back and forth. What had started out as a friendly mind game to pass the time had turned into a tiff between them. Chauncy didn't want it to continue any longer, so he spoke up with the answer he'd known all along.

"It's Marduk," he said simply.

The three SSOSA members stared at him. "How do you know?" Milos asked, stunned.

"Biblical archaeologist, remember? You were all right. This is something familiar to the Babylonians. Marduk was their chief deity and he is often shown wielding a lightning bolt, as in this symbol."

"Of course, a lightning bolt," Erick said. "The Golden Scepter fires lightning bolts. If we line up the symbols the last one should be Marduk. *Wunderbar*."

They turned their attention to the other symbols but had to abandon the game. The last leg of the journey was the dreaded vertical stairs carved in the granite. More than once Alexander threatened to quit but they managed to coax him up.

From the bottom of the spire it was difficult to see Julius' monastery due to the sheer verticalness of the site. But once they reached the pinnacle of the first spire the monastery was very visible.

The four men stopped as they saw a strange sight. The monastery was a gorgeous collection of structures, beginning with a front foyer with a cupola that led to several large rectangular buildings. The walls were whitewashed plaster that contrasted nicely with the red roof. It was a breathtaking image except for one problem: severe fire damage, with parts of the structure completely gone.

"There was a fire!" Milos said.

"I hope Julius is okay," Erick said, worry evident in his voice.

"Let us see if he is alive," Alexander ordered.

They made it across the rope bridge and were greeted by a man wearing monk's robes. "Good morning, I am Disciple James," the man said. "I am sorry to say the monastery is closed for the day. We are in the process of repairing the fire damage."

"Was Julius harmed?" Milos asked, stepping forward.

"The Teacher is fine. Thank you for inquiring, but he is not accepting visitors today."

Chauncy listened as the three SSOSA members tried their best to convince James to let them in. After a minute it dawned on him that *he* might have a way.

"Sir, please tell Julius that Chauncy Rollock is here to see him."

James turned his attention away from the other three. "I thought I recognized your face. You are supposed to be dead!"

"How did the news of my death reach here?"

"I personally walk down to Kalambaka to get the newspaper for the Teacher. Julius was very upset to hear about your death." James paused. "I think I will interrupt his solitude. He will want to see *you*."

As they entered the monastery the extent of the fire damage was more discernible. The foyer's cupola was more than half gone. Some of the burnt timbers were still sticking out of the dome like black gnarled fingers. Chauncy looked up and could see the blue sky and the sun light streaming in. The beauty of the sky was in stark contrast with the destruction below. Several monks were busy cleaning up the debris from the fire. The stench of burnt cloth, paper and wood was almost overpowering. Alexander, already wheezing from the climb, seemed to be having the most difficult time breathing. He found a chair, dusted off the soot, and sat down.

"Please stay here while I speak with the Teacher," Disciple James said. He walked down a side hallway, knocked on a door, and disappeared inside. Even though the door was thick they could hear a lively discussion from within the room. The door opened and an aged man walked out, helping himself along with a cane.

"I was not expecting to have to entertain three live guests and a dead man," the old man said with a smile on his face.

Erick stepped forward and held out his hand. "It is good to see you again, Julius. We were afraid you might not still be among the living."

"I am almost one hundred years old," Julius said. "I do not blame you for thinking I was dead."

Julius peered at the SSOSA members and finally at Chauncy. Chauncy was surprised at the brightness of his gaze. This man might be nearly a hundred but his mind had not been affected by the passing years.

"It appears I am not the only one that has cheated death. You are Chauncy Rollock, if I am not mistaken."

"It's a pleasure to meet you, Mr. Arcosanti. I'm sorry we've disturbed you during a difficult time," Chauncy said as he looked around at the debris. "But we desperately need your help. I'm afraid that danger is following us."

"I am aware of the help that you seek. You are here to ask me about the Divine Flame and answer your questions about the Golden Scepter. I also know who hunts you like animals in the night."

"He is a prophet!" Milos said, gesturing to the sky visible through the cupola.

"How did you know?" Chauncy asked.

"What did you expect when these three told you about me, Chauncy? Did you expect to find a lunatic with unkempt hair? Or perhaps a crazed hermit shouting scriptures over the Thessaly Valley just to hear his voice echo? Did you think I was a recluse with no knowledge of current events?"

"No, I never—"

Julius held up his hand to stop Chauncy. "I have suffered many losses lately. Part of my monastery and many of my books were

168

burned by a scorned enemy. Let us move past these tragedies and I can shed light on your questions." Julius turned and started to walk down another hallway. "Come, you must be hungry and thirsty after that climb."

"Who was the scorned enemy that burned your monastery?" Alexander asked as he got off his chair and shuffled after Julius.

"The bloodthirsty hunter, Hakan."

The four men following Julius were stunned. They expressed their surprise and their questions, but they were interrupted by Disciple James.

"Teacher, look what we have recovered," the disciple said, holding up a blackened and warped metal plaque.

They all looked at the charred plaque. The edges were burnt but the Latin lettering was still visible: *Destituo Omnis Tui Ante Falsus Cogitatum.*

"Abandon all your previous misconceptions," Chauncy translated quietly, almost to himself. It seemed to him to be a profound saying.

"I remember seeing this the last time we were here," Erick said, tracing the letters carefully with his finger. "It is the motto of your monastery, is it not?"

"The motto of my monastery, and of my life," Julius answered. "My mission was to learn and teach only the truth from the original sacred writings.

"And it still *is* your mission, Teacher," James said. He held the plaque close to his chest and got dirt on his robes. "My fellow disciples will restore the sign and place it at the front of the monastery when we rebuild."

Julius nodded gravely before continuing his journey. He was leading his four guests toward a wooden double door that seemed to take up the entire end of the hallway. When they reached the door he rested his hand against the wood, looked over his shoulder, and smiled. "The light will shine brighter and brighter for the just," he said as he opened the door with a flare.

Chauncy entered with a sense of awe. Julius' study reflected the Teacher's personality in every possible way. It was Spartan and obviously devoted entirely to books. The room had a large area rug with a few uncomfortable chairs congregated on top. The overwhelming smell was of musty paper, coming from the books stacked lovingly on shelves next to Julius' small, wooden desk. It reminded Chauncy, fondly, of Dr. Sova's study.

"I will have soup and bread served in here so we can talk without interruption," Julius said as he sat down. "I believe we should start with that."

He was pointing at the briefcase Chauncy held, so Chauncy went over and placed it on the desk. "We need your knowledge, Mr. Arcosanti," Chauncy said. "Time is running out and lives depend on it."

The aged scholar carefully opened the briefcase and touched the golden exterior of the scepter. "It is an instrument of great power and evil," he said very quietly. "You should have left it in Iraq."

"Yes, I've gotten that impression. Hakan has tried to kill me ever since I dug it up."

"Tell me, then, what you knew of Babylon before you went to work at Faruk Mayal's dig."

"You mean, from a scriptural standpoint?

"Is there any other standpoint?" Julius asked pointedly.

"I know that Babylon is one of the most influential nations mentioned in the Bible. They have more dealings with the nation of Israel than any other nation, with Egypt a close second. I believe that the Bible mentions Babylon one-hundred-and-ninety-times, or thereabouts."

Julius smiled. "Good, you do in fact have a brain. Yes, gentlemen, Babylon has more history and prophecy than any other nation except Israel itself. The first couple, Adam and Eve, were created in what today is known as Iraq, and what was part of the Babylonian empire for many decades. Noah built the ark in Iraq, the tower of Babel was in Iraq, Abram was from the city of Ur, which is in Iraq. Jonah preached in Nineveh, which is in Iraq. Babylon, from Iraq, destroyed Jerusalem in 607 BCE. The prophet Daniel was thrown into the lion's den in Iraq. Then we come to three Hebrew boys who refused to bow down to the golden image on the Plain of Dura, which is in Iraq. The same golden image that had a golden scepter, the golden scepter which you unearthed in Iraq."

"I never really considered how much Babylon was involved in the Bible," Milos said.

170

Julius continued to stare at the scepter as a few disciples served them their meal. "When King Nebuchadnezzar came to power, he had the golden statue built in his honor. He then had everyone in the jurisdictional district assemble to worship the idol, which carried *this* golden scepter." Julius touched the scepter one last time before closing the briefcase. "Think about it, gentlemen. What did he know about the statue that made him think he was worthy of worship?"

"He knew about the power contained in the scepter," Milos answered. "Why did he not use it in a display of power against his enemies?"

"Because Nebuchadnezzar went insane," Chauncy said, snapping his fingers. "Clinical lycanthropy, as was prophesied. Perhaps that caused him to forget about the power of the scepter when he regained his senses."

"That is one possibility," Julius said, smiling at Chauncy. "To tell the truth, we may never know why Nebuchadnezzar did not pass on the secret of the Golden Scepter. When King Cyrus conquered Babylon in one night, the scepter was not used to defend them. It is likely that nobody in Babylon knew what the statue on the Plain of Dura could do. Cyrus had the statue melted down into gold bullion, but the scepter part went missing. At long last it has been revealed to the world again."

"So this is the same scepter as the one from Babylonian times?" Alexander asked.

"Did I not just tell you that?" Julius asked.

"Yes you did, but Erick and I are convinced it is a hoax. Even today it would be extremely expensive and take many millennia to get even a gram of antimatter produced. It would be impossible for ancient Babylonians to have done this."

"It is most certainly not impossible," Julius thundered. "You forget that the ancients had no qualms about having slaves and working them to death, so money and time were not issues for the creation of the Golden Scepter. It was not, however, the Babylonians that did it. The antimatter technology came from the Greeks."

"Ah-ha!" Milos said, looking far too smug. "I knew it would be the Greeks behind it. My people are misunderstood and unappreciated geniuses."

"While that may be true, it does not necessarily mean that you follow in their footsteps," Erick growled.

"Did the Greeks sell out to the Babylonians then?" Chauncy interrupted before another argument could break out.

Julius shook his head. "No, the secret was stolen from the Greeks by the Divine Flame, and somehow stolen from the Divine Flame by the Babylonians. The cult went to retrieve the secret after the fall of Babylon, which is why the scepter disappeared."

"I have done a little bit of research on that group," Milos said. "But it is incredibly hard to track down sources. Where did you get your information?"

"Permit me to show you," Julius said. He got to his feet with difficulty and went to the door.

"Where are we going?" Alexander asked. He was also having a hard time getting up from his chair.

Julius turned and smiled like he was sharing a great conspiracy. "We are going to my library."

Chauncy grabbed the briefcase and followed after his friends. The more he learned about the Golden Scepter, the more impossible it all seemed, and the more important it became that he find out everything he could.

Chapter Twenty-Eight

The five men walked down a hallway, their footsteps echoing off the hewn-stone floors.

"Thanks to many generous monetary donations, we have been able to preserve the books that are in the library. We had to insulate the walls against the elements and keep many of the books in special cases. My next challenge is to find a successor who will be willing to preserve these books for future generations," Julius said.

The hallway ended in front of three stone steps that led to a large, thick wooden door. Milos and Chauncy pulled on the iron handle and the door opened with an audible creaking sound. The four men went up the steps and entered a dark room. Julius ordered the men to light the kerosene lamps that were on a table. As the kerosene lights flared up, the details of the room's interior became visible to them.

The room was the interior of a circular turret with a very tall ceiling. The rounded walls were replete with bookshelves. There were rows upon rows of shelves that reached the top of the turret. A rickety-looking ladder with wheels on the bottom was leaning against the round wall.

Julius slowly walked around the room and looked at the four men, the flickering light from the lamps casting a yellow pall on his face. Since Erick was tall and lanky, Julius asked him to retrieve a certain book that was on a high shelf.

Erick complied as he cautiously went up the rickety ladder and removed the book. Once he was down, Erick placed the book on top of a lectern that was in the middle of the room. The book was thick and had blue, intricate binding. Chauncy looked at the cover and noticed the dark Latin lettering on it. Translated, it read *Ancient Cults and Religious Orders of the Middle East.*

Julius walked up to the lectern and put his hand on the tome. "This book tracks the history of the Divine Flame cult, from before the fall of Babylon to their eventual disappearance when

173

Constantinople was taken by the Ottomans in 1453." He opened the book carefully and began to turn the pages. "There is no other like it in existence."

Chauncy and the others crowded around Julius to look at the contents of the book. The style was very much like an old illuminated manuscript, with intricate designs around the edges and brilliant artwork placed liberally throughout.

"We left off at the Greeks," Julius said as he continued to turn the pages with care. "Most scholars think that the concept of the atom was put forth by Democritus of Abdera approximately 350 BCE. In reality, the nature of the atom and of antimatter was discovered in 700 BCE, also by the Greeks."

"Yes, the genius of Greece. That is what my book is all about," Milos said, beaming with pride.

"Yes, you believe that you are *all* geniuses. May I continue?"

Milos sheepishly nodded.

"Good," Julius said. "Once the knowledge was discovered, the secret society of the Divine Flame was formed to protect that knowledge. Their ideology was cloaked under the guise of a religion, with theocratic creeds as if the gods themselves had formed the society. Their funding was provided by a clandestine group of scholars, scientists, and statesmen. However, as can happen in *any* imperfect organization, one member became corrupt and was bribed heavily by the Babylonians. Their spies had learned of the power that the Divine Flame protected."

"*Ach so!* So that is how the Golden Scepter switched hands and came to be on a Babylonian statue," Erick stated.

"I still do not entirely believe that the ancients could have had this advanced knowledge," Alexander said. "But the history makes perfect sense."

"You are actually incorrect, Erick: the Golden Scepter did not switch hands. The corrupt member took the scrolls with the instruments over to Babylon and it was King Nebuchadnezzar who had the Golden Scepter built. Neither the Divine Flame nor their Grecian government had yet attempted to weaponize the information. The Babylonians, though, conceived the military application immediately. The Divine Flame made several attempts to recover their lost secret; they managed to steal back the scrolls but there was too much security around the statue in the Plain of

174

Dura."

"That doesn't make any sense," Chauncy said. "If the Babylonians knew of the military power of the Golden Scepter, why would they put it on a giant statue where no one would be able to use it?"

"I have long believed that the statue itself was a siege engine designed to carry the Golden Scepter and prevent enemies from taking it," Julius answered. "Or perhaps there was some other way the Babylonians would be able to quickly retrieve the weapon for use. We will never know."

"You said earlier that it was Nebuchadnezzar's insanity that prevented him from using the scepter as a show of power," Milos pointed out. "But if the Babylonians had the scrolls, they did not need Nebuchadnezzar. They could have built a second, or third, or more."

"Maybe he kept the scrolls secret as well, and they did not come to light until the Medes and Persians took over," Alexander said.

"As I said earlier," Julius interrupted, "we do not know why Nebuchadnezzar did not share the secret of the scepter. The Medes and the Persians probably did not know the significance of the scrolls they inherited either, but the Divine Flame retrieved the scepter and the scrolls before anything could be done with the knowledge."

Julius paused for a moment before continuing. "Throughout the ages the Divine Flame endeavored to keep the scepter and its scrolls safely hidden away. They were not often successful in their attempts. The Romans took the Golden Scepter as part of their spoils of war when they conquered Syracuse and killed Archimedes. The Divine Flame got it back and thought that maybe they could hide it in Alexandria. They were unaware of the policy in place by Ptolemy III to confiscate and copy all incoming information to fill the Royal Library before returning it to the original owners. In direct retaliation for this unthinkable act, it was the Divine Flame that burned the library of Alexandria to keep their secret safe. They took their scrolls with them and let all of the stolen information be consumed by what, in their minds, was divine retribution."

"That changes the history books quite a bit," Chauncy said, not able to resist. "I always thought Julius Caesar burned down the library."

"You are saying it was Greeks who burned down the library, and not the Romans?" Milos asked, aghast. "I do not believe it!"

"The Divine Flame no longer identified themselves as Greek at that point. They were the Divine Flame, and that was it," Julius answered.

"Where did they hide the scepter and scrolls after Alexandria?" Chauncy asked.

"The scrolls and the scepter were taken to a vault beneath a nearby temple and kept there for centuries. In 391 CE Emperor Theodosius I ordered all pagan temples in Alexandria destroyed. That meant it was time for the scrolls and scepter to be moved again, and the Divine Flame chose Jerusalem as their new hiding place. They located an abandoned church, copied the secret scrolls into codex form, reorganized and rewrote their creeds to appear Christianized. They renamed themselves *Flamus Divinus Adventum*."

"That translation evokes the idea of the second coming of Christ," Chauncy said, tapping the book. "Did their plan work?"

Julius nodded. "It allowed them to survive for eight hundred years."

Milos snapped his fingers. "Up to the second Crusade, right?"

"You are correct, Milos," Julius said. He turned to a page that had an idealized illustration of a group Knights Templar. They were drawn as if they were ascending to heaven, with halos of light behind their heads. "The Knights Templar had been sanctioned to protect Christian pilgrims. They then became a mighty arm of the Pope to wipe out all heathens from the Holy Land. *Flamus Divinus Adventum* was declared one of those heathens. And so the might of the Knights Templar was directed to wipe the Divine Flame from the face of the earth. It was at this point that the high priest of the Divine Flame, the Exalted One, decided that they had run from trouble long enough. He took the Golden Scepter out of its hiding place and went out to meet the Knights Templar on the field of battle."

"That sounds rather epic," Erick murmured.

"It was rather epic," Julius said. "The battle lasted for several days."

"If they were *truly* using this scepter, why was the battle not quickly won?" Alexander asked, folding his arms across his chest. "They were using antimatter against knights in armor."

"Because the scepter, as powerful as it is, requires time to charge between shots," Julius said. "One scepter against hundreds of well-trained, well-equipped enemies. But even against that mighty force, the Divine Flame were almost the victors until they were ambushed by reinforcements. The cap end, the part that has been broken off, was the aiming and charging mechanism that allowed the scepter to work. Without it, the scepter would incinerate itself, which is almost what happened when the catapult struck. The attack vaporized all the nearby Divine Flame members, their prisoners and blinded nearly everyone else."

Julius paused to take a drink of water. "A cultist who had not been blinded recovered the broken scepter pieces and fled the battle. He returned to the Divine Flame who had been charged with defending the codex and told them the grim news. It was decided that the secret codex would be hidden in the catacombs beneath a real Christian church, while the surviving cultist was instructed to take the two parts of the scepter and hide them far apart. I do not know where the cap was hidden, but the rod was hidden in a royal grain bin that had once been used by the Divine Flame. That is where you found it, and that is why Hakan knew where to look. Once the codex and the scepter were hidden away, the Divine Flame died out as a public entity."

Chauncy leaned back and digested all of this information. "So the modern Divine Flame cult members knew about all of this. They brought the Divine Flame cult back to life and want to use the Golden Scepter again, this time against all of humanity."

Milos pointed to the book. "I was reading while you were explaining things, and none of what you just told us was in the book. Where did you find out about the hiding place of the secret codex and the Golden Scepter parts?"

Julius closed the book, a sad expression on his face. "That information came from the actual secret codex, which I had in my possession at one time."

The four men looked at Julius in shock. "You had the actual Divine Flame book?" Alexander asked. "With the details about how to make the scepter? Why did you not tell us?"

"And how did you get it in the first place?" Erick asked. "I thought it was hidden away forever."

Julius held up his hands for silence. "I did not tell you because it was not yet time, and also it is a sensitive subject. Eighty years ago a Bishop was involved in renovations of the Church where the codex was hidden. He noticed that part of the masonry was different from the rest of the catacombs and secretly opened it. He knew immediately that he could not be caught in possession of such a heretical book. His father was an avid collector of historical books, so the Bishop took the Divine Flame codex to him for safekeeping."

"You appear to have a firsthand knowledge of this," Erick said shrewdly.

"You are correct. The Bishop was my brother and the collector was my father. I found the book hidden in my father's basement and read it when I was young."

"And it contained the secrets of antimatter collection?" Alexander persisted.

"There were many diagrams and numbers in the book, but I did not understand them."

"Where is the codex now?" Chauncy asked. "You said it was in your possession at one time."

Julius took a deep breath. "The codex was discovered by one of my pupils who was not ready for the information it contained. He stole it the day he left. That pupil was Faruk Mayal."

Stunned silence settled on the room. After several minutes, Erick stirred. "So that is why Hakan tried to destroy this place. But if they know you are here, and knowledge of the scepter is here, what stops them from coming back to make sure you are dead?"

"It seems unlikely that they will return so soon," Milos said. "Hakan did just try to burn it down, what reason would they have for returning?"

"Mayal will come," Chauncy said, feeling sick to his stomach. His wife and son had gone to Turkey with the man. All that time he thought it was just Hakan who was a rotten apple. But to find out that Mayal was bad, too? He'd respected and looked up to that man as a pinnacle of the archaeological society. "He is famous for his determination and thoroughness, and now I know why. He will want to make sure the deed is done properly. Oh God, I hope my family is safe."

"We need to figure out what to do with this scepter, then, and we do not have much time," Alexander said. "We cannot let it fall into their hands again."

Chapter Twenty-Nine

She'd argued long and hard with Jake about leaving, but his logic was undeniable. They didn't know if Troy was even in Turkey any more, and Jake couldn't find the boy without more resources. So Anita was emotionally and physically exhausted. Travelling through different time zones and suffering with the thought of what might be happening to Troy was driving her crazy. She was used to being in control. But things were now out of control. The only positive thing in her life was the knowledge that Chauncy was alive. This knowledge helped buffer the shock of the kidnapping.

Jake and Anita landed at the San Diego International Airport. They drove a rented car from the airport to an area right behind La Jolla, a posh neighborhood of million dollar homes with spectacular hilltop views of the Pacific Ocean.

"Well, this is quite a change from Turkey."

Jake pointed up the hill at the mansions. "One day I'm going to be up there, but for now this is fine."

"What's our next move, I mean, how are we going to contact Chauncy? We don't even know where he is."

"He's travelling with Erick Hausen and Erick is a wizard with technology. There must be a way to reach him. As long as he has Internet access I can reach him."

Anita suddenly remembered her cellphone was off while she had been travelling. She reached into her purse and turned it on. As Jake continued driving down the winding roads behind La Jolla, Anita checked her email just to pass the time. Her eyes widened when she noticed an email from Troy.

"I got an email from Troy!" she exclaimed, causing Jake to swerve violently.

"Don't *do* that!" Jake hissed. "When was it sent? What does it say?"

"It was sent after he was kidnapped," she answered excitedly. "He's still alive, Jake. But the message doesn't make any sense. It says '*Help I'm in Mission de Al.*'

"Well, he's giving us his location."

Anita gave him a look that would have wilted flowers. "That's obvious. But what is Mission de Al?"

"I don't know, I don't recall any Mission de Al's in Turkey."

"There aren't any missions in that part of the world, Jake."

Jake grinned. "Of course. That does sound like a Spanish Mission name, doesn't it? Alright, we're almost to my house. We can dig through records and see what shows up."

Anita stared at the message on her phone, too preoccupied to notice the gorgeous view of the ocean. Her son was still alive and was asking her for help. She would do everything possible to answer that plea. They made it to Jake's house and he led the way down a long hallway. He stopped when he reached a door, pressed a hidden button and the door swished open. A well-lit staircase descended to the basement. Upon entering the basement, Anita thought that it looked more like a war room. There were technological gadgets and firearms strewn everywhere on large tables, along with large maps covering almost all the wall space.

"I didn't think people in California had basements, what with the earthquakes," Anita commented.

Jake walked over to his main computer and turned it on. "It is definitely an anomaly. I've spent a lot of money to make it as safe as possible." He sat down on his chair and began to furiously type away. "If Troy was taken to a Spanish mission, we have to find out which one starts with the letters A-L. One moment while I pull up a list..."

Anita brushed her blond hair away from her face and leaned forward. A long list of names showed up on one of the computer monitors and she felt her jaw drop open. "Is that the list of all the missions?"

"Unfortunately, that's just the list of the missions in Texas."

Her jaw dropped even further. "Just in *Texas*? I had no idea there were so many still in existence."

Another list showed up on the main monitor, and this one was considerably shorter. "Mission Basilica San Diego de Alcala," Anita said triumphantly. "That's it. It has to be."

Jake clicked on the information and grimaced. "Afraid not, Anita."

She leaned forward and groaned. "It's a museum. There are hundreds of tourists about. They couldn't possibly hope to keep a kidnapped child a secret."

"It's a pity, really, because that mission is only about fifteen minutes away. I just realized something, though. If this was the mission he meant he would have said B-A or S-A, for Basilica or San Diego. Also, look at these lists. A lot of the names are duplicated, at least in part. There's a Mission San Juan Capistrano in both California and Texas."

"But there wasn't another Alcala on the list. We would have seen it."

Jake laughed suddenly. "Ah, of course. This is a case, Anita, where we have to think, not outside the box, but outside the *lines*."

There was confusion written all over her face but it cleared quickly. "Of course. There are still plenty of missions in Mexico, aren't there?"

"Houston, we have liftoff! Mision de Alcala, an abandoned mission in Baja California."

"Wait, what if we're interpreting this all wrong? Isn't there a way to verify that he actually sent the email from Mexico?"

Jake took Anita's phone and then walked back to his computer. "I can check and see where it originated, yes."

Meanwhile, Anita walked closer to the map on the wall, pondering for a few minutes how Troy was transported to Mexico without being seen by the authorities. She hoped he was still in one piece. She knew the horror stories about kidnappings.

"I got it," Jake said as he stood up and pulled a piece of paper from his printer. "The email originated from an unsecured WiFi hotspot right where that mission is."

Anita looked at the map. "It's halfway through Baja. Is Ensenada or Cabo San Lucas closer?"

"It doesn't matter, really, as long as it's close to the beach. Which it is."

"So how are we going to rescue him?" Anita asked.

"Whoa, whoa, whoa, hold on there, tigress. Who said anything about us rescuing him? This is the point where we turn it over to the authorities."

"The authorities who might be working for Mayal?"

Jake clenched his jaw. "They might not *all* be working for him.

183

Come on—"

"I'm not taking that chance," she said firmly. "I know how you operate, Jake Thrasher. How much will it cost me to get you to rescue my son?"

"I thought we were going to tell Chauncy to give up the Golden Scepter and you'd get your son back."

Anita pointed at the map. "He's really close, and also, I'm not so sure about handing over something like that to terrorists. If there's a chance we can rescue my son *and* keep the scepter, I'm taking it."

Jake rubbed his temples with both hands. "Listen, Anita, I like you, I like Chauncy, and I even like Troy. But I'm not in the business of hostage extraction. That's best left to the SWAT teams."

"Like the GSG-9 team that Hakan infiltrated?" Anita demanded. "Or did you forget you told me all about your adventures with Chauncy?"

Jake swore silently; he *had* forgotten he'd told her about that. He was rapidly running out of excuses and he didn't think Anita would accept any of them anyway. "Twenty thousand. I won't do it for a penny less."

"It's a deal," Anita replied without batting an eye. "But I'm only giving you half up front, the other half when I see my boy."

Jake was honestly expecting stiffer resistance to his price. He should have asked for more. "Okay then, it's a deal."

"How will you get into Mexico?"

"I have a boat docked in the marina in downtown San Diego. I'll make it look like I'm fishing in the Mexican waters," he started walking toward the elevator.

"I'm going with you," she said in a commanding tone.

"Uhm, no you're not."

"Uhm, yes I am," Anita said. "They have my only son. I'm going to rescue him."

"Listen, I'm a professional. I don't take amateurs, they get in the way and gum up my plans."

"Jake, my son has my cell phone number and my email addresses. If he ever gets a chance to send another message, it's not going to go to you, it's going to go to me."

"Fine then," Jake said as he folded his arms across his chest.

"Get your own boat and go get him."

She glared at him. "I'm going to be there when you rescue him. I won't get in the way."

"You heard me, I said no because—" Jake stopped in midsentence and raised a finger. "Wait a minute. That's actually a good idea. Having a woman on board will make the trip look more legitimate."

"So, is it a deal?"

"As long as you stay on the boat you're good to go," Jake grinned. "I will be requiring that half up front right now."

Anita took her checkbook out and wrote a check for ten thousand dollars and handed it over to Jake.

"Excellent," Jake said as he stashed the check away. "Let's go."

Chapter Thirty

A stiff breeze swept across the waves as the sun disappeared beyond the Pacific Ocean. *El Maximo,* a sixty-five foot fishing boat, lazily bobbed up and down on the calm waters of the ocean near the Baja coast. The boat was in reality Jake Thrasher's disguised private reconnaissance vessel. He was on the deck busily preparing himself for the rescue of Troy Rollock. His assistant, Pascual, a burly Hispanic man with black, unruly, curly hair, was standing at the stern fiddling with a remote control box that operated the robotic arm.

Jake descended to the back of the fishing boat, went into the small locker room and changed into his waterproof black nylon bodysuit. It would keep him warm during the trip to the shore and it would help hide him in the darkness. He didn't want to turn the rescue into a bloodbath, although Anita was a little more ambivalent on that count. He'd selected a nice combination of smoke grenades, flash-bangs, and tranquilizer guns. All of them were high-tech, off-market and incredibly illegal. He strapped the black combat knife to his left ankle. Next was the waterproof equipment belt and backpack, and finally his combat helmet with the waterproof night vision set. Everything he would probably need for a quick and quiet hostage extraction.

"Hey man, are you ready?" Pascual asked in perfect English as he saw his boss walking toward him.

"*Si señor,*" Jake gave him a thumbs-up and smiled. "It's getting dark, I say we push off."

"How long will you be out?" Pascual asked as he casually looked down at his remote control box and pressed a button.

"I suppose it'll take five hours or so," Jake responded. "Unless I find a fish taco stand that's open all night. If so, add another hour.'

Pascual grinned. "Add an additional hour if you wash it down with a couple *Coronas*."

"Three, if a *señorita* wants to share a bottle with me," Jake

187

smiled wickedly.

"Dream on, dude," Pascual smirked. "Nobody wants an old man like you."

"You're breaking my heart," Jake sarcastically retorted.

Just then Anita came out on the deck, dressed exactly like Jake.

Pascual was slack jawed. Jake was angry. "What the…? Who gave you permission to snoop in my locker?"

"I changed my mind. I'm going with you," she announced.

No, you're not."

"Yes, I am. He's my son."

"That wasn't our deal, Anita," Jake said with quiet fury. "We had an agreement! I'm using tranq-darts but the bad guys are using real bullets, get it? You aren't experienced in this kind of stuff."

Anita walked up to him and looked at him square in the eyes. "And neither are you Jake. You were never a Navy Seal nor are you a professional in this kind of situation. You are a black marketer."

Jake noticed that Pascual stifled a chuckle. "So, what's your point?" Jack responded, not denying the accusation.

"You need backup. I have medical training and I can help."

Jake realized that there was no way he was going to win an argument against Anita's take-charge attitude. He quickly came up with a money-making idea to try and save his ego. "I'm charging you an extra ten grand if you come along."

"Fine, let's go."

"If you get killed, don't come running to me." Jake shook his head in disbelief. "I can't believe I'm doing this."

The conversation was interrupted as Pascual activated the robotic arm. It automatically raised itself up out of the hull. Attached to the robot arm was a blue Jet Ski. The arm moved over the starboard side of the boat and gently placed the vessel in the rolling swells. Jake used the robotic arm as a ladder and climbed down onto the Jet Ski, with Anita following suit. The arm unclasped itself from the small vessel. Once Jake and Anita were seated properly, he started up the engine. Water frothed madly at the back of the watercraft and they shot off toward the Baja peninsula, bobbing and skipping across the rough waves. This trip would be more difficult on the way back because they'd be going against the waves. But for now he practically glided across the water and they reached the shore within twenty minutes. Jake shut off the craft and covered it in a seaweed camouflage that wouldn't have worked during the day. He pulled his GPS from his belt and checked their bearings.

"Why didn't you just bring a cellphone?" Anita whispered.

"I did, but there's not a reliable amount of cell coverage out here," Jake answered. "Let's go."

They traveled quickly and quietly through the land, deliberately avoiding the main roads or the ranches that they connected to. They went up and down gullies for what felt like hours, fighting through soft sand and rock-strewn valleys. The stars were bright above, with no light or air pollution to block their celestial glow from reaching the earth. It was a strenuous path but almost peaceful in the cool night air.

They reached their destination a little over an hour after landing at the beach. They both crawled along the ground like lizards as Jake surveyed the situation with his infrared goggles. He spotted one solitary guard walking a post and carrying a rifle.

Jake activated the binocular function of his helmet and zoomed in and out, scanning the area and scrutinizing the various possibilities of entering the mission. He took a swig from his canteen and pulled off his backpack. After a few moments he assembled his air rifle that had been configured for use with his tranq-darts.

They continued to crawl forward toward the mission. When he reached a certain distance, he stopped and raised his hand indicating that Anita should stop as well. He rested his rifle on the ground and took careful aim at the guard.

Suddenly there was a rustling sound from the desert shrubs ahead to the left. Jake swung his rifle around and hesitated a split second. The infrared signature was far too small for a human. *Must be a dog*, he thought as he pulled the trigger. He heard the familiar sound of compressed gas being instantly released as the dart shot out into the night. The dog let out a loud yelp as he fell to the ground. He flopped like a fish on a boat deck for a split second before going limp.

"So much for a quiet entrance," Anita whispered at him.

Jake swore silently and turned his rifle back toward the mission. The solitary guard had heard the dog, alright, and was moving toward it. A brilliant idea came to Jake and he told Anita to stay put. He shimmied forward as quickly as possible without making noise. Thankfully the dog wasn't that far away.

The guard was kneeling down and checking on the animal when Jake struck. He grabbed the back of the guard's head and slid his knife up against his throat.

"Where is Troy?" he asked quietly in passable Spanish.

The guard trembled furiously and dropped his rifle. "In the wine cellar!" he answered, his voice barely above a squeak.

"And where is entrance to the wine cellar?"

"In the back, next to the kitchen."

Jake grinned and shot the man in the back. The tranquilizer took mere milliseconds to work and the guard fell to the ground with barely a sound.

Anita appeared suddenly beside him and he nearly had a heart attack. "I told you to stay outside!" he whispered fiercely.

"I found two cars in the parking lot," she answered back, not apologizing. "A newer-model Toyota Rav-4 and a Jeep that looks like it survived World War Two. I'm thinking the Jeep will be easier to hotwire."

He looked at her with newfound respect. Not only had she correctly gauged his next course of action, finding transportation, but she'd also correctly identified which one would be easier to take. "Good job," he said. "Show me."

They moved silently through the darkness and around to the parking lot. Jake crept over to the Jeep, opened the door and bent down under the steering wheel. It was almost child's play to rearrange the correct wires and get them ready to start the vehicle. With that out of the way they moved over to the mission. They stayed as close as they could to the walls as they approached the entryway. The ancient doors creaked open as they snuck in. Most of the pews were long gone making the room appear larger. Their footsteps echoed as they made their way through the church.

Jake ran to the right side of the altar until he reached an arched door. Slowly walking, he realized he was in the inner hallway. He motioned for Anita to follow. They ran in spurts, hiding under a series of arches that made up the hallway, trying their best not to make any noise. At the end of the hallway they turned left and found the kitchen. They finally made it to the hallway that would lead them to the wine cellar.

The guard at the cellar door never even saw Jake lean out and shoot him. He fell off his chair, his rifle clattering on the old stone floor.

"They're just a bunch of inexperienced kids," he whispered to Anita. He searched quickly through the man's pockets and found the key.

"Who is it?" a scared-sounding voice asked from below.

Anita's heart soared in her chest as she and Jake walked down the stone stairs. "It's me, Troy," she said, moving toward the voice. She embraced her son, cherishing the fact that he was alive and she was holding him.

"I'm so glad you got my message," he said.

"We need to get out of here," Jake said. "There were three more infrared signatures, and two of them are coming this way."

"Who are you?" Troy asked.

"Introductions can wait, kid," Jake said as he led the way back out of the cellar-turned-dungeon. The interior lighting was dim but still too bright to use infrared, so Jake crept up the stairs with extreme caution. It was because of his caution that he spotted the gun barrel around a corner. Jake shoved Anita and Troy down and leapt forward, pure instinct driving him. He grabbed the gun barrel just as the man carrying it turned the corner. He shoved hard to the left and with his right arm grabbed the guard. One quick move and the guard went flying twenty feet to the floor below.

"Bad neighborhood!" Jake shouted, turning around. Anita and her son were already running ahead of him. Another guard showed up. Anita didn't even slow down as she ran into him, her elbow extended like a battering ram. The man fell to the floor with a thud and Jake didn't even pause as he jumped over him.

"Where did you learn that move?" Jake asked as they continued to run.

Anita smirked as she rubbed her sore elbow. "I used to play tackle football after school."

***

Geraldo, miraculously, had no broken bones as a result of his fall. He picked up his gun and charged up the stairs, only to find Marcos panting for breath on the floor.

"What happened to you?" he demanded, helping his friend up.

"What does it look like?" Marcos wheezed, rubbing his throat. "They ran me over!"

"They've got the kid," Geraldo said. "We can't let them get away."

"Yeah, what if they kill us? That's not worth twenty grand, Geraldo."

Geraldo looked grim. "If they don't kill us, the Great One will. Let's go."

***

Jake, Anita and Troy made it out into the parking lot at a dead run. The old Jeep was clearly visible even in the darkness and they made a beeline straight for it. He tossed his pack in the back while getting in the driver seat. He put the wires together and the old vehicle roared to life in seconds. His passengers were already in so he put the car in reverse and stomped on the gas.

Nothing happened.

"What's the matter?" Anita demanded.

Jake swore loudly. "Pardon my French, but this has a bad clutch."

He wrestled with the gearshift and the clutch, trying hard not to keep swearing. Light spilled out from the church as the doors opened. "Duck!" Jake yelled. He practically stood up in his seat, jammed his foot as hard as he could into the clutch and wrenched the gearshift back. The Jeep finally moved backward just as a couple gunshots rang out. Jake spun the car around, pointed it in the right direction, and managed to get it into first gear without trying.

"We should have disabled the other car," Anita shouted over the cacophony of the engine.

"I wasn't expecting anyone to be awake to chase us out of here," Jake snarled back.

Jake had to almost break the clutch each time he wanted to switch to a higher gear. It made driving through the sand incredibly difficult. They only lasted a couple of minutes before he took them back onto a road. He was certain they would've dug themselves a grave had he stayed out in the sand.

Headlights appeared in his rearview mirror and he clenched his

192

jaw shut. "Troy, I need you to get my pack," he said over his shoulder. "And grab the flare gun before you give the pack to your mother."

He swerved the jeep down into a ravine near the road as bullets began to ricochet off the Jeep. He had enough speed going to risk the deep sand and it was better than getting shot.

"I always thought gunshots were louder," Troy spoke up from the backseat.

"This isn't Hollywood, kid," Jake answered. "Bullets don't hit with loud explosions. Good news is they'll run out of ammo before they puncture this old metal. Bad news is we're not bulletproof, so keep your head down."

Jake managed to get into a good gear to dig through the sand. He'd managed to throw off the enemy's aim, but in the process had lost his head start. The headlights were now blindingly close.

"Here's the pack," Troy said suddenly, handing the object to Anita. "You want me to shoot them with the flare gun?"

Jake couldn't help but grin. Not that long ago he'd been in an equally old Jeep, careening through the desert while another Rollock shot at followers. This was getting to be a bad habit, but he liked it. "You got it, Troy."

The first flare went wide but succeeded in making their assailants stop shooting and swerve. Jake tore his attention from the road and the rearview mirror and turned to Anita. "Find me the two silver boxes about the size of your fist," he ordered.

Jake looked in the rearview mirror just as Troy fired the second flare. This one landed a direct hit in the Toyota's grill and lit up the night. "Great shot! You take after your old man."

"These what you're looking for?" Anita asked, holding up two octagonal-shaped boxes that reflected the moonlight.

"Perfect," Jake said with a malicious grin. "See how they both have buttons in the middle? Press the buttons and throw both of them behind us. Or better yet, have Troy do it."

Less than a minute later both of the boxes were on the road behind them. With just a tiny bit of luck they'd be able to make the rest of the trip in peace.

***

The flare finally died down and Geraldo accelerated for all

Perla's car was worth. His continuous stream of swear words only got louder when their tires suddenly blew out. He held the steering wheel straight through sheer force of will and let off the gas, his heart sinking lower and lower as they came to an erratic stop.

He hopped out of the car and ran back where they'd just been. Sure enough, there were some kind of tire-spike strips lying across the road. He didn't recognize the boxes that the strips came from, but it didn't matter.

"Should we just disappear into the desert somewhere?" Marcos asked as he came up behind him.

Geraldo was sorely tempted. Hakan's wrath was not something to look forward to. But this was the life and the path he'd chosen. "We might as well see it out," he said with a sigh. "All the way to the bitter end."

The walk back to the mission was very quiet.

***

Three miles away from the beach, the Jeep started to sputter and cough. Jake banged on the steering wheel. "Come on! We got three more miles, don't stop now."

The Jeep unceremoniously stopped in the middle of the road. Jake hung his hands to his sides and laughed.

"What's so funny?" Anita asked.

"First it was the transmission, then the carburetor and now we are simply out of gasoline. I've never seen a worse piece of junk."

"So we walk from here," Anita said.

"It's only three miles. I've still got my tranq-darts and night vision, so nothing should bother us."

It felt like another couple of hours trudging through the desert when they finally heard the pounding surf ahead of them. Jake located his Jet Ski in a matter of minutes and pulled the cover off. The three people dragged the craft out into the water. Troy, not wearing the same suit as his rescuers, was already shivering as he climbed onto the back. Jake told him to hold on tight and they were on their way.

They fought several large waves, each one soaking them more than the last, before they finally made it back to the *El Maximo*.

The robotic arm at the boat was already extended into the water waiting to pluck the craft out. The bright spotlight from the boat created strange shadows on the restless water.

Jake attached the arm to the Jet-Ski and yelled out. "Pascual!"

The arm activated and brought them up to the deck. As soon as they got off the watercraft all of the floodlights switched on. Jake spun around, reaching for his rifle.

"Hands in the air," a familiar voice commanded from the direction of the lights.

Jake squinted and tried to see past the blinding effect. What he saw froze his blood in his veins. Four men in black outfits were pointing weapons at him. A fifth man, larger than the others, was walking toward them.

"Hakan," Jake said, the taste of defeat sour in his mouth. "How did you—"

"The Divine Flame has eyes and ears everywhere, Mr. Thrasher," Hakan interrupted, his voice openly gloating. He waved his hand and Pasqual stepped forward, smiling wickedly.

"Pasqual, you dirty—"

"He paid more than you," Pasqual said simply.

Jake filled his lungs to say withering words, but he was cut off by Hakan again.

"When we found out that young Troy had sent off a message," Hakan said, "I knew it was only a matter of time before his mother showed up. And here you are."

Jake looked over at Anita. They'd tasted victory only to have it snatched away at the last moment by a betrayal. He wanted to apologize, to acknowledge his failure, to say anything. But there was nothing that could be said to fix the situation. They'd lost, and that was all there was to it.

Chapter Thirty-One

Dr. Faruk Mayal's sanctuary was located beneath his mansion in Ankara, Turkey. The lighting in the room was kept purposely subdued, exactly as it had been when Hakan had been summoned here. Dr. Mayal was seated on the golden throne, dressed in his ceremonial garb which consisted of a black turban and a long, dark flowing robe. On the floor there were six men also clad in black turbans and robes. They were prostrated before their leader, the Most Exalted One.

He took a long deep breath then slowly exhaled. He made hand motions in the air as if he were mimicking the movements of a tornado. "Do you all see what is occurring? The scientific knowledge of the past and the knowledge of the present day are converging in a large whirlpool. Yes, we are at the center of the tempest. Nevertheless we will succeed. We are being used by God to accomplish His will. It is unstoppable and inevitable. The Hindu script says: *'The power of God is with me at all times, constantly doing all the work, using me as a mere instrument'*."

He stood up from his throne and slowly walked down the steps near the Embers. "I am an instrument of God to accomplish His will, and I have chosen only the best Embers from around the world to finish this task. That is why you six are here today. As prophesized, the scepter has been unearthed and all we have to do is take it from the hands of the infidels. This is our final mission. Babylon arises!"

Chapter Thirty-Two

"We can't destroy it, it's a priceless antiquity," Chauncy said for the sixth time. He was beginning to lose conviction. At first Milos had stepped in and agreed with him, but this time he was silent.

"It is a dangerous weapon," Erick said again. "How many times do we need to tell you that before you recognize it?"

"Why can't we just donate it to a really secure museum?" Chauncy asked. Deep down, he knew that he was just grasping at straws but he had to try.

"You know why we cannot do that," Alexander said, looking closely at Chauncy. "You are just trying to delay the inevitable."

"This is actual, physical proof of something I've been saying for years now," Chauncy argued. "Proof that ancient man was smarter than we are. It is also proof that the Greeks were incredible geniuses, right, Milos?"

Milos picked at his fingernails and didn't look at Chauncy. "This proof just so happens to be a weapon," Milos said quietly. "I would love to see my people shown as the intellectuals they are, but I cannot risk this weapon falling into the wrong hands. Let me finish, Chauncy. It is not just the Divine Flame that is a problem. If the world finds out about the Golden Scepter, *everyone* with a vendetta, or terrorist leanings, will try to get their hands on it."

"And there is no such thing as impenetrable security," Erick added.

"So we hand it over to the museum with the best security and it becomes their responsibility," Chauncy said desperately. "Not ours."

"Really?" Alexander asked. "That is really the argument you wish to use? It was not our fault the world was destroyed, it was the museum's for not having better security?"

"No," Chauncy said finally, feeling deflated. "No, I know you're right. It just...it goes against every fiber of my being as an archaeologist. We're supposed to preserve the past and share it with the world so that we can all learn. This is different, I know, but it's still hard."

"Making the right choice is often the hardest thing to do," Alexander said, rubbing his knees. "And it often comes at a price. But it is still the right thing to do."

"I know. We still need to figure out how to destroy this thing, though."

"The largest issue we face is that we do not exactly know how much antimatter is in the scepter," Alexander said. "I shudder to imagine that it could be more than a gram, but we cannot know for sure."

"So we really do not want to destroy it just anywhere, right?" Milos asked.

"Precisely," Alexander agreed. "One gram is equivalent to a sizable nuclear explosion. Going up the scale is simply frightening."

"There is another option," Erick said. "I have contacts in the private space industry—"

Chauncy laughed, interrupting. "You can't be serious. You want to launch the Golden Scepter into orbit? Won't it just come back down again eventually?"

"Not into orbit," Erick said stiffly. "Into space. The object is small and therefore can be launched outside the solar system relatively easily and inexpensively. Well, compared to launching a probe or something similar that far away."

"You're serious," Chauncy said.

"Very serious. As we have been saying, attempting to destroy the scepter will cause an explosion of unknown size and power. Hiding it will not work, because eventually it will be rediscovered. That leaves space. It is the only logical answer."

They argued for awhile longer, but in the end Erick won.

The following morning they were treated to a nice but simple breakfast on a veranda overlooking the Thessaly Valley. After they finished eating they had Disciple James show them a good hiding place for the scepter, a place where it would be safe until Erick made the proper arrangements. James showed them a secret basement where they stashed the relic before returning to the library.

200

Once that had been accomplished, they returned to the veranda. Alexander looked troubled and Chauncy noticed it.

"What's the matter Alex?"

"I still do not believe it," he exclaimed.

"What is wrong now?" Erick asked, irritated.

Alexander pounded his fist on the breakfast table. "I do not believe the ancients harnessed antimatter power. I want proof. I want Julius to show me how it was done."

"Alex, can you let it go?" Milos asked with a sigh. "Does it really matter if this is the same scepter or not? It is clearly a threat regardless."

"It matters to me," Alexander rumbled. "I have spent my entire life studying the atom and quantum mechanics. If what I was taught in school is wrong, I would like to be right."

They all went to the library, where Julius was overseeing the repair work. Alexander got straight to the point. "Julius, you keep saying that the Golden Scepter we have is the same scepter as the one in Grecian times, and that way back then antimatter was more understood. What you have failed to do is furnish proof. Did you see the equations in the codex of the Divine Flame?"

"I did see the equations in the book," Julius answered. He had clearly been expecting this conversation. "But I did not understand them."

"And with the book gone, there is no proof of any of this, then," Alexander said, a self-satisfied smile on his face. "I am still in the right."

"Excuse me, my friend, but you are not," Julius said, his face a mirror of Alexander's pompous expression. "Just because the book is gone does not mean that I have no proof. You recall that I said the Divine Flame captured some Knights Templar during the battle?"

"Yes, I do," Alexander said, the smile slipping from his face. "What does that have to do with anything?"

"The Divine Flame decreed that because the Templar were fighting for Christ, that they should die like Christ. So they flayed them, stabbed holes in their hands and feet, and finally wrapped them in shrouds. One moment."

Julius walked over and pulled a large scroll from a half-hidden cubbyhole. He unrolled the scroll on a desk, revealing an image that Chauncy instantly recognized. "You're saying the Shroud of Turin is a *Templar*?" he asked, incredulous.

"Heresy!" Milos barked.

"It is only heresy if you believe the Shroud to be the image of Christ," Julius said with authority. "But it is most certainly not."

"No wonder the church kicked you out," Milos said in disgust.

"An exile and a heretic I would rather be than to teach lies."

"You had best explain yourself," Milos said darkly.

"Such blind devotion with no proof," Julius said sadly. "Do you not remember the plaque above my door? Abandon all your previous misconceptions! I shall enlighten you, Milos. At John 19:39-42 the Holy Word of God says that Nicodemus, according to the custom of the Jews, washed Jesus' body with myrrh and aloes after his death. The Shroud has been examined many times and not once has anyone discovered evidence of either of those ingredients. Instead, the micro-chemical tests have revealed traces of vanillin, which is usually found in flax. Such a chemical is commonly found in *medieval* materials, but was not found in the cloth wrappings of the Dead Sea Scrolls."

Milos interrupted. "Myrrh and aloe might not last as long as flax, especially if they were absorbed by Jesus' dead body. That is not proof."

"I am not finished," Julius said sternly. "Next is the complex matter of the weave itself. Burial shrouds of other prominent men in Jerusalem during the time of Christ have been found, and they were made with a very simple weave pattern. The Shroud of Turin has a very intricate herringbone weave. Also of interest is the blood stains that were examined. The blood is AB, a type which did not exist before 700 CE."

"Jesus was wrapped in a special cloth because he was the Son of God," Milos interrupted. "And his blood was different for the exact same reason. You still have no proof."

Julius once again shook his head. "You continue to cling to your ideas despite mounting evidence to the contrary. I am still not finished, Milos Karakoles. The radio-carbon dating of the shroud has put the shroud around the year 1260. No, do not interrupt, I know what you are going to say. Yes, radio-carbon dating is not conclusive evidence, even in this case. Researchers have discovered evidence that the Shroud was taken from a church and venerated by the Knights Templar since 1204 CE, which is still nearly twelve-hundred years after the death of Christ. But finally, Milos, there are the results found in 1978 by NASA."

"You are speaking of the impression of the coins placed over the eyes," Milos said triumphantly. "I know of that report, Julius. The coins were discovered to be minted between 29 and 32 CE. That is the time of Christ's death, and only supports my argument!"

"You see, and yet you do not see. You have missed the most important part," Julius said. "The placing of coins on the eyes was based on a superstitious belief that when the souls of the dead traveled to hell, they would need to pay the boatman to take them over the river Styx. Do you really think Jesus or his disciples would teach such pagan ideas? Do you think Nicodemus, who was careful to wrap and prepare the body in accordance with Jewish custom, would break those customs, especially on a man whom he considered extremely important?"

Milos was silent. There was nothing he could say to that.

"This is all well and good," Alexander said rather sarcastically. "The Shroud is not of Jesus Christ. But what does it have to do with the scepter?"

"There are dozens, perhaps even hundreds, of theories about how that image came to be on the shroud," Julius answered. "But the evidence is there for anyone to see if they will only open their eyes. The orange pixels on the cloth that form the image of the dead man contain ion particles. The scientific report clearly states that the image was caused by ion association."

Alexander's eyebrows almost shot off his face. "You are jesting, surely."

"I am not. I can find the report for you, if you wish."

Alexander seemed to deflate. "No, there is no need. I believe you, but I do not believe you. How could the ancients have done this? It is beyond comprehension."

"What is ion association?" Chauncy asked.

"Ionized photons are used to interact with charged particles and for particle accelerators," Alexander answered. "Which is exactly what would have happened when the scepter was broken during the battle with the Knights Templar. The blast of ionized radiation that would have normally contained the antimatter instead flashed about and imprinted an image of one of the captives."

"Congratulations, Mr. Yubarov!" Julius said, reaching forward and touching his shoulder. "You have abandoned your previous misconception and have seen your way to the truth. The Divine Flame has had antimatter technology since at least the time of the Knights Templar, so there is no reason to doubt the rest of their history."

"How do you know all of this?" Alexander asked. "Was it in the Divine Flame book that Mayal stole?"

"Indeed it was. There were many secrets in that book, including the designs of Mayal's museum."

"There's something special about how he designed the museum?" Chauncy asked. "What is it?"

"Have any of you seen the pictures of the interior? It was in the newspapers not too long ago."

"I did," Milos said. "It looked like the Hagia Sophia, except with a large pillar beneath the cupola. It was kind of hard to miss."

"Exactly, which is so typical of Mayal," Julius said. "He claims that the pillar will eventually hold a very important artifact, the most important one in his collection. Any thoughts?"

"It is where he plans to put the scepter," Alexander said.

"Correct. The pillar is almost certainly reinforced steel and concrete, and it connects all the way up to the cupola at the top. The Golden Scepter is missing its firing end, and so Mayal has simply built an entire building to act in the same manner. It will be significantly harder to destroy the scepter or even to decipher where the attacks are coming from."

"And that design was in the Divine Flame book?" Chauncy asked.

"More or less. It is a design that was hypothesized by the Divine Flame about 500 CE. Why do you think cupolas are so prevalent in ancient architecture, especially once Islam adopted the design in 700 CE? It was by the secret prodding of the Divine Flame. A cupola makes a perfect design to harness and amplify the antimatter power of the Golden Scepter. The cult made sure that there would be cupolas all over the world in preparation for their eventual rise to power. Mayal just decided to build his own."

Disciple James came bursting into the library before Julius could continue. "Teacher, we have a situation. There is a large military helicopter coming this way."

"Do you think it's Mayal?" Chauncy asked, feeling his pulse increase. "I thought he wouldn't come back here so soon!"

The sound of the helicopter became audible and increased steadily. "We are about to find out," Julius said solemnly.

Chapter Thirty-Three

Chauncy ran to the foyer, moving much quicker than his older companions. The gaping hole in the cupola granted him a commanding view of the skyline. Even without the view he would've known the helicopter was right above them because of the incessant beating of the blades. As Chauncy covered his ears, the side doors of the helicopter opened and six men rappelled down to the courtyard and he lost sight of them. It looked like they'd been carrying heavy weaponry and that was all he needed to know.

He was turning around to warn his friends when the front door shattered. He didn't even see the men who came in and grabbed him under his arms. He tried to fight against the grip but he'd been caught off-guard. He was lifted and taken forcibly to the main library room where they dumped him unceremoniously on the floor.

He got to his feet and dusted himself off just as Hakan and Dr. Mayal walked into the room.

"It is the end of your journey, Mr. Rollock," Dr. Mayal said with a giant grin. "You have run long and evaded us well, but the game is over. And these three men must be the ones who led you here to the monastery."

Erick stood defiantly, his height eclipsing even that of Mayal. "And we are proud of that fact."

Dr. Mayal made a gesture at the three SSOSA members. "Embers, get these men out of here," he ordered his minions. "I have personal matters to discuss with Mr. Rollock and Mr. Arcosanti."

The Embers pointed their weapons at the SSOSA members, who were smart enough not to argue. Once they had been escorted out of the room, Dr. Mayal turned back and smiled at Chauncy.

"Your wife, son and friend Jake Thrasher are all alive and mostly well. Whether they stay that way is entirely up to you. But we will get to that in a moment." He turned and looked at Julius.

207

"Well, *Teacher*, we meet again."

"You have returned to the monastery," Julius said, a defiant look on his face. "I sincerely doubt that you have come to repent of your sins and return the book you stole from me, *Disciple*."

"For once you are completely correct. I have no need to repent nor to answer to you."

"That is because you have been blinded by your own ambition, Faruk."

"It is you who are blinded, Julius," Dr. Mayal said. "You kept the most powerful book in the world hidden in your basement, locked away from us, and when I dared to read its secrets you refused to share more with me."

"You were not ready for the information. You still are not, as your actions have proven."

Dr. Mayal shook his head mournfully. "You are an old, sad man, sitting here on a rock, reading your books and thinking you have God's favor. The whole time you had that most powerful book hidden in a cage. You had no right to keep it from the messiah!"

Chauncy groaned as he stared at the man in front of him. "So you think you're the messiah?" he asked carefully.

"There is no thinking involved, Chauncy: I *am* the messiah. Even as a child I knew beyond a shadow of a doubt that I was something special, that I was destined for greatness. The prophecies I learned here only reinforced those facts. Coming here to be taught by Julius was divine direction."

"So God told you to come here and steal the Divine Flame book, so you could destroy the world?" Chauncy asked.

"Has Julius been twisting your mind already?" Dr. Mayal asked. "I do not desire to destroy the world, Chauncy. I live and breathe on this earth just as you do. On the contrary, my burning desire is to *change* this world for the better."

"It is the job of any good self-appointed messiah to clean up the world," Julius put in sarcastically.

"Do not mock me, old man. The world has changed many times before, I will simply change it again. During World War II the use of the atomic bomb brought about a change in the way the world runs. Today the threat of a nuclear holocaust still haunts mankind, because rogue nations and terrorists are getting their hands on the technology for atomic weapons. It is only a matter of time before one of them drops a dirty bomb on New York City or London. Now, however, with the Golden Scepter I can change all of that."

"And how are you different from these terrorist groups and their dirty bombs?" Julius demanded. "You delude yourself!"

"You still refuse to see the truth that stands before you, Julius. Nuclear weapons create too much collateral damage and destroy the environment. The Golden Scepter, on the other hand, is highly precise. I can create change in this world by destroying only the people who refuse to obey my recommendations, not by killing their citizens. It is the leaders who have dragged this world into the abyss, and it is *only* those leaders that I shall destroy."

"And all because you are the messiah, right?" Chauncy asked pointedly. "What proof do you have?"

Dr. Mayal smiled at Chauncy before turning his gaze to Julius. "Teacher, what does 2 Kings 1:10 say?"

Julius' impeccable memory sprang to action. "That is where the prophet Elijah said 'If I am the servant of God then let fire come down from heaven.'"

"Fire coming down from heaven no longer means you have God's backing," Chauncy scoffed. "Otherwise, anyone with a napalm weapon can claim to have divine protection nowadays."

"It is only one part of the proof I have," Dr. Mayal said. "The prophecy at Genesis 49:10 speaks of Shiloh, or 'he to whom it belongs.' Shiloh is just one more name for the messiah. Do you know that prophecy, Chauncy?"

Chauncy's heart sank as he searched his memory of the scriptures. "It says that the scepter will come to Shiloh."

Dr. Mayal's eyes burned with fire. "Precisely."

***

The three SSOSA members were taken to a small room and locked inside. Almost immediately they began to plot a way out of their predicament. Milos climbed up Erick's back and looked out the window. The monastery was built right on the edge of the spire, which meant at least a three-hundred-foot drop if they went out that way.

They tried to break the doorknob off, but a guard showed up

and growled at them to stop it. Contingency plans, tactics, alternate methods were all passed between them at breakneck speed. Each plan they tried to come up with died at a massive drop or at the end of a SPAS-12 shotgun.

"We should have made a duplicate scepter," Alexander said. "One that would blow up when an enemy took it."

"*Ach so!*" Erick said. "That would have been good. It is a little late for that, though."

"I hate to say this," Milos said, looking forlorn, "but this may be the first time in history that we SSOSA members have no viable plan. We are beaten by thugs with guns."

Erick looked at his friends. They often argued and more often than not they engaged in petty insults, but when everything was said and done these men were his best friends. It hurt to not be able to save them. "Do you realize what René Sova would say if he were alive?"

Alexander snorted. "Of course I do. He would have shouted, 'Idiots, all of you!' And he would have been right."

***

"What makes you think the scepter is ever going to come to you?" Chauncy asked, trying to be defiant.

"It is really quite simple, Chauncy. I have your wife, your son, and your friend. It will be a simple matter to order their torture and death."

Chauncy squeezed his eyes shut but it didn't stop the tears from staining his cheeks. He was absolutely certain that he would endure torture and death to keep the Golden Scepter away from this madman. He even could have endured the death of Jake Thrasher. But he was equally certain that he couldn't endure the needless death of his wife and son.

Was this it, then? Were all the words in the scriptures merely empty promises? Mayal would have the Golden Scepter, he would rebuild Babylon and he would impose his will upon the nations. He tried to think of something, *anything*, that he could do. But he wasn't prepared for this.

"How do I know that you won't just kill us anyway once you get the scepter?" he asked. His eyes were still closed and tears were still coming. He felt broken in half.

"My dear Chauncy, why would I do that? You, your family and your friends are no threat to me. You could even shout to the media all you wanted about the Golden Scepter and its antimatter powers and absolutely nobody would believe you. Mathew 26:53: 'Do you not think I cannot pray to my God to summon twelve legions of angels to protect me?' I have legions of scientists and followers who can discredit anything you do to try and stop me. And if you prove yourself a true nuisance, I can send those same legions out to kill you. I do not want to. I want you to witness my triumph and come to understand how the prophecies about me are true!"

"I want proof that my wife and son are safe before I give you anything."

"Chauncy, a word?" Julius said. He turned to Mayal. "The *messiah* will not mind if I discuss something privately, will he?" Julius asked, his tone dripping with sarcasm.

Dr. Mayal chuckled and allowed them a few minutes to converse. Julius walked a few feet away. "He has all of us as well," he whispered in Chauncy's ear. "He will kill your family and then begin killing us to get to the scepter. Nothing will stop him."

"I can't just give it up to him," Chauncy said desperately. "Not now that I know what it can do. He'll be unstoppable!"

"Do you truly believe that he is the messiah?"

"Of course not," Chauncy replied without hesitating.

"Then you must have faith that the Almighty will fix this in the end, in His own way."

Chauncy stared at the floor, panic starting to grip him. He'd done everything he could to learn about the Golden Scepter and keep it away from the Divine Flame. And yet he'd just managed to get absolutely everyone he cared about captured by the ruthless cult. His entire world was falling apart around him and there wasn't a single thing he could do to stop it. "I'm not sure I have that kind of faith anymore," he said candidly.

Julius gripped his shoulder. "I have that faith, Chauncy. Trust in my faith even if you do not trust in yours."

Chauncy had a hard time swallowing. This wasn't supposed to be how it all ended. The good guys weren't supposed to lose. "It's in the secret basement," Chauncy spoke up to Dr. Mayal. "I'll show you."

Dr. Mayal laughed heartily. "How fitting. The very place that could not contain the knowledge of the Divine Flame proves equally unable to contain the Golden Scepter. Hakan, the basement is right over there."

Hakan found the basement with ease and moments later he returned to the library with the metal briefcase that held the scepter. "This is the moment we have been waiting for, Exalted One," Hakan said, grinning broadly. "Victory is ours!"

Dr. Mayal opened the briefcase and stared at the scepter, an almost lustful glint in his eyes. "Just one more prophecy that has come true. Perhaps, Chauncy, you will even join my Embers when you see my triumph. The great city of Babylon will be rebuilt. You will see the fire from heaven and the changes that I will bring, and you will know that I was right all along."

He closed the briefcase and turned to Julius. "As for you, Teacher, I will let you live out the rest of your days with your legacy: a half-burnt monastery full of moldy books. You could have had the greatness that I am now ascending toward, but you chose differently. A pity."

With that, Dr. Mayal spun on his heels and left the library, Hakan following closely behind.

Chauncy sat down heavily on a nearby wooden chair. "I have failed miserably."

Julius was still staring at the door through which Dr. Mayal had left.. "Do not be troubled, Chauncy you did everything in your power. The fate of the world is no longer in your hands."

Chauncy got up and went over to one of the windows, too nervous to sit. Down below was the gorgeous Thessaly Valley. The Apostle Paul had traveled the roads below during his third missionary tour, enduring hardship and pain and yet still pressing on. Chauncy Rollock had faced hardship and pain and had crumbled like a cracker. He didn't know how he was going to face his family as a failure.

Chapter Thirty-Four

Jake Thrasher leaned back and tried to get comfortable in the decidedly uncomfortable airport seat. His back ached from being cooped up in the back of a small car for too many hours. His head hurt from where the blindfold had been tied too tight. His wrists were on fire from the also-too-tight zip ties. But those physical ailments paled in comparison to the bruising his ego had taken.

They'd come *so* close. He'd been determined to be successful, to prove Anita wrong. Turns out he wasn't a Navy SEAL after all. Stupid Pascual. He would have to pick his associates more carefully in the future, if he chose any at all.

Jake looked to his left. Anita and Troy sat close together a few seats over, their eyes glued to the airport gates. The plane they were waiting for had just landed and the passengers were disembarking. Any minute now Chauncy would come down that corridor and be reunited with his family.

No thanks to Jake. He'd failed in his mission. He wasn't sure how he could face Chauncy after that. It was bad enough that he had to refund the rescue money, but to face the husband and father of his charges after a failure...

Chauncy appeared in the crowd of passengers. Anita and Troy were on their feet instantly, practically running to embrace him. Jake stayed in his seat and watched the tearful reunion, not wanting to interrupt. He felt a mysterious lump in his throat. Must be dry in here.

Eventually, Chauncy came over and held out his hand.

Jake stood and shook the proffered hand hesitantly. "It's good to see you alive and well, Chauncy."

"Thanks for taking care of my family," Chauncy said. There was a haunted aspect to his eyes that Jake had never seen before. The lines on his face were deeper as well.

"I didn't take care of them," Jake admitted. "I botched the mission bad."

Chauncy frowned, the lines on his face getting even deeper.

213

"You weren't the only one," he said hoarsely.

Jake looked over at Anita and Troy and the puzzle pieces clicked. "That's why we were released. You didn't give them—"

"I had to," Chauncy said, his voice resigned. "I couldn't lose my family."

So that was what the haunted look was about. Jake had never had kids so he couldn't relate. "Sorry I brought it up," Jake said, looking away. The anger and guilt visible in Chauncy's face was painful to see. "You'll get my refund in two-to-four business days."

"What's next for you, Jake?"

Jake snorted and looked back at Chauncy. They'd interacted very little in twenty years and somehow he still considered Chauncy a friend he could talk to. "I'm thinking of retiring."

"You? Retire? I always thought you'd die doing this kind of stuff."

"Yeah, well, I almost did die," Jake said.

"Sorry."

"Nah, it's okay, I let myself be talked into it. Anyway, I've got a nice little nest-egg saved up. I'm getting too old for this—"

"Stuff," Chauncy edited with a slight smile. "Well, take care of yourself, Jake Thrasher. I've got to look after my family."

They shook hands again and Jake watched them disappear into the crowd. He wondered if he'd ever see them again. He kind of wished he would.

Jake drove his rented convertible through the back roads of San Diego, the ocean breeze rushing through his hair. He pulled into his driveway and stopped. His eyes were drawn to the La Jolla mansions visible on the hill. They were so close and yet so far away: he didn't have quite enough money to afford one of those yet.

Maybe just a few more jobs, he thought with a smile.

Chapter Thirty-Five

Doctor Faruk Mayal stood at the lectern and surveyed the hushed, expectant crowd. It was the same lectern from which he'd given a rousing speech to the Institute of Antiquities of Ankara benefactors, but the setting before him was significantly different. At the previous event, his rare archaeological commodities had been the focal point of the gathering. Today, the alcoves that contained those commodities were darkened and closed off from viewing. There would be no startled awe or exclamations about golden helmets.

His attire was also quite removed from the tuxedo he'd worn. He was now adorned in the garment of the High Priest and Exalted One of the Divine Flame, the first time that most in the crowd had seen the outfit. The long black robe was embossed with gold and purple designs on the trim and a flaming handprint covering the chest.

The crowd was also different. There were no rich but oblivious benefactors in sight, hoping to raise their social standing by supporting antiquities. The men and women still streaming into the main room were the upper echelon of his Burning Embers, people whom he'd trusted throughout the years. They knew exactly why this entire structure had been built, and why they were present for this ceremony. It was a purposely low-key event, with no media invited, but the number of individuals was still impressive.

Geraldo Esperanto and Marcos Campana, recently promoted due to their fine work in Mexico, were the last to arrive. Mayal nodded gravely at them before drawing in a deep breath.

"Burning Embers of the Divine Flame, I welcome you," he said in Akkadian, the language of the Babylonians. "Today marks our ultimate triumph and ceremony. You are here because you are the best and brightest of my followers. Your devout faith has seen you through years of doubt and uncertainty and will finally be rewarded."

The leaders of his Embers were not prone to outbursts but he could see the powerful emotions coursing through the crowd. "I see in your eyes the same emotions I am feeling," he continued in English. "Our aim has been accomplished. Some of you have sought this goal for only a few years, while others have spent decades in tireless, faithful service. I have spent my entire life in pursuit of this goal. Ladies and gentlemen, my Embers, welcome to the Grand Sanctuary."

He raised his hands in a showy display as a low rumbling sound of stone on stone was heard. The walkway in front of him slowly descended, creating a staircase leading away from the pillar. Several people gasped but they were drowned out by a short round of applause. "Descend to the room below and we shall all revel together in our victory," Mayal ordered.

The crowd quickly obeyed and filed down the wide staircase. Mayal followed at the end of the crowd and couldn't help but smile as he saw the cylindrical room. The floor was highly polished marble, imported from Carrara, Italy. The curved walls were polished stone with inlaid Babylonian tile art. Every few feet there was a statue of a Babylonian deity, framed by red silk drapes. Where aboveground there was just a pillar, down in the sanctuary it was replaced by an immense, twenty-five-foot tall statue of Marduk atop an ebony column, its arms spread out and holding lightning bolts. Above his head, at the ceiling, there were four large-screen TVs pointed toward the seating areas where the Embers were even now sitting down.

At the opposite end of the room from the stone staircase waited Hakan Ramush. He was wearing the royal garb of the Great One, a less-ostentatious version of Mayal's outfit. Mayal smiled warmly as he approached his second-in-command. Hakan may have failed several times in this last endeavor, but in the end he'd returned with the scepter intact. Mayal never had a more faithful, loyal, and successful servant than Hakan. He was proud of the loyalty and competence he'd inspired in these men and women.

Mayal stopped a few feet away from Hakan, who bowed low. The Great One then stood, turned and unlocked a large vault built into the wall. He pulled an ornate and ancient wooden box from the recess, a box rescued from the pawnshop in Hamburg. The sacred symbols of the Divine Flame seemed to stand out from the box as Hakan held it forward and opened it.

Mayal reached forward slowly, a tingle running through his arms. He'd walked the path of a messiah for decades now, quoting scripture and prophecy, digging into the past to predict the future. The fulfillment of all those prophecies was right there in front of him. His fingers curled around the golden object and his heart skipped a beat. He was holding his life's dreams and aspirations, and it was everything he could have hoped for.

With a flourish, he turned around and held the object above his head. "I present to you the Golden Scepter!"

A cheer erupted from the crowd, a roar of pride and accomplishment that shook the very walls. He let the applause run its course, his heart swelling, almost bursting with a sense of destiny. He lowered the scepter and looked at it.

"With this scepter we shall rebuild the sacred city of Babylon," he said. "The wrongs of the past and the present will be righted. We shall bring enlightenment and understanding back to the world, knowledge that has been hidden for nearly a thousand years. The Divine Flame shall burn bright once more."

More applause broke out as he walked across the room to the statue in the middle. Marduk looked down at him and Mayal felt a sense of approval. He unlocked a door on the ebony column and placed the Golden Scepter very carefully inside, double-checking that it was oriented properly. He closed the inner door by pulling two levers, creating an airlock-type seal, before shutting the ebony outer door. The tiny cameras within turned on and began to broadcast to the TVs, showing the entire room an image of the Golden Scepter encased in the column.

"We were unable to recover the aiming mechanism of the Golden Scepter," Mayal said as he walked back to where Hakan stood. A podium with a laptop rose from the floor and Mayal began to type commands. "Even though we knew where to look, from our own history books, the broken piece was never recovered. To rectify that, I had our brightest scientists build the entire pillar to act as an aiming device. As you can see, miniature robotic arms will be used to turn the rings so that the scepter may fire."

He paused his speech as he manipulated the arms by typing in the proper commands. The first ring slid into place, closely followed by the second. The third ring was a little stuck, the passage of time having dulled the mechanism somewhat, but it also fell into place.

"Our first target will be something simple: a cell tower on a mountain a thousand miles away. Once we have tested the Golden Scepter and made certain it works properly, we will begin to change the course of history. Embers, today is the start of the most important era in history."

The roar of the Embers made it sound like their first attack would level the White House or Buckingham Palace. He smiled and decided to let them revel in their moment of triumph. They had all waited many years for this. The penultimate ring clicked into place and another hush fell on the crowd.

The final symbol lined up. An eerie sound, like a million cats wailing, burst forth from the column. The wail was followed by a low rumble as the power of the Golden Scepter was unleashed for only the second time in history, nearly a thousand years after its first usage. Mayal held his hand over his heart and held his breath. The image on the TVs switched to a view of a mountain. A pillar of smoke was all that remained of the cell tower. The power of the Golden Scepter was real. This was truly a day to remember!

The cheer from the crowd was even louder as the Divine Flame witnessed their first victory. Dr. Mayal breathed a huge sigh of relief and closed his eyes, awash in the glow of triumph. After all of the years of studying and analyzing the scepter and its power, he'd known that anything could've failed. Nobody had recently tested the scepter...until now. It worked perfectly, and the prophecies were true. It was now time for him to take his place as the Messiah of the Divine Flame and show the world leaders where they'd gone wrong.

Another low rumble that quickly grew louder erupted from the pillar and Mayal opened his eyes. That wasn't supposed to happen. Hakan appeared at his side and Mayal turned to him. "What is wrong?" the Exalted One hissed quietly.

"I do not know," Hakan said, his voice trembling.

The rumble became a howl as cracks began to appear in the ebony column. Unnatural yellow light began to show from the cracks and the Embers broke into panic, trampling each other as they rushed for the exit. The walls began to buckle and dust filled the room, making it difficult to see. Mayal and Hakan stumbled like drunkards as the floor shook violently. The statues along the walls crumbled to the floor, their glory shattered to pieces.

The largest statue in the room, Marduk, began to splinter and break. The lightning-bearing arms bent and swayed a moment before they cracked off and plummeted to the floor, impaling Hakan and killing him instantly.

Mayal stared at the limp form of his most devout follower and felt a numbness wash over him. The fractures in the ebony column widened and the light grew brighter as Mayal stared at the place where the Golden Scepter was housed. This couldn't be happening. He'd read the prophecies and deciphered them personally! He knew every verse and phrase by heart. He was *destined* for greatness.

The howl became a shrieking bellow and the statue bent and warped. In the last second before the statue shattered Mayal wondered if he might have been wrong.

A light flashed through downtown Ankara, bright enough to be blinding even in the midday sun. The ground rocked and twisted as a quake shuddered through the earth. It was over in a moment, almost as if it had never happened. A large crater and rising cloud of black smoke were all that remained of the Divine Flame.

Chapter Thirty-Six

Milos Karakoles looked up from his book and smiled as Disciple James entered the room. "Is that the newspaper?"

James plopped it down on the table. "Read page five," he said simply.

Milos picked up the paper. He read page five twice before he could truly believe it. "Looks like the Golden Scepter didn't work exactly as Mayal planned."

Julius Arcosanti walked slowly into the room just then, a large smile on his face. "The true God stepped in. Has your faith been restored, Milos?"

Milos looked at the newspaper, especially the picture of a crater where Mayal had vanished. "My faith was never shaken, Teacher."

Julius sat down across from Milos and peered closely at him. "Your SSOSA friends have returned to their normal lives, yet here you remain. Why is that?"

Milos looked down at the book he'd been reading. It was an early copy of the Bible, a translation from before the King James Version. "We of SSOSA pride ourselves on our intelligence, logic and reasoning prowess. You have opened my eyes to truths that I did not know, and yet I should have known them. I want to stay until my errors have been corrected."

"It is a noble goal to have," Julius said with a solemn nod. "It is the same goal I had. I have been thinking it is time to change, however."

"Why would you change?" Disciple James asked, shocked. "You have the truth!"

"Yes, I do. But I think it is time that I began to spread it farther. I chose this monastery, Milos, James, because it was difficult to get to. I wanted to weed out the unworthy with an imposing entrance requirement and by locking them away from the world. After seeing what happened with Faruk, though, I do not believe it is right to do so. Only now do I understand Christ Jesus' prayer to not take his disciples *out* of the world, but to protect them *because* of the world."

Julius paused and looked off into the distance. "I am old and set in my ways, and this decision is difficult for me. I will stay here, but I will leave the future of the monastery to one who is younger and eager to help. James, I have been training you for many years. Are you ready for this challenge?"

James held his head high. "I will do my best, Teacher."

"I am no longer the Teacher here, James," Julius said quietly. "You are."

Milos stood up to shake James' hand. "Congratulations, Teacher. What do you plan to do?"

"I think we should have Internet and telephones up here, for starters," James said. "Spread the invitation out farther, maybe install an elevator. I have a lot of ideas and plans."

Milos left the room quietly as the two men began to discuss the future of the monastery. It made him think about the recent conversation SSOSA had. They really were just old men playing games. But if Julius was willing to change his ways, maybe SSOSA should as well. Maybe open up membership, accept apprentices and train them to use their minds. If Mayal had seen fit to kill them, SSOSA would have ended on the spires of Meteora and no one would continue the tradition. That would be sad.

He started down the mountain, heading toward the closest telephone. It was time to make a call to Erick and Alexander. It was time to make sure that the traditions of SSOSA would survive into the future.

***

Chauncy Rollock stood at the end of the driveway and stared at the charred debris that had once been his house. It was one thing to hear the news about it burning down, but it was a completely different thing to actually see it with his own eyes. The motifs and styles Anita and he had carefully chosen were now little more than ashes, ashes that had long been blown away by the Wyoming winds. It left a hollowness in the pit of his stomach that he wasn't sure how to deal with. The furniture, the paintings, and the designs were all gone. So too, it seemed, were the many dreams their young, naive selves had dreamt while inside those walls.

He looked to his right and to his left and felt a smile creep upon his face. He pulled his wife and his son closer to him and squeezed them tight. Maybe those old dreams were dead, maybe they weren't. It didn't matter. He could have new dreams now that he was once again complete with his family and the threat of the Golden Scepter no longer cast a shadow upon the world.

"How do you want to rebuild it?" he asked, the words almost catching in his throat. He didn't dare allow himself to think about how close he'd come to losing his family.

Anita stirred. "I don't know that I want to," she said quietly. There was still pain visible on her face. Chauncy didn't know if it was because of the house, or if she was also trying not to think about how their family had almost been destroyed. "The winters are so harsh and we're so far from everything. I think I want to move somewhere else and start fresh."

Chauncy considered that. Wyoming was his birthplace and until now it seemed like it would always be his home. But maybe it *was* time to start fresh. Rebuilding here might just bring up reminders of the ordeal they'd gone through. Mayal and Hakan had left deep cracks in his faith. He needed time and distance to recuperate.

They talked for a few minutes about possible places where they could move, but they all knew that it was just idle talk for right now. Each of them was filtering through their emotions and saying their own goodbyes to their house. They would be able to decide on a new place to live soon enough, but not right now.

Troy pulled away and looked up at his father. "You want to know something, Dad?" he asked.

Chauncy let go of Anita and bent over so he was eye-level with Troy. He didn't have to bend nearly as far as he used to. "Sure I do, Son," he responded, smiling. "What's up?"

Troy waved his hand to encompass the rubble of their house. "I don't think I want to be an archaeologist when I grow up."

Chauncy chuckled. "You know, I don't think I want to be one either," he said softly.

He looked at Anita and saw the knowing smile on her face. They both knew that the lure of antiquities would be with him always. "Well, at least not for awhile," he amended.

The Missing Capstone

A short story by Dyego Alehandro & Alex Zabala

Cairo, Egypt
1994

A loud horn and equally loud Arabic swearing jolted Chauncy awake. He looked out the windshield and was mildly surprised to see an elephant blocking the road. The elephant morphed into a camel after several blinks and he sunk further back into his seat. He was exhausted. He'd been in the air or in airports for almost twenty-four hours. His body demanded sleep but he didn't want to nod off again. He was in Cairo. *Cairo*! His first impression of the city had been a distinct disappointment; it was as modern a city as Denver or New York, two of the cities he'd traveled through from Wyoming. Like most Americans he knew, he'd pictured Cairo as being nothing but the old buildings of Ancient Egypt.

But he'd gotten into a taxi and given his destination anyway, unwilling to let his broken expectations keep him down. He'd apparently fallen asleep a long time ago because *now* the city looked like he'd imagined it. The buildings were older, smaller, and definitely more Egyptian in architecture. Uneasiness began to spread through him as he looked around. He'd heard horror stories of cab drivers who drove their clients into dark alleys to be mugged.

"Are you sure you know the way?" he asked in very garbled Arabic.

"I speak English," the cabbie replied, his accent just as garbled. "Yes I know the way."

Chauncy sat back and tried to relax. After all, he was finally in Cairo. The entire trip was a pre-graduation gift from his parents: a round-trip ticket to anywhere in the world. When he'd chosen Egypt they hadn't batted an eye; why would their son, studying archaeology, have chosen anywhere else? If they'd known the *real* reason he was coming here they probably would have canceled the whole deal.

He stared at the address scrawled on a worn piece of paper with a mixture of excitement and foreboding. One of his college buddies had listened to Chauncy's crazy idea and had immediately stated he knew who could help: Jake Thrasher. The fact that his friend had already traveled the world four times instead of studying gave credence to the idea that he might know the right person for the job. But it was that same fact, and its associated lack of discipline, that gave Chauncy the foreboding. Would Jake Thrasher actually know how to help, or had Chauncy's friend been really drunk when he'd offered up the name?

The farther they got from the fancy part of town the more Chauncy's dread grew. The old was mixed with the new out here, and as they traveled it increasingly became the old. The driver made a sudden turn down a dusty street and came to a stop.

"Here you are, sir," he said. "Your arrival."

Chauncy stared out at the old, non-descript building and felt his heart heading somewhere near his ankles. The blinking neon sign declared that it was *The Old Banshee Bar*. Or, at least, it would have said that if it wasn't missing most of its letters. Now it just looked like it was called *TOdneBar*. He took a deep breath, paid the driver and got out of the car, clutching his backpack and attaché case to his chest. The taxi drove off in a cloud of dust and Chauncy knew he was going to strangle his 'buddy' when he got back. There was nothing to do but go ahead with this. He was already here and there wasn't likely to be anywhere else to go before the sun set.

He walked into the bar and was immediately assaulted by the smell. A hundred different types of cigarettes and cigars vied for supremacy in the air. Even with all that smoke haze Chauncy could still detect the telltale smell of alcohol and men who didn't have easy access to indoor plumbing. The sound of a dozen different conversations in at least three different languages filled the room. In the background he could hear the bar stereo playing something from Gloria Estefan and he felt a little bit better. Maybe somebody here spoke English after all.

"Hey!" the bartender shouted, proving Chauncy's guess. "You American?"

He nodded and walked over to the bar. "Yes I am. Is that a problem around here?"

The bartender snorted and smiled. "Not always. What are you

226

doing so far from downtown Cairo?"

"I'm looking for somebody."

"Oh, like a girl?" the bartender asked with a wink and a broader smile. "There are quite a few nice ones here who'd be fascinated by an American for no extra charge."

Chauncy grinned and felt a little more at ease. There were some things that were universal no matter where you went in the world. "No, I'm looking for Jake Thrasher."

"That worthless bum? What do you want with him?"

Chauncy rubbed his jaw. His fears had been right. "Why'd you call him a worthless bum?"

"Because he is," the bartender said matter-of-factly. "He does nothing but sit around this bar all day."

Yep, I knew it, he sighed to himself. Thousands of miles and dollars across the world just to call on the village drunk. He felt like an idiot but the next question had to be asked. Might as well go all the way. "Where can I find him?"

"He's over there in the corner," the bartender said, pointing the way. "You sure you don't want a girl instead?"

"I'm sure. Thanks for the help, barkeep."

Chauncy peered through the murky depths of the bar and could almost make out a person sitting alone in a booth. It could just as easily been a pile of luggage but he headed in that direction anyway. He finally got close enough to see that it wasn't, in fact, a pile of luggage and found himself pleasantly surprised. The man was well-dressed in a dinner jacket, white shirt and bolo tie. He was probably in his mid-forties, was Caucasian and was clean-shaven. Best of all, his eyes looked alert and intelligent. Maybe things weren't as bad as he'd feared.

"I've been expecting you," the man said, his voice slightly accented. "Glad to see you made it in here alive. Welcome to Egypt."

Chauncy sat down and breathed a sigh of relief, the first time he'd done that since landing in Cairo. "It's nice to meet you in person, Mr. Thrasher. I'm glad you got my letter."

Jake smiled wanly. "Tell you what. If we dispense with the pleasantries I'll order you a drink. What'll you have, Chauncy?"

His mind raced over the various popular Egyptian drinks. "I'll have a Sakara, Jake."

Jake whistled over a waiter, placed the order, and then folded his hands across his chest. "You've come all the way from Wyoming just for me and your letter didn't say why. Why?"

He instinctively clutched his attaché case tighter and glanced furtively around the bar. "I really don't think I should be saying this in public. Especially in...such a seedy location."

Jake readily agreed. "This place does seem to attract the low-life, doesn't it? Tell you what, I'll take you to my place and we can talk. My vehicle isn't too far from here."

The waiter brought their drinks but Jake waved them away and started out of the bar. Chauncy followed quickly, not wanting to be alone in this place anymore. The glaring sun was just beginning to set beyond the horizon, casting sharp shadows everywhere in sight. The people looked even more sinister than when he'd first arrived. Jake led the way down narrow, dusty side streets, a meandering path that Chauncy immediately lost track of. If Jake turned out to be a waste of time there was no way Chauncy would be able to find his way back to civilization. He fervently prayed that he'd make it out of this alive.

Jake led the way to an empty field and Chauncy felt his eyebrows creeping up his forehead. "What is this, the Red Baron?" he asked incredulously.

Jake smiled as he climbed up into the two-seater biplane. "Technically, Red Baron was the nickname of the pilot, not his plane. And Manfred Von Richtofen flew a Fokker triplane. This obviously does not have three wings. Climb in."

"But...but..."

"I told you my vehicle was nearby," Jake said. "I never said what kind of vehicle it was. Climb in."

Chauncy could hear a distinct note of amusement in the other's voice. He really didn't want to spend more time in airplanes. He *especially* didn't want to fly in an ancient relic flown by what might or might not be a drunken bum. But, once again, there wasn't anything he could do about it. He climbed into the back seat, shuffling his luggage into a very uncomfortable resting location.

"Where did you get this old thing?" he asked.

"A customer couldn't pay for a job with cash and offered me this. I've had a pilot's license since I was seventeen so I jumped at the chance to own a Boeing Stearman. Now sit back and enjoy the ride."

The engine sputtered and coughed for a few seconds before blazing to life in a deafening roar. Jake taxied the vehicle down a dirt runway before cutting into full gear. The small biplane was airborne in seconds and climbed away from the setting sun. Chauncy quickly forgot all his worries and fears and looked down at the city below. The buildings looked like small brown boxes and off in the distance a silhouette made his heart skip a few beats. "Are those the pyramids?" he shouted over the noise.

"Sure are!" Jake shouted back. "Just hang on for a few minutes and you'll get a close-up view."

The magnificent ancient structures seemed to glow brighter as they approached and Chauncy could scarcely breathe. These buildings were the reason he'd chosen archaeology as his major. These buildings were the reason he was here in Cairo. He was looking at his life's aspirations from a vantage point he never thought he'd enjoy.

Jake circled the pyramids three times, long past the point where the sun had set and the spotlights had turned on. Chauncy felt a strange sort of sadness as the plane turned one final time and started away from the pyramids. His trip had not been a total waste. Even if he never got the information he needed and failed in his quest, even then he would never consider this a failure. He'd seen the Giza plateau from the air and just for a few minutes he'd gazed into the past.

The engine sputtered and then suddenly quit and Chauncy wished he'd never come here. He screamed as loud as he could as the plane suddenly started down.

"Shut up and let me concentrate!" Jake yelled as he desperately pushed buttons and pulled on levers.

Chauncy squeezed his eyes and his mouth shut. He felt his stomach lurching and trying to exit his body through his head. He didn't want to crash. He didn't want his body splattered across the very soil he'd just recently been admiring. The faces of his friends and family flashed through his mind and he absently realized he was praying.

The engine sputtered back on with a jolt and the plane leveled out. By the time they landed, ten or fifteen minutes later, Chauncy still hadn't unclenched his jaw. Jake apologized for the condition of the plane and promised to have it checked out first thing in the morning.

Chauncy didn't talk much as Jake led the way down a dusty, narrow street. He finally stirred when a familiar neon sign flashed in the darkness and caught his attention. "You've got to be kidding me," he said tiredly. "You nearly killed me just so you could bring me back *here*?"

Jake grinned. "Yep. This is my place. I live upstairs."

"We just wasted precious time and raised my blood pressure for nothing?"

"I seem to recall you enjoying the view of the pyramids," Jake said with a bit of extra steel in his voice. "Besides, there's nothing we can do at night, not in Egypt. Relax."

Chauncy felt like arguing but deep down he knew Jake was right. He *had* enjoyed the view of the pyramids. "Yeah, sorry."

"Don't worry about it. Now let's get upstairs and you can tell me all about your little errand."

Δ Δ Δ

Jake's apartment was a welcome relief compared to the exterior of *The Old Banshee Bar*. It was small but very nicely decorated, and it seemed designed from the ground up to be as comfortable as possible. The armchairs and sofa looked deep enough to swallow somebody whole, the ceiling fans were large and almost silent, and the window shades looked like they would block most of the harsh sunlight.

"You never got your drink in the bar; would you like one now?" Jake asked as he pointed Chauncy to a chair.

"I'm parched," Chauncy admitted. "I'll take anything."

Jake walked over to the kitchen and Chauncy looked around some more. The living and dining room were connected to the kitchen in one big open area, but there were two doors to the side that he guessed led to the bed and bathrooms. It was cozy and posh and he really liked it. It was so many levels above the bar below.

He felt his face burning a little as he suddenly realized something. He cleared his throat. "I must apologize that I called your bar a seedy location. I didn't know you owned it."

Jake laughed as he poured an amber liquid into a couple of glasses. "And you'll notice I agreed with you and said it attracted lowlifes. That's how I like it. Makes a good front for my real business. Which brings me to my point: what do you need my services for?"

Chauncy accepted the glass and took a sip. It was a rather excellent scotch. "I'm here to prove my doctoral thesis and impress a girl at the university," he said with a grin.

"Ah, young love," Jake said. "Who is she?"

"Her name is Anita Forester. She's brilliant and she's gorgeous. We share a few classes in Atmospheric Sciences."

Jake raised his eyebrows. "Weather? I thought you were working on archeology. What's she going to be, a weathergirl?"

Chauncy mock-glared at Jake. "No, she's going to be a nurse. She picked a few weather classes so she would better understand how weather affects people, especially those with arthritis. I picked it because it will help me get an idea of how ancient cultures would have reacted to weather and climate changes."

"Noble reasons," Jake said and Chauncy couldn't tell if he was being sarcastic or not. "Please continue."

"How much do you know about the pyramids of Giza?" Chauncy asked.

"Surprisingly little, considering how close I live to them," Jake answered as he sat down. "They're big and a tourist attraction, both of which I tend to avoid."

Chauncy patted his attaché case. "I have more details about the pyramids in here than most people will ever know. My doctoral thesis is about the Great Pyramid, or the Khufu Pyramid. Do you know anything about the missing pyramidion, or capstone?"

Jake shrugged. "Ah, capstones. I know a little about them. They are very rare. The Cairo museum only has four of them. I once—nevermind. What about the missing capstone?"

"The Great Pyramid is more than it seems," Chauncy said. His eyes lit up as he talked about his favorite subject. "It's the most precisely-built structure in history. Its pyramidion would have been significantly larger than any of the others and it would have been covered in gold or electrum. I'm convinced that it was removed for a specific reason."

"Isn't it generally assumed that it was looted?"

Chauncy snorted. "Do you have any idea how much it would have weighed? Not to mention the difficulty involved in climbing all the way to the top of the pyramid in order to get to it. No, the capstone was not looted, at least not by normal grave robbers. The whole reason I've come here to Cairo, and to you in particular, is…I think I know where it is."

Jake actually sat up a little straighter. "The Great Pyramid's missing capstone. Do you have any idea how valuable that would be?"

"It would be one of the greatest finds in recent archaeological history," he agreed. "I'm hoping that selling it will help finance your part of my mission."

Jake chuckled and finished off his drink. "I sincerely hope you brought some real money with you, Chauncy. If I worked only on the *promise* of finding lost artifacts…well, let's just say that I would have died of starvation decades ago."

"How much will your services cost me?"

"I don't know yet. You've carefully avoided telling me where this capstone is supposedly located."

"You'll forgive my caution, I hope," Chauncy said a bit defensively. "This is not an ordinary business transaction."

"I can agree with that, but I still need an idea of what I'm going to be doing before I can name a price. I'm still not entirely certain why you haven't just gone out and found it yourself."

Chauncy braced himself. "The Egyptian Museum rejected my requests for official backing. That means the only chance I have of finding the capstone—"

"Is to do a little digging of your own," Jake interrupted. "*Illegal* digging. Right?"

Chauncy seemed to shrink a little. "I haven't even graduated yet. There's no way anybody will accept my views on the subject, especially on such a lost cause. This is the only way I can prove my thesis."

Jake waved his hand in dismissal. "I do this sort of thing all the time. I can pave the way for you, and we can do it as quietly as possible. Where are we digging?"

Chauncy perked up at the mention of 'we.' "So you're in?"

"I need money before I do anything, Chauncy. I need to know where we're going."

Chauncy braced himself. "We need to go to Abydos."

Jake's eyebrows tried to reach escape velocity. "Abydos. That's just a *little* bit outside of Cairo."

"I know, I know," Chauncy said. "But my friend spoke highly of your skills. Quite frankly, you're the only chance I've got at this. And yes, I just weakened my bargaining position considerably by admitting that."

"There may be a slight problem," Jake said as he leaned forward. "Abydos is over 500 kilometers away. That's two hundred kilometers beyond my normal operating range. Even worse, it's right on the border between the Sohag and New Valley Governorates. It's been a hotbed of rivalry between several black market groups for years. I'm not on good terms with any of them.

"So...what does that mean?"

Jake rubbed his jaw and gazed at nothing in particular. "What exactly is your plan? Just go someplace in Abydos and start digging?"

Chauncy stiffened a little. "Give me a little more credit than that. I was hoping to rent a house, and *then* start digging."

Jake couldn't help but chuckle as he finished off his drink. "I sometimes miss Americans. Do you know where in the city you would like to rent a house?"

He rummaged around in his backpack and pulled out a small map of Abydos. "This is the temple of Seti I, not a bad tourist attraction. But it's far too new to be of interest to us. Seti I was nineteenth dynasty, Khufu was fourth. The temple of Ramesses II is also too new. Less than a mile northwest, however—"

"Is the much older Osiris city/temple complex," Jake said, nodding.

Chauncy looked up, surprised. "You know that?"

"Let's just say I'm familiar with the area. Why do you think the capstone would be in there?"

"I don't," Chauncy said. A conspiratorial grin spread across his face. "But this area has been home to tombs and temple complexes since before the first dynasty. The ruins we can visit right now are a remake of the original temple sites, and they were done in the *sixth* dynasty. I'm convinced that an earlier area, further north and closer to the Nile, is home to Khufu and his capstone."

"And 'further north' is, of course, buried under the town."

"Exactly."

Jake leaned back with a sigh. "I'm going to need more than conjecture on this one. Why do you think it's going to be in a specific spot?"

"I've spent most my academic career studying ancient cultures," Chauncy answered. "And especially the Egyptians. There are patterns, even mathematic norms, to the way they built things. There are also certain similarities between Abydos and later constructs, especially Thebes and the Valley of the Kings. If the capstone isn't exactly where I think it is...it's probably not anywhere. I wouldn't be wasting my time and money if I wasn't absolutely convinced."

"Speaking of money, let's talk finances."

They negotiated for a couple more hours before coming to a mutually acceptable agreement. Jake told Chauncy to make himself at home and disappeared outside, running some kind of errand. Chauncy walked to the guestroom and flopped down in the bed as his mind swirled slowly. He tossed and turned in the unfamiliar bunk, halfway across the world from where he normally slept, and wondered if this trip was going to be worth it. The outrageous price of Jake Thrasher's services would only be paid off if his theory was correct and they managed to sell the capstone. But what if he was wrong? What if the capstone was never in Abydos and he was wasting his last Spring Break before graduation? He'd spent all of his cash and two golden rings he'd planned to give to Anita, just getting Jake to agree to this deal. If things went poorly he would be stuck in Cairo without a way out. Heck, he might be stuck all the way south in Abydos without a way out. He'd have to get word to his parents and they'd have to foot the bill and bring him back, and he'd have to tell them why he'd *really* come to Egypt and that wasn't a conversation he was looking forward to. And he wouldn't have a finished doctoral thesis nor a way to impress Anita.

A million questions played through his mind but he didn't know the answers to any of them. Doubt coursed through him but he had to try and shut his brain off and go to sleep. *Sufficient unto each day*, he quoted silently to himself. Maybe tomorrow would bring some answers. Or maybe it would just bring more troubles.

Δ Δ Δ

"Wake up!" a voice bellowed in his ear.

He rolled off the bed and was standing before he even realized what was going on. "What time is it?" he asked Jake.

"It's 1 pm and time to get moving. Breakfast is ready; I suggest you eat whether you're hungry or not. We're not going to be getting food for a long time after we leave."

Chauncy stumbled through the hallways to the dining room and sat down at the table. He somehow managed to eat, get showered and dressed, grab his luggage and follow Jake through the streets of Cairo while still partially asleep. When they reached their destination he snapped awake really fast.

"Oh no," he said, shaking his head and putting up his hands. "Oh no you don't. I'm not flying in that thing again."

Jake grinned as he carried his luggage up to the red bi-plane. "Relax, Chauncy, I didn't waste my morning like you did. Three separate mechanics checked her out and she's in better shape than when I bought her."

"I don't want to go in that plane again," Chauncy said, sleepiness making him more stubborn than usual.

Jake sighed. "It's three hours flight to Abydos in this plane. Driving would take us seven hours or longer. *Walking* will take you a week. Have fun."

"You wouldn't."

"I've already got your money, Chauncy. Doesn't matter to me how I spend it."

Chauncy sprinted to the plane and made sure he was strapped in before Jake was. He glowered at the pilot, who ignored him and got the plane started up. Chauncy was listening closely and he had to admit that the engine sounded more vibrant and steady than it had yesterday. It lifted gracefully into the air and headed due south. He was saddened that they weren't going to fly by the pyramids again, but he was still ecstatic that he'd been able to see them in the first place.

Slowly the edges of the city came into view. To his right was the Nile River and its associated greenery, but everywhere else was the bright sand and dirt of the desert. He settled in as comfortably as he could, adjusted his goggles, and traced the Nile River Valley as it snaked its way through the dusty land.

It was close to twenty minutes later when he finally realized his eyes weren't playing tricks on him. The Nile was definitely moving farther and farther away on the horizon.

"Where are we going?" he shouted over the noise of the engine.

"Abydos, like we agreed," Jake responded.

"Wouldn't it be safer to follow the Nile?"

"Ha! You're afraid we're going to crash, aren't you?"

"Of course I am!"

"Well, sit back and try to relax. Following the Nile would take longer than a straight shot. You're on a tight schedule, right?"

Chauncy grumbled to himself and watched with increasing horror as the Nile became nothing more than a shimmering mirage at the edge of the horizon. If the plane crashed they would end up in the middle of a desert halfway between the Red Sea and the Nile River, equally far from any good water sources.

He closed his eyes and tried to not think about that. Before too long the droning of the engine coupled with his jet lag put him right to sleep.

The changing pitch of the engine snapped him back awake. He looked around in horror, not remembering where he was or how he'd gotten there. The ground was rushing up to meet him and he only barely managed to stifle a scream. It was a dirt runway in the middle of a green field. They were landing. Jake's plane had actually managed to make the trip in one piece.

They touched down safely and within a few minutes Jake was talking to a local man standing next to a rickshaw. Chauncy was still too woozy to try and translate but he caught a few words here and there. The tone got darker and the volume increased, and with it Chauncy's heart rate went up. Were things not going well?

The conversation continued for another minute before the other man nodded and disappeared. Jake turned around, his expression halfway between relief and agitation.

"Is everything okay?" Chauncy asked.

"The situation is both better and worse than I was fearing," Jake replied. "Hesso is down in Luxor as usual, but Ian will be in town in five days and we'll have to meet with him."

"Who's Ian?"

Jake took a deep breath as he began loading up his luggage into the small vehicle. "Ian Moore is leader of the strongest gang that currently vies for control of the Sohag Governorate. Don't let his suave British manners fool you. I'd rather be dealing with Hesso."

Chauncy climbed into the rickshaw after loading his own luggage. "And who's Hesso?"

"Hesso Khalid Mustafa Al-Kanaan is the undisputed underground leader of the New Valley. He's a brutal little Arab who wields considerable power, but at least with him you always know exactly where you stand. Ian is the kind of man who'll smile and wave as he plots to nuke your house."

Chauncy swallowed. "And how is any part of this situation better than you expected?"

Jake started the rickshaw after several tries and began negotiating the narrow streets of Abydos. "It could have been worse. They could both have been in town, fighting one of their little border wars. I just wish neither one of them was here. We've only got about two hours of sunlight left and I'm hoping to get into our target abode and make some merchant contacts before then. Now please be quiet and let me concentrate."

The sun sank inexorably to the west as they snaked through the tiny, confusing streets of the town. At a certain point Jake pulled onto a street that dead-ended right at the desert. Chauncy could see the ancient ruins of the Osiris temple complex in the distance and he felt his heart skip a few beats. This place was even more ancient than the Giza pyramids. Jake stopped the Rickshaw in front of one of the ubiquitous multi-story adobe-style buildings on the street. "Welcome to your new home," he said as he climbed out.

Chauncy didn't waste time staring at his surroundings. He was overheated, tired, and felt all-too-conspicuous. The air inside was stale and dusty and Chauncy tried to limit his breathing. "This doesn't look like a home," he said, careful to use as little oxygen as possible.

"It's not. It used to be a textile shop. The top floor is the dwelling. Get settled in wherever you want, but I would suggest sleeping on a higher floor. If we're going to be digging this up, we'll want someplace to go to get away from the dirt. I'll be back in an hour or so."

237

"Where are you going?" Chauncy asked nervously.

"I've got to arrange some work crews for tomorrow and buy us some supplies. You didn't expect to just start digging by yourself, did you?" he asked with a snort. Without waiting for an answer he went back outside. Chauncy spent the time trying to find the least dusty of the rooms and setting up his cot once he did. He got his supplies all organized and spent the rest of the time reading the documents in his attaché case, just to refresh his memory.

Jake returned with good news about work crews, and even better news about food. He cooked dinner over a small camping set and then invited Chauncy to join him.

"So tell me more about the Great Pyramid," Jake said as they ate. "Tell me why you think it's the most...whatever it was you said when we first met."

Chauncy smiled. "It's the most precise structure ever built. Its sides are aligned within twelve points of the compass, for starters. How did the ancient Egyptians know that? We only just recently got the Global Positioning System in place!"

"You're not going to suggest it was aliens, are you?" Jake asked, not even trying to hide his scorn.

"No, it wasn't aliens. It wasn't Atlantis, either. Or any of the other hackneyed theories people like to spout because they don't understand something. The simple fact of the matter is that ancient humans were better and smarter than we are. It would take today's machines and workforces decades to build the pyramid. Heck, in the 70s the Japanese tried to do a small-scale version of the pyramid and failed miserably. But it's not just the compass alignment that makes Khufu's pyramid special. There are so many other things about the structure."

Jake leaned back in his camp chair, the only sitting furniture they'd been able to find on short notice and funds, and took a long drink. It was obvious that he was preparing himself for a long discussion that he wasn't particularly interested in. "Go on."

Chauncy's enthusiasm dimmed. "You're not very keen on this subject, are you?"

Jake barked a laugh. "Not really, Chauncy. I deal with the here-and-now, and also with the up-and-coming. I keep my mind on market fluctuations, legalities and territory disputes. Ancient history has no bearing on my business. No, don't sulk. I'm willing to listen because *you're* so interested in it. Who knows, you might be right and then I'll be forced to appreciate history. Also, the more I learn about your crazy ideas, the more I know about what kind of price we can fetch for the capstone."

Chauncy was only slightly mollified, but he decided to continue the discussion anyway. "Well, you can also find the Fibonacci Code in the measurement of the triangular sides of the pyramid. It's a mathematical sequence, I won't go into the details, but it's an equation that can be found in nature. You can find it in a pine cone, the design of a flower petal, the circular pattern of a hurricane and even galaxies. All you need to know is that it is very precise. The pi equation, or 3.14, can also be found all over the pyramids measurements."

"So Khufu wanted a really precise tomb," Jake said, taking another drink. "What of it?"

"That's the most interesting part about all of this," Chauncy said. "There was never a mummy in Khufu's Pyramid. The Sarcophagus found in the 1600s was cracked but empty, with no signs that Khufu or anybody else had ever been buried here. And that's what led me to my conclusions. There was never *supposed* to be a mummy in the pyramid, because it wasn't supposed to be a tomb. It was a machine!"

Jake raised an eyebrow. "A machine?"

Chauncy retreated a little bit. "Yeah, sort of. It's complicated."

Jake finished off his drink and stood up. "An interesting theory, but I think I'm going to get some sleep. We've got an early start tomorrow."

Chauncy stayed in his chair for at least another hour. He spent the whole time going over everything he knew about the pyramid, including the things he hadn't yet told Jake. He knew he was right; he *had* to be. His academic reputation, his money and perhaps even his life depended on his having gotten everything right. By the time he went to bed he had convinced himself once again. The numbers didn't lie.

Δ Δ Δ

The next few days melded together for Chauncy. He'd been on three archaeological expeditions before but none of them had been like this. For the first time he was digging *within* a structure, instead of outside in the elements. They had to dig in a tight circle so that they didn't undermine the old building. He was not fluent in the language of the diggers which meant that there was no light conversation to keep the day going. Well, there *was* light conversation, but he wasn't involved in it. They were also digging for a specific goal, which was definitely different. Usually they'd go through each inch of dirt with a fine-toothed comb in order to locate any single artifact, carefully catalogue it, and then proceed. It would be weeks, months or sometimes even years before they'd make this kind of progress. Every fiber of his archaeologist body screamed at the speed in which they progressed, but the logical and frightened part of his mind knew that his time was limited. If they didn't find the buried structure that he was expecting...well, he didn't want to rely on Jake Thrasher's good humor to get him out of Cairo.

And so he dug along with the workers, his body shaking with exertion and suppressed emotions. Even indoors the heat was unbearable and he was forced to spend more and more time resting and drinking water. He knew the diggers were talking about him each time he took a break. He could catch snippets of Arabic words that he knew weren't polite. Each time he vowed that he would just give up now and face the consequences, but each time he knew he couldn't. He had to prove his theory, and not just to himself. He had to prove it to the smarmy Jake Thrasher, to the egotistical professors back home, to his parents, and especially to Anita. He hadn't told anyone but Jake about his plans, but everybody back home knew he was fascinated by crazy theories. They'd scoffed at him when he suggested the pyramids might not be tombs. Well, he would show them, and he'd get his doctoral degree on top of it. *Doctor Rollock*. It had a nice ring to it.

It was day four, the day before they'd have to go talk to Ian Moore, when they found it.

"Stop digging!" Chauncy shouted in his broken Arabic. He waved his hands frantically as his heart rate skyrocketed. The stone they'd come across could be anything but he had a feeling otherwise. He dropped down to his knees and brought out his big brush. It was the first time since they started that he'd brought it out. He carefully brushed away the dirt and sand and felt his heart skip a beat. A limestone block about three feet wide and four feet long lay before him, a block that hadn't been seen by humans since the time of the Egyptian Dynasties. These were the moments he lived for, the moments that had convinced him to become an archaeologist. He was actually looking into the past, but not *just* looking. He was brushing it off and touching it. He felt connected to those brilliant, ancient engineers.

"Looks like you were right," Jake said from above, shattering the spell. "Do you think this is a one-off block, or attached to something?"

Chauncy slowly took his hands off the block and faced the present reality. He had to throttle his instincts to catalogue this. He was being a rogue archaeologist, but he had no other choice right now. "Give me a minute to find out."

He scooped out the dirt with a small garden shovel and felt a grin spread across his face. The large block had another one directly beneath it. "I think this is it," he told Jake, unable to contain his excitement. "We'll need to dig in a grid pattern around this block. And we'll have to do it carefully. Translate, please."

Jake barked out the orders and the workers began to carefully shovel out the ground around the block while Chauncy stepped back. Time seemed to drag to a crawl as a structure began to be revealed in front of him. They found a sealed doorway about three hours later and it was all Chauncy could do to keep from running up and down the streets shouting "Eureka!" His enthusiasm was only slightly dampened by the fact that the work crews were leaving for the day.

"I set out a specific time frame when I hired them," Jake said. He actually sounded sad. "We'll have to wait until tomorrow."

Chauncy stared at the door and shook his head. "No. I'm not waiting until tomorrow. I'm going in tonight."

Jake stared at the sealed door. "You know, I'm not superstitious, but don't these things usually come with a curse or booby traps?"

"I don't really care," Chauncy said. "This is what I came here for."

"You sure this is it? Don't get me wrong, I think it's great that we've uncovered an unknown structure. I can probably sell this house for a huge amount to a museum. But do you think the capstone is in here?"

Chauncy kneeled down and pointed to a set of hieroglyphs on the lower-right-hand side of the door. "This is promising. See it? It's a lined disc, a chicken, a snake, and a chicken."

"You're reading it backwards."

"That's how you read hieroglyphs. This is Khufu's name."

"And Khufu is—right, pyramid of Khufu. Whole reason we're here. So finding his name on this door is—"

"The most exciting thing I've ever come across," Chauncy finished, standing back up with a huge smile on his face. "One way or another, I've been vindicated. Even if the capstone isn't here, we just discovered a tomb, or a temple, or *some*thing new at Abydos with Khufu's name on it. This proves the ivory statuette wasn't a fluke, and now we have three things associated with the name of Khufu. I'm going down in history."

"*We're* going down in history," Jake corrected. "Let's get this open. And while we're doing that, you're going to tell me the parts about the pyramid that you haven't gotten around to yet."

Chauncy carefully traced out the edges of the doorway and felt his ears burning. "What do you mean?" he asked, as innocently as he could.

"Come now, Chauncy, I've dealt with much better liars than you. You've been holding something back the whole time. Yes, yes, the pyramid is a precise structure, good for it. You mentioned it was a machine and then immediately regretted it. I could see it in your face. So tell me what kind of machine the Great Pyramid is."

Chauncy took a deep breath and wished he hadn't; the dust down here was ancient and thick. After a moment of choking he was finally able to speak. "How about we trade secrets. Why are you living in Cairo instead of America?"

There was silence and for several heartbeats Chauncy was afraid he'd crossed a line.

Jake let out a long sigh. "Well, why not? It's not like it'll hurt anybody. A senator and a congressman decided to raise their bribe requirements to levels I wasn't willing to pay. They were just the end of a long line of reasons the US government and I didn't get along. The congressmen made it rather impossible for me to stay, so I found a new life here."

"Easier to bribe people here?"

Jake made a strange choking-laugh-sound. "Most of the bribery here is done in blood. But we're straying off-subject. What kind of machine was the pyramid?"

Chauncy found the spot he was looking for: two small indentations on either side of the door. "Get me a crowbar and I'll tell you."

Jake reached into his satchel and brought out two crowbars. They placed their tools in the small indentations and Chauncy looked across the way at Jake.

"We're about to open a door to the past," he said, feeling both elated and saddened. "This is what I live for, Jake."

"Any solemn words you'd like to say?"

Chauncy grinned. "Take a deep breath and close your eyes."

With a great exertion they pulled the door off as a rush of ancient air mingled with the modern sky for the first time in millennia. They waited a few minutes for the dust to settle down before grabbing their flashlights and entering the long dark hallway.

Chauncy walked carefully, trying to watch everything at once. Booby-traps might be an invention of Hollywood and action-thrillers, but that didn't mean there *couldn't* be any. He was struck by how many hieroglyphs filled the walls, the floor and even the ceiling. There was a story being told here and he only wished he could spend a decade or two studying it.

"It was the limestone coating that first tipped me off," Chauncy said as he brushed his fingers across the wall. "Almost all of it is gone now, looted or lost through the ravages of time. But when the pyramid was complete it would have been covered in a white limestone, a type called *Tufa*, which lacks magnesium. That means it has highly insulating properties."

"Insulation," Jake said from behind Chauncy. "Electrical or weather?"

"Electrical. It's like the entire pyramid except the capstone was covered in a wrapping, like electrical cords are covered except their ends. The blocks *inside*, however, are a different type of limestone. That limestone is slightly conductive, allowing electricity instead of hindering it. Also, the granite used in the internal chambers is a specific type that contains a slightly radioactive substance which causes ionization of the air. And finally, the capstone itself would have been made of solid electrum, which is a gold/silver alloy that is extremely conductive."

"Huh," Jake said. He sounded a little more interested than last time. "So the pyramid has the properties of an electrical device. Doesn't prove anything. Last I checked, the battery wasn't invented until the 1700s or something. How would the Egyptians have generated electricity?"

Chauncy looked over his shoulder. "I was wondering when you would ask that question. Do you know about the subterranean chamber in the pyramid?"

"Don't have a clue."

"Well, nobody knows why it was built. There's no real reason for it, at least not in conventional thinking. But if you expand your horizons just a little bit it becomes obvious. The subterranean chambers have shafts dug down into limestone aquifers where water from the Nile runs past them. Running water produces an electrical current that was then sent all the way up to the capstone."

They came across another sealed doorway, this one covered in as many hieroglyphs as the rest of the chamber. Chauncy stopped his dissertation and carefully studied the Egyptian symbols. "Well, I've got good news for you," he said. "There are no booby-traps."

"How do you know?"

"Because Khufu placed a curse instead. This is really it, Jake. They didn't curse just *anything*. Something really important is behind this door."

"You don't believe in curses, right?" Jake asked a bit nervously.

"My first dig was cursed. I'm still here. The indentations are in the same place. Take another deep breath!"

They popped the door off and a rush of air blasted past them into the new chamber. "Negative air pressure," Chauncy said once they'd caught their breath. "Very interesting."

"How so?"

"I don't know. Let's see what's in here, shall we?" He stepped into the room, his heart beating and his palms sweating. A long stairway leading down greeted his flashlight beams. He started down the steps, testing each one to make sure it would hold his weight. He had no doubts, really. The pyramids had lasted this long and these steps looked like they were made of the same type of limestone.

He stopped suddenly. *The same type of limestone*...he took the rest of the steps much faster. Every few feet he felt the air getting thicker, more ionized. He could hardly contain his excitement as he reached the bottom and stared into the chamber that awaited him.

The chamber was an almost perfect cube, perhaps thirty feet in every direction. Perfect design was evident in the evenly-space pillars that filled most of the room. The walls were again absolutely covered in hieroglyphs. But none of that was nearly as important as the large, gleaming pyramid that sat on a pedestal in the exact center of the room.

The missing capstone.

"I don't believe it," Jake said with difficulty.

"Neither do I," Chauncy said, feeling like he was in a trance.

"Do you feel the electricity in the air?" Jake asked. "It's...it's almost a physical presence."

"I know," Chauncy said. "And that's what the Great Pyramid really was, Jake. It was a power generator for the entire Egyptian kingdom. We can feel the energy here in this tiny room, imagine it amplified by the *entire* Great Pyramid."

"But that's impossible," Jake said as he walked slowly forward. "Wireless energy...it's impossible."

"Not really. Nikolai Tesla did it in 1917. He built a tower that was powered by aquifers and generated electricity. There's even pictures of him holding a lit lightbulb that isn't attached to anything. The Egyptians figured it out four millennia ago."

"So if we put this capstone back on top of the pyramid, will it generate power again?" Jake asked as he took a few more steps forward.

Chauncy stepped up next to Jake and felt the sudden increase in electricity. "I don't think the pyramid will ever work again; the limestone skin is gone. Hold it a minute. You feel that, right?"

Jake nodded. "Every step we take it feels like we're being pushed back. How is the capstone generating power in *here*? This isn't a pyramid."

"No, but the limestone is the same, and we're not that far from the Nile. There must be aquifers here too. I can't believe it. I spent all that time and all of my money on this one giant gamble. I mean, I knew it made sense, and I knew everything was as it should be...but to actually see the capstone...to actually feel its power..."

He paused as his flashlight illuminated the series of hieroglyphs on the pedestal. He took a few steps forward and felt all the hair on his body stand straight on edge. He had to be reading these wrong. He had to be.

"What's the matter?" Jake asked. He was practically rooted in place.

Chauncy looked between the hieroglyphs and at the capstone, shaking his head. "I was right, Jake, but I was also very wrong. See this inscription here? It's talking about the Uraeus *Was*-Staff projecting the power of the pharaoh anywhere in Egypt, destroying the enemies of the gods."

"Uraeus, I know that word. That's the rearing cobra, isn't it, usually seen on a pharaoh's headdress?"

"I really don't want to know how you know that, Jake. But yes. The Uraues was said to protect the pharaoh by spitting fire or lightning. A staff that can spit fire or lightning and destroy the enemies of Egypt. If you combine that with a giant pyramid that generates power..."

"You get the world's first super weapon," Jake finished with a heavy sigh.

Silence descended on the chamber. Chauncy stared at the inscriptions, re-reading the hieroglyphs over and over again. He played his light over the rest of the hieroglyphs but it only made it worse. Everywhere he looked there were gloats and descriptions of the power of Ra captured by the pharaohs and used to enforce the rule of Khufu.

"I had this idea," Chauncy spoke finally. "This idea that the pyramid was a great achievement that powered the Lighthouse of Alexandria and other great works. That the pyramids were a source of good and wonder in Egypt, and that by finding the capstone I would somehow contribute to that greatness. But that's not what it was at all. It was a weapon, an establishment of fear. No wonder Khufu's name isn't found all over Egyptian records. They wanted to forget what he'd done."

"Everything can't always be the way we want it to be," Jake said quietly, an odd tone in his voice.

A silence descended again as Chauncy stared at the capstone. The pinnacle of Egyptian technology hadn't been the wondrous object he'd imagined. The gleaming capstone was tainted now with blood and horror and he knew he'd never be able to look at it the same way. He sat and stared at it for a long time, trying to sort through his feelings.

"Well, isn't *that* quite the dish," a new voice spoke up.

Chauncy spun around so fast he nearly fell over. A short and impeccably-dressed man was standing in the doorway. "Who are you?" he demanded.

"Chauncy Rollock, I'd like to introduce you to Ian Moore," Jake said quietly. "He owns your capstone now."

Chauncy stuttered as he suddenly caught sight of the pistol in the Englishman's hands. "B-bu-but but this is *my* find!"

"Not quite, good chap," Ian said, his voice surprisingly jovial. "It's in my turf and it was found by my crews. Thrasher, this is quite a mint. Thanks for pointing it out to me."

"Jake?" Chauncy asked, his world spinning. "Why, Jake?"

"I told you I wasn't on good terms with anybody in this part of Egypt," Jake said with a shrug. "This is my way of squaring the balance."

"You can't let him have it," Chauncy insisted. "You know what it is now. You really want *him* to have access to it?"

"I'd suggest you belt up," Ian said, his tone suddenly losing its joviality. "Thrasher, what should I know about this thing?"

Chauncy's feet suddenly unbolted from the floor. He couldn't let the key to a super weapon end up in the hands of a gang leader. It didn't matter that the capstone might never work that way again. It didn't even matter that Ian had a gun. This was *his* find, this was *his* capstone. He leapt toward the Englishman with an incomprehensible snarl. The gunshot echoed through the room so loudly that it hurt his ears. The cold, hard limestone hurt even worse as he hit it hard. Shockwaves of pain ran out from his foot and he curled up into a little ball.

"You really have no choice, Chauncy my lad," Ian said quietly into his ringing ears. "If you tell me what I want to know, you'll die a quick and painless death. If you don't, I'll leave you in here to die slowly. Pick one."

Chauncy gripped his foot as hard as he could, trying to use

247

pressure to stop the pain. It didn't seem to be working. He breath came in short gasps and he couldn't think of anything to say. He was never going to see his parents again, never see Anita or the university. He really had come all the way out here for nothing.

"The capstone might not be real," Jake said. "Chauncy was about to see if it was. If it isn't, it's worthless."

"Why wouldn't I want the real one?" Ian asked.

"Because it's worth a lot more than I originally thought," Jake said. "But only if it's real."

The buzzing in Chauncy's mind quieted for a moment as he strained to pay attention to the conversation. What was Jake *talking* about? He wasn't about to see if it was real. He had no doubts on that score.

"And how do you know if it's real?"

"The real one will be perfectly smooth to the touch, but a fake one will have little holes and imperfections."

Chauncy was well and truly lost now. He hadn't said anything like that. He tried to figure out what was going on but the pain in his foot made thinking difficult.

"Why don't you check that for me?" Ian asked, his voice suspicious.

"You'd really trust *me* to tell you that?" Jake asked.

"Fine, I'll see if it's real. Terribly sorry, Chauncy, but it looks like I'll be leaving you here."

Chauncy suddenly understood. He twisted his body around and curled into an even tighter ball. The blast was visible even through his closed eyes. Electricity filled the chamber and washed over him like a dust storm, knocking him several feet from where he lay.

He opened his eyes and looked around. A hand appeared in his vision and he looked up to see Jake offering him assistance.

"You going to stab me in the back again?" he croaked.

"Pretty sure I just saved your life, Chauncy."

Chauncy took the proffered hand and got to his feet. Or at least, he got to *one* of his feet. The second he tried to stand on the shot one he nearly fainted. He looked over at the crumpled form of Ian Moore. "We need to bury this, Jake," he said through gritted teeth. "We need to bury it so that nobody can ever find it again."

He expected a struggle or at least a mention of how valuable the capstone was. But Jake Thrasher merely glanced at the pyramidion and nodded his head. "I know. Come on, we need to get that foot of yours looked at."

They walked slowly out of the chamber and up the stairs, leaving behind the missing capstone forever.

Δ Epilogue Δ

"You were really going to sell me out to Ian Moore?"

Jake swallowed the last of his scotch. "Either him or Hesso. It just made good business sense to trade a capstone and a starry-eyed American for a great rep in that part of Egypt."

"And yet you changed your mind. Why?"

"Because you were right, Chauncy. If it had just been a capstone I wouldn't have batted an eye. But a super weapon? I wouldn't want that in Ian's hands. I wouldn't want that in *anybody's* hands. The world is volatile enough as it is right now."

Chauncy chuckled and stared at the cast on his foot. He'd never have expected Jake Thrasher to have that kind of world view. "You planning to make a move for Abydos, now that Ian is gone?"

"What do you mean, 'planning?' I already worked out a deal with his gang and struck an accord with Hesso. I own half of Abydos now. How do you think I got the capstone buried and the textile shop torn down on top of it?"

"Of course. What was I thinking? How are you going to make sure the workers don't talk about the find?"

"Pretty simple, really: they work for me now. I also told them it was a fake, so there's no real reason to mention it. Bury it beneath some concrete, tell the workers it's not worth anything, and tell them if they talk about it you'll kill them."

"Yeah, pretty simple," Chauncy said before lapsing into silence. He stared into the dark amber liquid in his glass and was amazed at how the swirling drink mirrored his thoughts. "It's funny, really," he said after a long pause. "I came all the way over here and spent all of my money to find that capstone. I broke several Egyptian laws and several of my own rules about proper archaeologist procedure, not to mention breaking my foot. It was going to get me my doctorate and get me the girl of my dreams.

249

Now I won't get either, all because stupid Khufu wanted a super weapon."

"Would you rather have a doctorate and a girl, or the secret of a killer lightning generator buried forever?" Jake asked.

"Good point. There must be *something* I can do to impress Anita, though. Something different, something crazy. Any thoughts?"

"Why not get your picture taken on top of the Great Pyramid?" Jake asked. "You might not get the capstone, but you can stand where it used to be. Would make for a beautiful shot and you'd impress Anita with your daring."

Chauncy sat up straighter. "Hey, that's a great idea! But isn't climbing the pyramid illegal?"

They stared at each other for a minute before bursting out in laughter.

-About the Authors-

Dyego Alehandro is an author who has been writing since a very young age. He enjoys creating his own cover art and has received many accolades for his work. His hobbies include playing Legos, board games and PC games with his wife. He lives in Phoenix, Arizona and really needs to move somewhere that has rain.
You can read his Smashwords interview here:
https://www.smashwords.com/interview/ArcaniArts

Alex Zabala lives in Arizona with his wife Anita. By day he is a professional landscape contractor and by night an author. He started writing when he was 45 years old. He calls himself a 'late bloomer' in the authoring business. However, he says when it comes to developing hidden talents it is 'better late than never.'

-Other Books by the Authors-

The Chauncy Rollock Series
Treasure of the Mayan King
The Golden Scepter

Solo Books by Alex Zabala
El Tesoro del Rey Maya (*Spanish translation of Treasure of the Mayan King)*
The Incident in Montes Azules (*2015 release*)

Solo Books by Dyego Alehandro
The Avarice Dynasty Series
Avarice Dynasty: Evasion
Avarice Dynasty: Illusion (*2015 release*)
Avarice Dynasty: Dissension (*coming eventually*)
Avarice Dynasty: Invasion (*coming sometime after eventually*)
Avarice Dynasty: Ascension (*coming after that*)

Celestial Shadow Series
The Deeping Call (*2015 release*)
Within Voices (*coming eventually*)

-Connect with the Authors-

Dyego Alehandro
Friend me on Facebook:
https://www.facebook.com/dyego.alehandro
Follow me on Twitter: https://twitter.com/ArcaniArts
Enjoy my blog of random musings:
http://www.dyegoalehandro.com
Favorite my Smashwords page:
https://www.smashwords.com/profile/view/ArcaniArts
Collect some pins: http://www.pinterest.com/dyegoalehandro/

Alex Zabala
Enjoy my blog: http://www.alexzabala.com

www.ingramcontent.com/pod-product-compliance
Lightning Source LLC
Chambersburg PA
CBHW071143170626
46809CB00002B/754